Death
at the
Dinner
Party

BOOKS BY EMMA DAVIES

EMMA DAVIES

Death
at the
Dinner
Party

THE ADAM AND EVE MYSTERY SERIES 2

bookouture

Published by Bookouture in 2022

An imprint of Storyfire Ltd.
Carmelite House
50 Victoria Embankment
London EC4Y 0DZ

www.bookouture.com

ISBN: 978-1-80314-293-7
eBook ISBN: 978-1-80314-292-0

1

Francesca Eve was floating, letting the water hold the weight of her body. Thoughts came slowly, ebbing and flowing, as sunlight bounced on the rippled surface of the pool, dancing shadows across the ceiling. Fran watched them for a moment, transfixed. What must it be like to wake up every day, knowing you could take a swim before breakfast? A swim any time you wanted? No queuing up at the local pool, no worrying that everyone could see your wobbly bits; your own stretch of cool, blissful, and utterly private water. And this house had two, one inside and one out. She closed her eyes, breathing deeply, evenly, letting time trickle past and—

A wave of water crashed over her as a slight figure bombed into the water beside her.

'Adam!'

He raced away and just for a moment she thought about giving chase, but Adam had fifteen years on her and would reach the end of the pool long before she did. Instead, she returned to her peaceful reverie, and began to swim leisurely widths, leaving him to his more youthful acrobatics. These quiet moments would probably be the last she would have for a while and she intended to make the most of them, but already she could feel her thoughts turning to the day ahead and the spell was broken.

She waited until Adam had climbed from the pool and wrapped his towel around himself, before doing likewise once his back was turned. The semi-naked body of someone nearly old enough to be his mum was embarrassing enough. The fact that Fran was also a friend of his mum's made it much, much worse.

Turning, she took one last look at the frescoed ceiling, at the huge palm-filled urns, and the stunning view to the gardens beyond.

'Well, there isn't much I'm going to miss about this place,' she said. 'But I will miss this. It's going to be a busy morning though,' she warned. 'All hands to the deck for one final push and then we'll be done.'

It was Sunday and her and Adam's third day at Claremont House, a couple of million pounds worth of beautiful Georgian architecture, set in acres of rolling Shropshire countryside. And Fran was chief cook and bottle washer for the weekend. Her business cards promised exclusive catering, although her own description was often far more accurate a depiction of reality. Nevertheless, exclusive catering was what she had been hired to provide this weekend, and that was exactly what she had delivered.

Adam turned to smile at her. 'It's been sort of fun though,' he said. 'Despite some of the appalling food.'

The very first time she met Adam, he had complained about the use of anchovies in some of her canapés – hors d'oeuvres he had pinched, she might add, so it served him right. This weekend she had well and truly got her own back. *Just try the caviar*, she'd said, *I think you'll really like it...*

'So, you won't want any cinnamon rolls for breakfast then?' she asked, teasing. 'No croissants? No pains au chocolat?' They were almost at the end of the pool, walking towards the staircase which would take them back to the main part of the house.

Adam considered the question carefully. 'I know how much you hate waste,' he replied. 'I'll see what I can do.'

Back up in her room, Fran showered quickly, checking her watch. She'd lost count of the number of times she'd done that over the course of the weekend. Too many *to* count... The weekend-long house party was all about abundance and lavish indulgence, where nothing was too much trouble or seemingly outside the budget. Since her arrival on Friday, Fran had certainly fulfilled the brief, but she had never worked so hard. Now, with just breakfast and lunch still to provide she was on the final straight and already looking forward to home.

Home meant snuggling under her husband Jack's warm arms, feet up on the sofa, drinking one last cup of tea before bed. It meant squishing Martha to her, smiling as her daughter squirmed in protest before submitting completely and hugging her right back, the embarrassment of teenage years forgotten, if only for a brief instant. Home meant a warm, friendly, bay-fronted Victorian house which was charming, often messy, and in need of some decoration, but utterly the centre of Fran's world. And gorgeous, incredible, jaw-dropping and other-worldly as Claremont House was, that was exactly the problem. It *was* other-worldly and Fran much preferred the one she normally lived in.

Twenty-five minutes later she was dressed and ready for work.

There was no sign of Adam yet, although she could hear sounds of movement from his room next door. Adam was a computer game designer and here to undertake some research for the setting of a new game he was working on. Agreeing to his request that he accompany her this weekend had been somewhat of a risk, but he'd been true to his word and hadn't put a foot wrong.

Her clients had scarcely noticed him, but then they'd scarcely noticed her either so that wasn't altogether surprising. And importantly, there would be nothing in Adam's finished game which would allow the owners of Claremont House or their guests to identify themselves. It had all worked out perfectly.

Slipping down the back stairs opposite her room, Fran made her way to the kitchen where Rachel would already be hard at work. The woman never seemed to stop and had earned Fran's gratitude countless times over during the course of the weekend. Not least of all because as housekeeper she might well have felt threatened by Fran's presence, even resentful, but she had been helpful, grateful and best of all, enormous fun. It had made what could have been a very awkward situation into, if not exactly an easy time, a far better one than Fran had hoped for.

Neither of them had had much sleep and Rachel looked tired. No worse than Fran, but without make-up, with her hair still hanging loose, and without her professional persona in place, it showed. Yet still she greeted Fran with a wide smile and a wave at the teapot which had hardly been empty the entire weekend.

'Morning,' she said. 'Did you sleep?'

Fran pulled a face and tucked her wiry curls back behind her ears. 'Not a wink. You?'

Rachel shook her head, eyes flicking to Fran's before dropping once more. 'I never do on these weekends. I'm always listening out in case anyone needs something. Or gets sick. That's happened before, and everyone was pretty well-oiled last night.' She pulled out a scrunchie from the pocket of her jeans and tied her shoulder-length hair into a loose ponytail. Yesterday it had been coiled into a low bun, as it had been for most of the weekend, but it suited her down, framing her face perfectly, with its rich chocolate colour, thick and glossy.

Rachel smiled again. 'Never mind. That was then, this is now. Just brekky and lunch and then...' She sighed. 'Freedom.'

'For me, maybe, not you.'

'Normality then,' replied Rachel. 'And if past experience is anything to go by, Mimi will be off to a spa somewhere for a few days to recover from the excesses of the weekend, while "his lordship" will hotfoot it back to London at the first available opportunity. It will be beautifully quiet and I'll be able to remind myself that most of the time, being here is really quite pleasant.'

Fran gave her a sideways glance, smiling at her nickname for Mimi's husband. 'Well, good. There's that at least.' She looked around the vast kitchen, spotless even after the relative chaos that last night's dinner had wreaked. 'Right then, let's have a cup of tea and finish the rest of the clearing-up. What's still left to do?'

'Not that much actually. I've already reset the dining room. Mimi is very particular about it so I did it as soon as I came down. It would be just my luck for her to get up early and bemoan the fact that it hadn't been done. So, there's really just a little straightening up to do. Derek has drained the last of the water from the ice sculpture and dismantled the stand, so it's ready to be collected, whenever the company calls.'

'In that case I think we should have some breakfast of our own before we start work on everyone else's. I don't suppose any of the guests will be up that early.'

'Only Mr Chapman, he'll be out for his usual morning run, nothing stops him.' She checked the clock. 'I'll make him a cup of tea in a bit, but otherwise, I imagine it will be quiet for a while. Mimi won't be too long though. Don't be fooled by her appearance last night, she's very good at seeming just as inebriated as everyone else, but she won't have drunk much, she never does. She takes her role as Mrs Chapman very seriously – only when there's an audience, obviously. This contract is worth a pile of money, I mean huge... She won't let anything stand in the way of that.'

Fran smiled. 'I lead such a sheltered life. I had no idea business was still done this way.'

'Oh yes, Mr Chapman has been cultivating his prospective clients for months, this weekend is just the icing on the cake. The final sweetener which he hopes will seal the deal. They all stand to make just as much money from this as he does, but it's all about putting on a show.'

Fran raised her eyebrows. 'They've certainly done that.' She thought back over the last couple of days, to the extravagance of the food, the wine, the champagne, not to mention the activities which had been staged: the clay pigeon shooting, the pampering sessions for the women; whatever the guests enjoyed had all been provided.

A movement behind her made Fran turn, and she smiled when she saw who had entered.

'Lovely sunny morning again, ladies,' said Derek. 'Are we all ready for one last hurrah?'

Rachel was already pouring tea into mugs. 'I'll bring you a bacon sandwich in a bit, Derek, but here's your tea. Have you checked the list of when everyone is leaving?'

Derek nodded, gratefully accepting a mug. 'I'm off to do that now. Once I've had my sarnie, I'll go and rake the drive, too. We'll give them just as good a send-off as we did the welcome, don't worry.'

Fran noticed the hint of a blush accompanying Rachel's smile as she nodded at the man who was her perfect counterpoint – where she took care of everything inside the house, he took care of everything outside, including her client's collection of cars. Over the course of the weekend, Fran had thought more than once that they were a couple, but she had never seen any evidence to confirm it; they were never anything less than professional. It was a shame, she thought, if friendship was all they shared. They were both so obviously in love with one another. She had even teased Rachel not long after she had introduced her to Adam, commenting on how good-looking he was, but she could see now how irrelevant that had been.

Fran pushed up her sleeves once Derek had left to attend to his own duties.

'What will you have for breakfast, Rachel?' she asked, as the housekeeper began to open cupboards. 'I've got loads of croissants left. How about we go continental? Pastries, fresh figs and hot chocolate?'

Rachel positively beamed. 'Perfect,' she said, taking down several packets. 'I'll just make his lordship's tea and then I'll be with you.' She glanced at the clock again. 'He should be back shortly.' Her gaze took in the rest of the kitchen. 'You haven't seen his blue glazed mug, have you? It's his favourite.' She frowned. 'I usually leave it on the side there ready.'

Fran shook her head.

'Never mind, I probably just forgot to collect it, I expect it's in his study. Back in a sec.'

Fran swallowed a mouthful of tea and began to remove a selection of fruit from the large double fridge in one corner. She would need to serve it at room temperature for it to taste its absolute best. She turned on the oven as she passed, already thinking about the selection of pastries she would provide; made by herself and freshly cooked, they were all but irresistible.

'Fran...?'

She turned at the sound of Rachel's voice, much quieter than usual.

The housekeeper was standing in the doorway, her face an odd mixture of uncertainty and shock. Her normal rosy complexion was pallid, her mouth open.

'You okay, Rach? You look like you've seen a ghost.'

Rachel's eyes widened even further and her hand touched

her chest. She swallowed. 'Can you come with me?' she half whispered, half croaked, air catching in her throat. 'There's been a...' She trailed off, eyes closing as she leaned against the door jamb.

Fran took a step forward. 'Rach? What's the matter?'

'It's Mr Chapman, he...' But the housekeeper couldn't finish. Instead she almost stumbled back out into the hallway, leaving Fran with no choice but to follow, fully aware that her heart was beginning to skitter in her chest.

From the kitchen they entered the rear hall, a service area for the rest of the house. A staircase rose from the cellar right to the top of the building, on either side of which was a doorway through into the main hallway of the house from which the principal rooms could be accessed. Emerging into the lower hallway, they turned towards the study opposite the dining room. Both doors were closed as was usual first thing in the morning. She pointed to the study door.

'In there,' she said, lowering a trembling arm to her side. 'He's in there.'

Fran's own hand shook as she turned the door handle. Rachel hadn't seemed prone to flights of over-imagination; neither was she easily upset, but something had taken both her colour and her voice. Mustering what courage she could, Fran slowly pushed open the door.

She didn't see Mr Chapman at first. He was lying on the floor, just beyond his desk, on the far side of a room where something furious had erupted. It was evident in the books which had been torn from the shelves, the curtain which was half hanging from its rail, and the picture frame which had been ripped from the wall and now lay in pieces on the floor. And it was most certainly evident in the pool of blood which had seeped from Mr Chapman's head onto the carpet where he had fallen. His glasses were still in place, crushed and broken. One of the lenses had popped out, coming to rest a little distance away. A dark red smear of something had slid down one side of it. Fran seemed almost transfixed by it, but perhaps that was simply because she didn't want her eyes to linger on the side of Mr Chapman's head where the dark hair was matted with... She turned her head away.

'Is he dead?' Rachel was still standing in the entrance to the room, her breathing ragged.

Fran nodded, straightening, her eyes locked on Rachel's for a moment before she carefully retraced her steps to the doorway. She took Rachel's arm and closed the study door behind her. Wordlessly, they returned to the kitchen where Fran sat Rachel down at one of the chairs on the long island unit, placing a mug of tea in front of her.

'Drink that,' she said softly. 'Honestly, it will help.'

Holding on to the countertop for support, Fran slid her phone from her pocket and searched through the contacts. She was looking for a number she thought she would never need again. One that she'd left there, just in case.

It was still only a little after seven in the morning, but Fran's call was answered within three rings.

'Helen Bradley.'

Her voice still made Fran almost wince.

'Hi, Nell...' She licked her lips, swallowed and tried again. 'I'm not sure if you remember me, it's Francesca Eve here, we met a few months ago when—'

'I remember, Fran. And what can I do for you this early on a Sunday morning?'

Fran's head went blank. 'Um... there's been an accident. Where I work. Am working. At Claremont House near Shrewsbury.'

'An accident?'

'No, actually. No... I don't think it is.'

'Well, Fran, either it is or it isn't. What's happened? I must say I didn't think I'd be hearing from you again. Not after last time.'

'No, me neither, I... I'm sorry, I know it's early, but the owner, Mr Chapman, is dead and... I don't know what to do.'

There was a pause from the other end of the line.

'Then don't touch anything... Oh, and Fran?' The voice was much softer this time. 'Put the kettle on, I'll be with you as soon as I can.'

Fran ended the call just as Adam appeared in the kitchen. He looked exactly as he had the first time they'd met; jeans, a tee shirt and, despite the warmth of the morning, a multi-coloured beanie hat pulled down low over his black curls. That day had been just over a year ago, but as Fran stared at him in horror, the time in between fell away.

'You're never going to believe this,' she said. 'But there's been another murder.'

2

DCI Helen Bradley was just as terrifying as the last time Fran had seen her. The fact that it was still only half past seven on a Sunday morning made no difference to her appearance, or her attitude. She arrived at the front door in a pin-sharp suit with matching bag and jacket thrown over one arm, her chestnut bobbed hair tucked back behind her ears. Her make-up was impeccable. Even though Helen scared the pants off Fran, it was weird how much she liked her.

'Morning, Fran, I hope you're not going to make a habit of this. Ringing me up to tell me someone's been murdered. Though presumably you haven't already solved this one?' Helen didn't wait for a reply. 'Come on then, show me where he is. And leave that front door open. My two DCs will be arriving any minute.'

Fran shot a glance at Rachel, who was standing beside her in the hallway. 'Um...'

Helen followed her look. 'We can do the introductions in a minute. I want to see the body first.'

Fran swallowed. 'Okay, he's down here, in the study.'

'And no one's been in there?' Helen was scrutinising her face.

'No, only Rachel... she was the one who found... I went in as well, just to check. I didn't touch anything and no one else has been in. I don't think anyone's up yet.'

Helen looked around her. 'Anyone?'

'Yes, Mrs Chapman, she's his wife, and the guests. There are people staying here for the weekend. Five of them.'

'Oh, good grief. Well, that's going to make rather a difference to how we do things, but it can't be helped.' She looked at Rachel, who flushed bright red, but managed to nod, then smiled at Fran. 'Right, where are we?'

'This way. That first door there.'

Helen scrutinised the hallway. 'We're going to need to preserve this whole area as a crime scene, so that's something at least. Much easier than if the room was in the middle of the house.'

Fran swallowed as Helen quickly donned a pair of gloves she took from her suit pocket and pushed open the door. Fran could hardly bear to look.

'And no one's touched him, or moved him?'

Rachel cleared her throat. 'No, I just left when I saw...'

Helen's gaze swept back and forth, taking in the detail of the room. She hadn't moved from her position by the door but her eyes narrowed as she peered closer at the wall where the picture had been torn down, at the shelves from which the books were missing, like gaps in a row of teeth. 'You two stay here,' she said and, in a sudden movement, she crossed to Mr Chapman's inert body. Placing her feet carefully, she knelt on the floor, arms bent upward, hands into her chest. She lowered her face until it was only inches away from his, holding it there motionless for a moment before sitting back on her heels.

'Well, you're right, he's dead.'

Fran winced.

'Head bashed in by the look, lots of bone fragments. More than one blow I'd say. So, unless he fell, hit his head on something, got up, and fell down all over again, which is not very likely, I'd say someone beat him to death.' She frowned, and got carefully to her feet. 'Tell me what you did when you came in here.'

Rachel flushed. 'Erm, nothing... I was just fetching Mr Chapman's mug, his favourite one, he has tea in it every morning and I thought he might have left it here.'

'And had he?'

Rachel pointed to the desk. 'Yes, it's there.' She pointed to a large light blue mug. 'I didn't pick it up though, I... well, I stopped. That's when I saw him.'

'Did you touch the mug?'

Rachel shook her head.

'Or anything else?'

'No. I only took about three steps into the room.'

Crossing to a spot a little distance away, Helen bent down, peering at the carpet.

'Why is this floor wet?' she asked.

Rachel looked at Fran, horrified. 'I don't... I don't know.'

Helen peered at her. 'So, you didn't drop anything here? When you found the body?'

Rachel shook her head. 'No, but there's an empty glass on the desk.'

Another stare. 'Okay. So, what time did you find Mr Chapman?'

'I'd only just come down,' answered Fran. 'So, it would have been a little after seven.'

'And what time do you start work, Rachel?'

'Um, six...' She dropped her head. 'I was a little late this morning though, so about ten past.'

'And, as far as you know, no one else has been into the study?'

'No, there's Derek, but he—'

'Derek?' Helen's head jerked up.

'He's the caretaker, and chauffeur... he does a lot of things.'

'And where is he?'

Rachel pressed her lips together. 'I don't know exactly. Probably in the garage, or... he lives here too, the coach house, it's the red-brick building at the side, but he has workrooms too, in the outbuildings around the back.'

Helen nodded. 'And would he be responsible for security here?'

'Yes, that's right. He does a check first thing every morning, he will have already been round.'

'And found nothing?'

Rachel shook his head. 'No, he would have said.'

'When does he come on duty?'

'Six, the same time as I do.'

With one final sweep of the room, Helen picked her way carefully back towards them. 'Right, ladies. Out we go.' She pulled the door closed behind her, and peeled off her gloves, smiling at Rachel. 'I'm Detective Chief Inspector Helen Bradley – Nell – and you are?'

'Rachel Allen... I'm the housekeeper here.'

For a moment Nell held her look and then her face softened. 'Has anyone made you a cup of tea yet, Rachel?'

'Yes, Fran, she—'

'Excellent. We'll go and have another in a few minutes, just as soon as my—' She broke off at the sound of tyres on gravel. 'Excellent, right on cue.'

It took a minute for the two officers to collect what they needed from the boot of the car, but Nell began speaking again before they had even finished climbing the steps to the front door.

'This is Detective Constables Owen Holmes and Clare Palmer.' She gave them both a tight smile as they approached, looking a little awed by the grandeur of the house. Fran knew exactly how they felt.

'Morning,' began Nell immediately. 'Right then, we've got a body in the study, this room here. A Mr Chapman, owner of the house. It will be pretty evident how he died when you get in there, but I've only just got here myself so, pathologist please, quick as you can, plus the usual.' She looked behind her. 'And get the hallway taped off. We're lucky he died in the study, this is a bloody big house and I don't want folks traipsing around any more than they have to. Get a uniform on it, please. No one is to come down here.' She paused for a moment to check that her officers were still with her before continuing.

'This is Rachel, the housekeeper, who found the body and, as yet, one of the only three people up and about.'

'Oh...' Fran made a small noise in her throat, colouring as all eyes turned to her. 'Sorry, no, there's four people up and about.' She paused, preparing herself for the inevitable response to her next statement. 'Um, Adam's here as well. He's been helping me. He's in the kitchen.'

Fran almost buckled under the weight of the look Nell gave her. She turned back to her detectives. 'My apologies. One of only four people up and about. Fran here is a hired caterer, brought in for the weekend. Francesca Eve, would you believe... and also Adam Smith.' She took in the slightly raised eyebrows of her officers. 'I know, that's what I thought... The fourth person is the caretaker, a man called Derek. So, first things first – Rachel, can you go with DC Holmes and fetch Derek from wherever he is, and bring him back here, please?'

'I could ring him,' offered Rachel. 'Or text, that's how we usually keep in touch and—'

'Thank you, but no, go on foot, please. Oh, and when you get back, come to the kitchen. Owen, I want a tour of the building with Derek, please, starting from this point here. He's already checked security this morning apparently, but in view of events I want another, please. Windows and doors checked for anything unusual, any sign of a break-in, locks being tampered with. Anything Derek thinks doesn't look right. We've got a houseful here, guests all enjoying a weekend in the country. Needless to say, none of them are going anywhere now. There's a Mrs Chapman as well, still in bed, knows nothing at the moment. So be thorough, but don't waste time either. I want as much done as we can before the wife gets hysterical. I'll talk to her, and the others too, but don't let's wake them up yet, I want to surprise them.' She nodded. 'I think that's it for now. I'm going to the kitchen... which is where?' She looked at Rachel.

'Past the staircase, through the door on the left and it's the room opposite.'

Nell nodded. 'So, I'll be in there, taking Fran with me for the moment. Clare, you stay here and coordinate everyone arriving, and if any of the guests or the wife appears then—' She swivelled her head. 'What's that room there?' She pointed to the room on the right, just opposite the staircase.

'The drawing room,' supplied Rachel.

'Right, let me know, and then shepherd anyone in there until we know what we're looking at here.' She stared at DC Holmes. 'Go on then, off you go.'

Fran had scarcely heard anyone speak as fast and as precisely as Nell Bradley, seemingly without ever taking a breath. There was a softer side to her too, which Fran had discovered the last time they'd met, but she certainly wouldn't want to get on her wrong side.

Adam had been sitting at the kitchen's central island unit, perched on a stool and nursing a cup of coffee. He scrambled to his feet the moment Nell entered the room.

'Hello, Adam, nice to see you again, and please, don't get up on my account.' She smiled at him sweetly. 'Actually, you might prefer to be seated while I read you the riot act. And no, before you ask, you may not see the body.'

Adam put a hand to his chest, indignation written all over his face. 'Why would I possibly want to see a dead body?'

He might protest but it was a legitimate question. Adam was... hard to describe. Fran and he had met a little over a year ago when his mum, a client of Fran's, had been accused of murdering one of the guests at her own birthday party. Adam, having no one else to turn to, had sought out Fran's help in clearing his mum's name and together they had uncovered the identity of the real murderer. Incredibly intelligent, with a ready wit, cheeky smile, and at times unorthodox approach to solving problems, he possessed a rather unique talent for getting to the bottom of puzzles. One that Nell had been simultaneously impressed and frustrated by.

Nell glanced at Fran. 'I've been told that you're here help-ing, Adam, which I assume means in a catering capacity. That being the case I don't need to ask if you've left your lock picks, listening devices and other "gadgetry" at home, do I?'

Adam flashed Fran a somewhat nervous look. 'Is that a rhetorical question?' he asked.

'It should be. But in your case, no, it isn't. So, have you left those things at home?'

Adam nodded, twice. But he'd retaken his seat so his hands were on his lap, underneath the table. Fran couldn't be sure his fingers weren't crossed.

Nell held Adam's look for several more seconds, before smiling and taking a breath. 'So, why are you here?'

'Helping Fran,' said Adam. 'I promise.'

Fran prayed he wouldn't mention the other reason she had let him join her. Nell would most likely take a very dim view.

'And I wasn't going to come, but Fran promised there'd be cake, so...'

'And has there been?'

Adam looked wary. 'Yes.'

'Excellent. So, to get things straight, I am happy for you to eat cake and help Fran in any catering-related capacity, but you are not, I repeat not, to interfere in my investigation in any way. You are not to interview guests, or hunt for clues, or bug people's conversations because, apart from anything else, Adam, you being here at the time of death also means that you're a suspect. Have I made myself clear?'

The look on Adam's face made Fran want to howl with laughter. You'd never know it, but Nell had a soft spot for Adam, they all did. You couldn't help it, he was just so endearing.

Nell suddenly grinned. 'My day just gets better and better. Now, cup of tea, anyone? Let's make one for Rachel, she looked as if she was about to fall down.'

Several minutes later Rachel reappeared, just as Nell was fishing teabags from a row of mugs while simultaneously trying to look around the impressive space she found herself in. It was one of the things which Fran had noticed about Nell quite early on; that she could make herself instantly at home in any situation. Given what she did for a living, Fran supposed she had learned to. Fran had the same ability when it came to kitchens.

'This is quite some place,' Nell remarked. 'How long have you worked here, Rachel?'

Rachel had taken a seat at the island, perching nervously on a stool. 'Um, a little over ten years.'

'And do you like it here?'

'It's a beautiful house.'

Nell's eyes narrowed. 'And the owners, Mr and Mrs Chapman, they're good employers, are they?'

Rachel swallowed, darting a look at Fran, who was standing by the cooker. 'Yes, I... There's never been any problems.'

'Good. So, you didn't kill Mr Chapman then?'

'No!'

Fran had never seen anyone's face drain of colour quite so fast. She had forgotten just how brusque Nell's manner could be. Necessary, but daunting all the same. Poor Rachel didn't know what had hit her.

Nell held Rachel's look for just a moment, and then she smiled. 'Apologies, but it's a necessary question. One I shall be asking you again, no doubt. You and Fran are also suspects, obviously, as is Derek, so let's make that clear from the start; you're no different from anyone else in the house. However, my team and I are going to need a lot of help while we're here and it would be good to know I can rely on you for that. I trust that's okay?'

Fran didn't dare argue.

Nell smiled again, placing a mug in front of Rachel before handing another to Fran. 'I bet this one hasn't told you about the last murder she was involved with, has she?'

Rachel looked up, startled.

'Thought not. How long ago was it now, Fran? Not long.'

'No, erm, just over a year.'

'Really? Is it that long? Anyway... I get a phone call from one of my DCs. "Ma'am, you're never going to believe this, but that Becky Pearson case, we've got the murderer in custody, a taped confession, and two people downstairs who solved the whole thing." He was right, I almost didn't believe him, but it was true. A woman at a party Fran catered for dropped down dead. Not at the party, weeks later, poisoned. Very nasty. And Fran here, along with Adam, her trusty sidekick, worked it all out. They caused me no end of problems, I can tell you. Civilians working on a case, you can imagine what *my* boss said about that, and then I had to go and bloody thank them, 'cause they were right, they had worked it all out. One very nasty piece of work, confessed, tried, and now safely behind bars. It's going to be a very long time before she sees the light of day.'

'She?' queried Rachel, eyes wide.

'Yes. Revenge. A dish served incredibly cold, as it happened. Killed someone else as well.' She pursed her lips. 'So, there you go. Nowt so queer as folk, as they say.'

Rachel nodded and buried her face in her mug. It was all just beginning to hit her.

Almost immediately, Nell drew in a long breath. 'So, Rachel, tell me about Mrs Chapman.' Her eyes narrowed. 'Only, her husband is lying in the study with his head bashed in and she's... what? Still in the Land of Nod. A heavy sleeper, is she?'

'Um... I don't know. But there was a party last night. Everyone had quite a lot to drink and besides...' Rachel toyed with the handle of her mug.

'Yes?'

'She and Mr Chapman have separate bedrooms, adjoining, but she might not have realised he wasn't there.'

There was a long pause. 'I see,' said Nell eventually. 'Okay, well, at some point she's going to wake up, as, presumably, are the other guests. And that's when it all begins to get a little more complicated. Could you make me a list of everyone in the house, please?'

'They'll be wanting breakfast,' replied Rachel, nodding. 'We're supposed to be serving them, but...'

'Quite right,' replied Nell. 'They're going to have to wait but have some yourself, Rachel, if you can face it. And...' She tipped her head to one side. 'Once you've had yours, could I ask you to make something for my DCs? Derek too perhaps. It might make you feel better if you've got something to do.'

'I could make some toast, or...'

Nell smiled. 'Excellent idea. Adam can help you. And while you're doing that, Fran and I can have a little chat. Is there somewhere we can go? Somewhere private, but where I can also keep an eye on things?'

Fran looked back at Rachel. 'Perhaps the morning room?' she suggested. 'You can see the front door from there.'

'The morning room it is, Fran. Bring your tea.'

It was by far Fran's favourite room in the house; seemingly always bathed in sunshine. As its name suggested, it faced east, and took full advantage of the rising sun. By contrast, the kitchen had been dark and far more suited to the morning's sombre mood than this bright space which was flooded with dancing light. It overlooked the garden too, and the view from the windows was filled with green and growing things. It didn't seem right, somehow.

Nell took a chair which gave her a view straight down the hallway to the front door. She would also be able to see anyone who went either up or down the stairs, as well as into the study. She beckoned for Fran to sit down.

'Good vantage point, this,' she commented. And Fran knew exactly what she was driving at. Because if you had been sitting there, at the right time, perhaps in the dim light of evening or the darkness of the night itself, you could see anyone entering or leaving the room where Keith Chapman had been bludgeoned to death. Nell was already fishing for potential witnesses.

She folded her legs elegantly to one side and looked steadily at Fran, her hands held in front of her, fingers steepled and just touching her chin. 'So, tell me,' she said, 'the housekeeper... Apart from Derek, she was the first one up, and she found the body. What's your impression of her?'

Fran blanched. 'A good one,' she replied without hesitation. 'Salt of the earth. A bloody hard worker, friendly, diplomatic and, before you ask, no, I don't think she killed him.'

Nell licked her lips. 'Fair enough,' she said. 'Well, Fran, I don't know what to say. This is... unusual, isn't it? I really didn't expect to be seeing you again.'

Fran dropped her head. 'I didn't expect it either,' she said. 'But—'

'But... given that you are here, I'd be foolish not to make the most of it. I need to get a handle on this, and quickly. It's going to take a huge amount of time to take everyone's statements, process them, analyse them. And, at the moment, I don't have much to go on – no murder weapon – I don't even have the time of death until the pathologist gets here. But I think you might be able to help me. You know the people here, enough to have formed an opinion of them, anyway. You know the house, and you know as much about the events of the weekend as anyone. What's gone on here, Fran?'

She shook her head. 'I don't know. Honestly... Everything seemed fine. People were enjoying themselves, some more than others admittedly, and it was late when I finally got to bed last night. Everyone had already gone up, fit and well as far as I could tell. I got up again this morning and... well, that's when Rachel found him, Mr Chapman.'

'So, you didn't hear any disturbances in the night?'

'No, none, sorry.'

'Okay... So, run through the set-up for me. Tell me briefly about the weekend. Who's here and why?'

Fran wriggled, feeling swallowed by the depths of the comfy chair. She sat a little more upright, mug balanced on her lap.

'I was asked to cater for the party about three months ago, by Mrs Chapman. In fact, I was engaged for the whole weekend – arriving on Friday and, well, I guess this won't be happening now, but leaving some time this afternoon once all the guests had departed.' She looked to Nell for confirmation but she remained expressionless. 'Mr Chapman is a property developer, although not simply houses, we're talking big stuff – huge developments; shops, offices, the lot. Every now and again, when he has a new project and is looking for backers, he hosts these weekend house parties. Five or six guests who he wines and dines before deciding who he wants to go in with him. That's pretty much it. There was a cocktail reception on Friday, a whole host of stuff going on yesterday, culminating in a swanky dinner in the evening and then today, well... that's it, I think.'

'And is this the first time you've worked with them?'

Fran nodded. 'The request came via a contact form on my website, but I've since learned that Mrs Chapman had been given my name by a woman whose daughter's wedding I catered for last Christmas.'

'And what do you think of them? Rachel evidently doesn't like them.'

Fran looked up. 'Doesn't she? How do you know that?'

'Because when I asked her if she liked it here, she said it's a beautiful house. It is, but that's not what I asked.'

Fran blushed a little. She had asked the exact same question two days ago and received the same answer. Fran had spotted it too, but that didn't mean Rachel was guilty of anything.

'I don't think she meant anything by it, just that—'

'Fran, this is off the record,' said Nell, leaning forward. 'For now... You'll be asked all this again for your statement, and you can be diplomatic then as long as you tell the truth. Right now, I just want to know what you really think of them.'

Fran took a deep breath. She didn't like to speak ill of anyone, particularly someone who had died, but neither did she want to hide the truth. It had been hard to keep up with Nell's train of thought since she arrived. Her mind moved fast, and her mouth even faster, but it was clear what she was thinking: that someone in the house had killed Mr Chapman, and if that was the case then, in all likelihood, the murderer was still among them. She was also very well aware that, despite what she might say, as far as Nell Bradley was concerned, nothing was off the record, not if it had relevance to the case.

'I think the Chapmans are used to getting what they want,' she said, feeling around for the best way to explain. 'I mean, you only have to look at this place to see how wealthy they are, and the point about this whole weekend has been to demonstrate not only their status, but the power that gives them. It's been very evident from things they've said *and* done. Jobs like these are few and far between and I'm grateful to be asked – their name on my list of clients is going to show my business in a good light – but, no, I don't like them. Morals of alley cats.'

Nell was clearly thinking. 'Hmm... what's more than likely then, when we get to the bottom of all this, is that we're going to discover it's yet another dirty squabble over money. The root of all evil. It is, you know.' She took several sips of her tea, staring down the hallway as she did so. It was clear where her mind was; focused on the room which contained all the questions. And the answers.

She glanced at her watch. 'We're quite likely to get interrupted, but take me back to when you first arrived, Fran. This was on Friday, was it?'

'Yes, around nine in the morning.'

'And what happened then? Talk me through it.'

3

FORTY-EIGHT HOURS EARLIER – FRIDAY

'And so you see, Francesca – may I call you Francesca? – that really is the essence of this weekend. I want our guests to feel utterly at ease. I never want them to feel thirsty or hungry, and it will be your job to second-guess their every need. If they have to ask for anything, it will reflect extremely poorly upon my skills as a hostess, and that simply cannot happen. You are here to make me look good. Mr Chapman too, of course, although...' Mimi Chapman glanced out of the window. 'His requirements are a little different from mine.' She twisted a heavy gold bracelet at her wrist. 'So, Francesca, may I assume we have an understanding?'

Fran held her look. 'Oh, absolutely,' she replied, with a smile that was one hundred per cent fake.

Fran had dressed carefully for this initial meeting: smart, professional, but other than a touch of lipstick, she wore no other make-up. Her skin didn't need it, but what was more important was that one, she felt comfortable, and two, on no account should she outshine her client. Not that she needed to worry on that score. Mimi Chapman dressed appropriately to her surroundings and if you lived in a three-million-pound house (Fran had done her homework), Mimi's cream silk blouse and trousers were entirely representative of the wealthy life-style she led.

On their arrival at Claremont House, Fran and Adam had been met by a woman called Rachel. Introducing herself as the housekeeper, Rachel had led them along a sumptuous hallway into a room which overlooked the rear garden. Indicating that they should take a seat, Rachel withdrew almost immediately, and the full fifteen minutes which Mimi had kept Fran waiting had given her plenty of time to assess her surroundings. And form an impression of her client.

Mimi's appearance, therefore, had been no surprise, and neither had her manner. From the top of her expertly-dyed golden-blonde hair to the red soles of her Louboutin shoes, Fran had very quickly grasped the measure of Mimi Chapman. And while a part of her was fully prepared to feel overawed, under-dressed and utterly unworthy in Mimi's presence, the better part of her smiled in understanding. Fran might be small, with unruly short dark hair, a face full of freckles, and a smattering of grey hairs (not many), but generally she was happy with her lot.

Fran smiled again. 'May I assume you were happy with everything I sent you?' she asked. 'In particular, the menu choices themselves?'

Mimi studied a long pale-blue fingernail. A tiny gold star adorned its tip. 'Fine, fine... You come highly recommended, Francesca, I trust you know what you're doing. Now, I must get on. Wait here and I'll ask Rachel to collect you, assuming I can find her of course.' She flashed her perfect smile at Fran and glided from the room, completely ignoring Adam – she hadn't even looked at him in all the time they'd been speaking.

Fran watched as Mimi left, the beginning of a wry smile turning up the corners of her mouth, and she raised her eyebrows at Adam in amusement. They wandered through to the adjoining conservatory to wait for Rachel, where double doors were open to the garden, the heavy scent of old-fashioned roses filling the air. This really was a heavenly spot. Later, she would take a tour of the gardens and see where were the best places to serve drinks and lay out refreshments, but for now she was happy enough to bask in the surroundings and, above all, stay calm: she had a busy time ahead of her.

Rachel arrived nearly twenty minutes later, full of apologies, which Fran batted away. 'It's fine, please, don't worry,' she said. 'I'm sure you have a million-and-one things to do. It isn't just us who's going to be busy this weekend.'

Rachel smiled. 'Shall I take you up to your rooms first, or show you the kitchen? Which would you prefer?'

'Whichever suits you.'

'Let's go upstairs then maybe...' She checked her watch. 'Would you both like a cup of tea?'

'Love one,' replied Fran, taking a last look around the room. 'It's a beautiful house. Have you worked here long?'

'Just over ten years,' replied Rachel, indicating that she and Adam should walk on ahead.

Her reply surprised Fran. Rachel didn't look much older than her, and that would mean she had started work here around her thirtieth year. It struck Fran as odd for someone so young to have stayed for that length of time.

Rachel smiled at her reaction. 'You're right, the years *have* rather crept up on me. I never intended to stay that long but I needed somewhere to live when I came here, so it suited me.' She lowered her voice. 'Disastrous love affair, so it was as much out of necessity as anything else.'

'You must like it here, then?'

'It's a beautiful house,' she replied.

They had reached the bottom of a wide mahogany staircase which turned sedately to the upper level of the house and an impressive galleried landing.

'You'll get the layout here pretty quick,' said Rachel. 'It's basically in two halves. This half is where all the principal rooms lie and through there,' she pointed to an archway just beyond the stairs, 'is the other half.' She grinned. 'The lesser half. There's a rear hallway where you'll find the kitchen, utility rooms, and a smaller sitting room. It also leads outside and to the coach house, which is where Derek lives.'

'Derek?'

'He's the chauffeur, gardener, handyman, whatever-needs-doing-man.'

Fran nodded, giving Adam a smile. 'I hope you're remembering all this.'

'There's also a second staircase, which would have been servants only in the good old days but which now leads down to the cellar and right up to the attic. Those are the stairs you'll normally use, but we'll take these for now.'

Fran followed her up, pausing midway, arrested by an enormous painting which filled the wall. It was a riot of colour, vibrant and immensely striking.

'Beautiful, isn't it? Some of the paintings aren't my thing at all, but I love these. Mr Chapman collects them, they're by Smith-Cline. There's another in his study, which is worth a fortune. I mean, most of the paintings here are, but I wouldn't give them house room, if I had a house, that is...' She smiled. 'You know what I mean though, but this one is lovely.'

'It's stunning.' Fran pulled her gaze away and carried on up the stairs, where another wall was filled with artwork. Huge botanical prints this time, lush ferns and larger-than-life monstera leaves. Everywhere she looked there was a feast for the eyes. And the feet. Fran didn't think she had ever walked on carpet with such a deep pile.

Rachel pointed to her left at the head of the stairs. 'So, in clockwise order, guest suites three, four and five, and through there,' she pointed to another archway on her right, 'is the principal suite. Guest suites one and two are also to the right, just around the turn of the bannister. That's where we're heading. There's a door through to the rear half of the house, just as there is downstairs and, beyond it, are three more bedrooms, another bathroom and the back stairs to the top level of the house, which is where I am.'

'Okay, I think I've got that.'

'Don't worry, if either of you take anything up to one of the private rooms, I'll make sure you know where you're going.'

'I wanted to say thank you for the list of guests you sent me. It was really helpful,' replied Fran. 'I've been able to do some homework and it makes my job so much easier, just knowing a few simple details.'

Rachel's cheeks dimpled. 'You're very welcome. There have been some last-minute room changes, there always are, but I've made a list for you, it's downstairs. Anyway, let's get you to your rooms and then we can get the kettle on.'

Rachel walked the length of the landing and then, turning a corner, pushed open the door which led through to the rear part of the house. Following her, it was evident to Fran that this part of the house, while still luxurious and beautifully furnished, slightly lacked the wow factor of the area they had just passed through. She smiled to herself – she was definitely below stairs when it came to ranking.

Her room was still incredible though. Or rather *rooms*, plural. A sitting room lay through an interconnecting door from the bedroom, beyond which was an ensuite bathroom roughly the size of her living room at home. She had a sudden almost overwhelming desire to throw herself on the bed simply to see how soft it was. Perhaps she would, once she was alone again.

'Adam, you're in the room next door. Shall I give you both a few minutes to settle in?' asked Rachel. 'And I'll get Derek to bring up your things, he shouldn't be long.'

But Fran shook her head. 'There's really no need. I might need a hand with one or two bits of kitchen equipment I brought, but Adam can help with those and the rest of our things. We travel pretty light. Besides, you and Derek both have enough to do without waiting on us.'

Rachel looked about to argue, but Fran cut her off. 'Please, I'll feel awful if you do.'

There was a slight dip of the head. 'Okay, but we're here to help,' she replied.

'As are we, Rachel.' Fran smiled. 'It's a beautiful room.' She nodded to the flowers which stood on a small table in front of the window. 'You?'

Rachel nodded. 'Fresh from the garden this morning.'

'Thank you. It's all lovely.' She took another look round her. 'Right, I'll just pop to the loo if I may and then we'll be with you for that cuppa. Where do I find the kitchen?'

Rachel pointed through the open bedroom doorway. 'Down the back stairs and it's the room immediately opposite, you can't miss it. How do you both take your tea?'

'Just milk for me, please,' answered Fran with a smile.

Adam simply nodded. He was still a little awestruck.

She waited until Rachel and Adam had both left before running headlong at the bed, throwing herself on top of it and grinning like a loon as she bounced around for a few moments. This weekend was going to be one of the hardest of her career, for people who, if she wasn't much mistaken, would be less than forgiving should anything not go according to plan. But it wasn't without its pleasures either and Fran was determined to make the most of it.

Ten minutes later, with Adam following behind, Fran pushed open the kitchen door and got her first glimpse of what was to be her domain for the next two days. It was big and impressive, particularly if you liked black marble, which Fran didn't, but what was more important than looks was the kind of space it would be to cook in. Was it a cook's kitchen or did it just look nice? If she was lucky, it would be both.

Rachel was sitting at one end of a long island unit which ran virtually the whole length of the room. Beside her sat a man of similar age, with what Fran could only describe as one of the friendliest faces she'd ever seen. It was round, and cheeky, with expressive dimples and topped with receding dark hair, the whole combination giving the impression of openness and honesty. Fran liked him instantly on sight.

He got to his feet as Fran came into the room. 'You must be Francesca,' he said. 'And Adam. Welcome to Claremont House.'

Fran held out her hand. 'Fran, please. Francesca looks good on my business cards but that's about all the use I have for it. You must be Derek?' She smiled.

Beside her, Adam looked, if not altogether relaxed, then at least not as if he wanted to run away either. When she'd first met him, he had been very unsure of himself around people. He hadn't had an easy time of it when he was younger, his intelligence hampering development of friendships among a peer group who had seemingly little in common with him. It had also clashed with an education system that hadn't known quite what to make of Adam, the result of which had been expulsion and an end to formal education. All of which had contributed to his living an almost hermit-like existence. Until he'd met Fran, that is, and his mum had almost been accused of murder. That had brought him out of his shell pretty smartish. He still saw the world differently from a lot of people but, as Fran was finding out, that was often more of a help than a hindrance.

'Guilty as charged,' said Derek. He moved around the island to shake both their hands in turn. 'Come and sit down. Are you a biscuit sort of a person?' he asked Adam, indicating a plate full of cookies.

'I'm a biscuit and especially a cake person,' he replied. 'Apparently I have hollow legs.'

Fran smiled. Her initial assessment of him still held.

'As am I,' added Fran, with a rueful look towards her stomach, which was not her greatest asset. 'In fact, I brought a stash of biscuits with me and some cakes. For the use of, obviously. I'll fetch them in a bit.'

Derek flashed Rachel a glance. 'I think we like them, don't you?' He took a swig from a mug in front of him. 'You'll let me help you with your things though, will you? Not because I think you can't manage, nothing like that. But it's my job and I reckon everyone should get a proper welcome.'

Fran dipped her head, answering for them both. 'Then, thank you. I don't have a great deal with me, but there's some kitchen equipment I brought in case—' She looked around at the bank of cupboards which lined one wall. 'I wasn't sure what you would have here. So, tell me, Rachel, what sort of a kitchen is this?' She had already deduced that it wouldn't be the easiest place to work in.

Rachel wrinkled her nose. 'One that's a pain in the arse,' she replied, smiling. 'This...' she tapped the island, 'is in entirely the wrong place for starters. Because everything you need is in these cupboards here, but the cooker is over there. You have to walk around the damn thing every single time. I hope you've got some comfortable shoes, you'll end up walking miles.'

Fran nodded. 'So, do you usually do all the cooking?'

The housekeeper nodded. 'But more often than not it's just for me and Derek. Mrs Chapman doesn't eat much, or she isn't here... let's just say she's out a lot. And Mr Chapman stays in London most of the time. But I don't do fancy stuff,' she added. 'Not like you're going to be doing.' She searched Fran's face. 'So, you won't be stepping on my toes, nothing like that. I'm happy to help, but...' She looked at Derek again. 'I was actually relieved when Mrs Chapman said she was getting someone in, I wouldn't want the pressure.'

'Thanks, Rachel, I'll be very grateful for your help.' Fran eyed the bank of cupboards again, which stretched to the ceiling. 'Not least of all because I won't be able to reach half of what's in those. Did all my orders arrive okay?'

Rachel nodded. 'I've put everything in the pantry for now. I didn't know where you'd want things, but I'll help you move stuff to wherever it needs to go.'

'Sounds good.' Fran took a biscuit and dunked it in her tea. 'And this is lovely, thank you.'

Derek picked up his mug and drained the contents in one swallow. 'Thanks, Rachel, I must get on.' He turned to look at Fran. 'If you have your car keys on you, I can make a start with your things, if you like. While you finish your tea.'

Fran couldn't help but smile. 'Which was your cunning plan all along, wasn't it? Something tells me we were never going to be allowed to carry our bags up to our rooms.'

But Derek merely smiled, catching Rachel's eye as he did so.

Fran fished in her pocket for her car keys and handed them over. 'There're just two bags, in the boot: the black one is Adam's and mine's the tatty brown one. And also, two boxes on the back seat which are for in here, if that's okay.'

Derek nodded. 'And would you have any objection to my moving your car? I can bring it around the back for you, to the courtyard. You can get to it through the back door then, save having to go all the way around.'

Rachel cleared her throat. 'What Derek is trying to say is that he needs it off the front driveway because Mrs Chapman doesn't like...' She trailed off. 'And Derek needs to rake the drive.'

Fran looked up, astonished, but she bit back her comment. 'Of course, move it where you like, Derek. I'm sorry, I wasn't thinking.'

'No worries, I'll catch you all later.' And with that, he was gone.

Fran was beginning to realise there was going to be a whole

lot more to this weekend than just providing exquisite meals. She sipped her tea.

'I can see I'm going to need your help, Rachel,' she said.

'Oh?'

'Because I'm used to catering for lavish parties, weddings, big bashes at country houses, but...' She toyed with the handle of her mug. 'I don't want to say anything I shouldn't, but I get the feeling that your employers are... perhaps a little more particular than some. Would that be right?'

Rachel took a biscuit and pulled it apart to get at the cream inside. 'I've never worked as a housekeeper for anyone other than them so I wouldn't know, but yes, Mrs Chapman can be a little... difficult sometimes.'

'Then I shall rely on you to keep me straight,' said Fran. 'And tell me what I should or shouldn't do. I can see how important this weekend is, and I don't want anything I do to reflect badly on you or Derek. So please, just tell me if I'm doing something wrong.'

Rachel smiled. 'Thank you, I will. But I'm sure you'll be fine. It's good you're here early anyhow. There'll be plenty of time to go through things in a bit.' She tucked her hair behind her ears with another glance at the clock. 'I must go and get changed,' she added. 'Mrs Chapman likes me to be in uniform by ten. Will you be all right here for a few minutes?'

'Perfectly. We'll finish our tea and then have a nosey, if that's okay? Just the kitchen though, we won't wander anywhere else.'

Fran watched as Rachel left the room and then got to her feet, smiling at Adam, who was grinning from ear to ear.

'This place is incredible,' he said. 'And just what I've been looking for as the setting for my new game. It's like a house in an Agatha Christie book. Where there's a billiard room and a study and the butler did it with a candlestick. Okay, so there're going to be aliens in my version, but you get the idea. I think it's going to be perfect.'

Fran looked around, trying to orientate herself in the space where she would be spending so much time. 'That it might be, but as far as the catering goes, this room looks lovely, but the lighting is poor, the sink's in entirely the wrong place and, as Rachel already said, the island unit should have been offset so that the cooker is easily accessible. Still, we'll manage; the house *is* beautiful, and the setting's incredible. I'm not sure how much spare time we'll have though, Adam, or how much you'll be able to explore. Once the guests arrive, that's going to be it, I think.'

Adam shrugged easily. 'That's okay, I'll pick things up.' Fran didn't doubt it. She might have a photographic memory when it came to her work, but Adam was one of the most observant people she knew. Or rather, he saw things that most people missed.

She was still poking about in the vast array of cupboards when Derek returned, carrying both of her boxes at once. He set them down on the island unit and then handed her back her car keys.

'I've scribbled down my mobile number for you,' he said, pulling a piece of paper out of the top pocket of his shirt. 'That way you can message me if you need anything doing. Anything at all.'

Fran had left her phone upstairs with her handbag but she thanked him, smiling at his receding back. Now she was all set. She had her things, and she knew the lie of the land: it was time to get down to business. First things first, however.

'Shall we get our bags unpacked before we do anything else?' she suggested. 'I know we haven't brought much with us, but the guests are due from early afternoon and with the champagne reception planned for this evening, it'll be very late by the time we can even think about getting to bed. I don't know about you, but I'll want to just fall in it, without having to sort out my stuff first.' She didn't say so but having her own things in place would help settle her nerves too.

They quickly finished their tea and headed up the back stairs to their rooms.

It was as she was hanging up her dress for the evening in the wardrobe that Fran heard raised voices, or rather *one* raised voice, coming from the hallway outside her room. Fran may have only met her once, but Mimi Chapman's tone was unmistakable.

'Is it, or is it not, your job to attend to such things?'

Fran didn't quite catch the reply and, without thinking, stepped closer to the door.

'Then why is that room not ready?'

'I'm sorry, Mrs Chapman. I had prepared that room, but I hadn't realised it had been used since.'

There was a pause.

'And what do you mean by that? If you're insinuating—'

'I'm not, I'm sorry. I'll attend to the room straight away.'

'I should think so. For heaven's sake, must I do everything in this house? Rachel, I really hope I don't need to impress upon you again the importance of this weekend. Can you imagine the embarrassment if Mr Knight had arrived to find his room in such disarray?'

'No, clearly, I... Well, I would have checked it again before his arrival.'

'Would you? Would you really?'

'Yes, I... Like I said, I thought the room was already prepared. I didn't think that anyone had used it.'

'Rachel, may I remind you that I pay you to keep this house in a manner which I believe I have set out for you on many occasions. Is that not right?'

'Yes, Mrs Chapman.'

'I do not pay you to make assumptions. I pay you to follow my instructions, and my instructions have always been that all the upper rooms in the house are to be set straight by ten in the morning, unless anyone has made a prior arrangement. Had I made any such arrangement with you?'

'No, Mrs Chapman, but...'

'Yes?'

Another pause. 'Well... that isn't your room, and I—'

'This is my house and as such, I can sleep in any bed I damn well please! Get it sorted. Quickly!'

Fran jumped back as movement passed her door, her cheeks burning on Rachel's behalf. Nobody deserved to be spoken to in such a way, but she was racked with indecision. Fran was being paid to cater for a weekend house party and whatever the politics of the house were, they were also none of her business. But her impressions of Rachel so far had all been good and Mimi's treatment of her really hadn't sounded fair.

She stood stock-still until she was sure there was no further movement outside and then eased open her door. The hallway was empty, but the doorway to a room on her far left now stood open. She crept forward.

The entrance to the room gave only a view of the window opposite, underneath which stood a small table similar to that in her own room. It too held a vase full of fresh flowers. But she could definitely hear movement coming from within. Taking a breath, Fran stepped inside.

'Rachel?'

The housekeeper swung around from where she was busy stripping the bed.

Fran hesitated, caught by the look on Rachel's face. 'Sorry... is everything okay?'

Almost immediately, the beaming smile was back in place. 'Yes, perfectly.'

'Only I heard... It sounded like Mrs Chapman chewing your ear off. I wondered if you were all right.'

'Yes, I'm fine. She does that. Every now and again. I expect she's just a bit on edge over the weekend.'

Fran looked around, at the sheet on the floor which Rachel had obviously already stripped from the bed. Otherwise, there was nothing at all which appeared out of place, just like the rest of the house.

'Can I give you a hand?' she asked.

Rachel shook her head firmly. 'Thank you, but I can't ask you to do that. I should have checked the room, but it's no matter, it won't take long to remake the bed.'

Fran frowned. 'Yet this isn't Mrs Chapman's room. Does she sleepwalk or something? Why was she sleeping here?'

A faint trace of a smile crossed Rachel's face. 'I don't think she was sleeping.'

Fran stared at her, colour suddenly flushing her cheeks as she realised what Rachel was implying. No, not implying...

'Oh my God, she's having an affair?' whispered Fran. 'Who with?'

Rachel stopped what she was doing, a pillow in her hand. 'I don't think that's quite the right question,' she replied, ripping off the pillowcase. 'Not so much who with, but who with *this* time...'

4

Nell gave a chuckle. 'Sorry, I shouldn't laugh, but is there anything more clichéd than the rich society wife who plays around?' She frowned. 'Doesn't mean they're murderers though. Did you find out who she'd been sleeping with?'

Fran shook her head. 'No, Rachel's far too discreet, but I got the feeling it was someone she'd met up with before.'

'How so?'

'I don't know really, more an impression than anything else. Judging by the way Rachel reacted to having to change the sheets, it was something she'd had to do on more than one occasion; like Mrs Chapman often played musical beds.'

'So, this would have been on the Thursday night, the day before you arrived?'

Fran nodded.

'And where was Mr Chapman while his wife was having such a fine old time?'

'I'm not sure. Not in the house though. He didn't arrive until some time mid-afternoon on Friday, although Derek would know exactly when. He took Mr Chapman's bags inside and then brought the car around to the stable yard at the back of the house. The Chapmans don't like cars parked out the front, apparently.'

Nell tutted. 'Bad luck, that's where mine's staying. So, is that when you met Mr Chapman?'

'No, I didn't see him until the evening at the cocktail reception. I think he stayed in his room until then.' Fran gave a thin smile. 'Makes him sound like a teenager, doesn't it? But when I say room, it's not just the one room, obviously, there's a whole suite of them, all interconnecting.'

'Quite. And the guests – when did they arrive?'

'During the same afternoon. Not all together, but, again, Derek could tell you exactly when. He met some of them off the train. One couple came in their own car, I think, but Derek would have greeted them when they arrived, Rachel too. I was busy in the kitchen and I—'

'Hang on a minute. Where was Mrs Chapman when the guests were arriving?'

'I've no idea,' replied Fran. 'Again, in her room, I suppose.'

'So, she didn't greet the guests?'

Fran pulled a face. 'No, neither of them did. They didn't all meet up until the evening.'

Nell nodded. 'Is it me or is that odd?'

'Yes, that's exactly what I said, it's...' She trailed off as Nell held up a hand.

'Sorry, Fran, I'm getting ahead of myself here. Let's go back to when you were speaking with Rachel about Mrs Chapman bed-hopping. What happened after that?'

FRIDAY AFTERNOON

Fran watched from the kitchen window as Derek brought Mr Chapman's car around to the courtyard. She had no idea what model it was, but it was dark-blue, sleek and, she had no doubt, very expensive.

'So, what's Mr Chapman like?' she asked, turning around.

Rachel was busy with more floral arrangements and her face was a picture as she tried to come up with words which didn't reveal exactly what she thought of him. She tipped her head to one side.

'Let's just say he isn't how you imagine,' she replied. 'But compared with Mimi, he's polite, reserved and very quiet. He's also hardly ever here.'

'I don't get that,' said Fran. 'This is such a beautiful house, why wouldn't you want to spend all your time here?'

Rachel shrugged. 'I know, but sleepy Shropshire is not where the business is at, so London it is. He uses this place for entertaining mostly.'

'And he's a property developer, is that right?'

Rachel stared at her, a deep rose-coloured peony in her hand. She touched one of the velvety petals thoughtfully before nodding. 'It's a bit more than that, but yes, I guess that's what you'd call it.'

For a moment Fran thought she was going to say something else, but she didn't, merely placed the bloom in a vase and picked up another. Fran watched her carefully. Rachel's movements might appear nonchalant but Fran had a feeling they were anything but.

'You don't approve, though... Or have I got that wrong?'

There was the faintest trace of a smile. 'Keith Chapman doesn't just do up the odd house here and there. Instead, we're talking massive developments, redevelopments really of whole areas, things that affect a lot of people. I just don't like the way he destroys things that get in his way. You'll meet him later,' she said, before Fran could say any more. 'He usually pops in to say hello, but he's not one to chat so a quick visit will be all. Then he'll disappear until later this evening.'

Fran nodded. 'And what about the rest of the guests, when will they be arriving?'

Rachel put down a sprig of eucalyptus. 'I'll get the list for you,' she replied, crossing to a drawer in the island. She returned with a slip of paper.

'Only Mr and Mrs Dawson will arrive under their own steam. Derek will collect the others off the train.'

'Okay.' Fran checked the list again and frowned. 'But they're mostly arriving mid-afternoon. That seems very early for an evening reception which doesn't start until eight.'

'Hence the need for the rolling refreshments.'

Fran's head shot up. 'What rolling refreshments?' She glanced at Adam.

An anxious look crossed Rachel's face. 'The refreshments for the drawing room. The sandwiches, tea, biscuits... that sort of thing.'

Fran stared at her. 'Nope, still blank. As far as I'm aware, I'm to provide a cocktail reception this evening with canapés and an informal selection of food – a buffet, in other words. No one said anything about refreshments this afternoon.'

Rachel's jaw clenched. 'Can you give me a minute to pop these flowers in the study and then I think you and I ought to go over what you *think* you're providing this weekend, and with a fine tooth comb an' all.'

She bustled from the room, leaving Fran staring at Adam, her stomach churning as she frantically ran through the list of provisions she had either brought with her or had delivered. *Oh God, what if there isn't enough?* What if there were things she needed? Fran was used to making allowances for unexpected things which cropped up while she was working – power cuts, dishes of food dropped – events which could cause havoc but that she built in contingencies for. But she had never had to produce food she wasn't aware was even required.

She was still running options through her head when Rachel returned, closing the kitchen door firmly behind her.

'Right... Fran, I'm sorry. This shouldn't have happened, but... we've had this sort of thing before, and I should have checked with you days ago that you knew what you were doing.'

'Rachel, this isn't your fault. You've already given me more help than I asked for, you weren't to know.'

Rachel gave her a grateful smile. 'Well, anyway, it doesn't matter how we got here, let's see what we can do next.' She sat down at the island unit and pulled out a pad and pen from a drawer. 'Sit down and let's go through it.' She glanced at the clock. 'We've got plenty of time, don't worry.'

Fran took a seat, picking up her own notebook first. In it were all the notes she had made over the last week or so. 'So, shall I tell you what I've been asked for?' she said.

At Rachel's answering nod, she flipped over a sheet of paper. 'Starting with this evening, there's the cocktail reception with accompanying food, not a sit down, a buffet. Then tomorrow, I'm to serve breakfast, provide picnic hampers for lunch and then the evening is when all the stops come out. A champagne reception with appetisers, five-course dinner, and then on Sunday, breakfast and a buffet lunch as everyone will be leaving at different times. That's it,' she finished.

To her relief, Rachel was smiling. 'Well, thank God, you've got most of it. I had a horrible feeling that the hampers for tomorrow wouldn't have been mentioned. The only thing which is missing is the hospitality for the afternoons, both days. Although I say only things...' She broke off. 'I know it's still a lot of work.'

'What kind of things are expected?' asked Fran.

'I think the best way to describe this weekend is like an open house. The guests arrive this afternoon, Derek will bring them in, I'll show them to their rooms, and then, essentially, the house is theirs to use as they see fit until this evening. So we lay out tea and coffee in all three reception rooms, that's the drawing room, the morning room and the dining room, together with some light biscuits or cakes, sandwiches too if you like – things to stave off hunger pangs, you know. Guests just take what they like. From wherever they like. So we have to keep an eye on it too and provide top-ups if necessary. It's a pain 'cause it's usually just endless rounds of collecting cups, washing them, and replacing the tea and coffee as it gets cold.'

Adam tutted. 'But that's—'

'Incredibly wasteful, yes.' Rachel held his look. 'And we do the same thing tomorrow afternoon as well so that after the morning activities have finished and the picnics have been eaten, there's something to bridge the gap until dinner.'

Fran's head was spinning. 'Can I ask you something, Rachel? Did Mimi, Mrs Chapman, even look at the information I sent over?'

Rachel smiled. Warm and full of understanding.

'Ah...' Fran nodded. 'I thought not.' She was beginning to see very clearly what the weekend was all about. 'I haven't even budgeted for any of this.' It was the only thing she could think of to say, she was so shocked.

'Well, that, at least, is one thing you won't need to worry about. Whatever extra expenditure is incurred, just add it to your total bill and don't be stingy neither. It will be paid, I can assure you. Mrs Chapman doesn't care about the detail.'

Fran nodded. At least that was something. 'I'd better have a look at what provisions I have. I can make biscuits and cakes in my sleep but I wasn't expecting this, I may not have enough of certain things.'

'Derek will fetch whatever you need.' Rachel smiled. 'He will, honestly. And he won't mind either. And Adam and I can help. I'm only a basic cook, but I can do baking. I make a mean shortbread.'

Adam nodded. 'I can fetch and carry,' he said. 'And wash up...'

'Perfect,' replied Fran. 'I'll hold you to that. Okay, a list is what we need. And then I guess I'd better make a start.' She paused a moment. 'I'm still a bit confused though.'

'Go on.'

'Just that when the guests arrive, Mr and Mrs Chapman will both be here by the sounds of it, and yet you make it sound as if you'll be the one greeting them. They won't even see their hosts until later.'

Rachel nodded. 'Yes, that's right. At the reception.'

'Is it just me, or is that really weird?'

'Yep... but that's how they always do it. It's all part of the theatre, isn't it? The show.'

A frown wrinkled Fran's brow. 'Sorry, I'm not sure I understand.'

'Mr and Mrs Chapman are very important people. And if the guests weren't aware of that before today, then they'll soon catch on. They've all been invited because they're Mr Chapman's chosen ones, you see, the ones he's selected as potential investors. I imagine under more normal circumstances it would be the other way around – that it would be up to Mr Chapman to impress his guests in the hope that they might *want* to invest in his latest project. But no, this weekend is all about them impressing him so that he can decide who gets to invest. They'll all be vying for his seal of approval. Therefore, it wouldn't do for the Chapmans to be available at all times. They have to maintain the allure, you see, the illusion that they're so precious their guests are only permitted access to them in measured doses. Like I said, it's all part of the game, the show.'

Fran swallowed. She was beginning to regret ever accepting this job. She was also beginning to understand the frequency with which Rachel checked the large wall clock over the doorway to the utility area. It was approaching eleven and

Rachel was right, they did have plenty of time, but Fran would need to get a move on.

It took only a few minutes to make a list of the extra things which Fran would need. Instead of bringing all the required food with her, Rachel had suggested that Fran have it delivered direct to Claremont House before her arrival, and so that's what she'd done. By the time she had even set foot in the kitchen, Fran's butcher, fishmonger and greengrocer had already delivered her order. All Fran had to do was turn up, with a couple of boxes of her own, and she was ready to go. It was something else she had to thank Rachel for.

Not only had all the provisions been delivered, but Rachel's earlier comment that she had simply left all the deliveries in the pantry didn't even begin to cover the amount of thought Rachel had put into the task. Admittedly, the pantry was an enormous room, so there was plenty of space to spread out, but Rachel had also cleared one of the fridges so it only contained what Fran had ordered. It had been filled, carefully and in well-ordered sections so that Fran could see everything at a glance. Meat, separate from fish, separate from dairy produce, and fruit and vegetables too. Everything had its own space. In similar fashion, lined up along one long counter were dry goods: flours separate from sugars, herbs and spices separated out too. Neat, logical and as well as Fran could have done it herself. She picked up a tub of brownies she had baked the day before, plus one holding Florentines and carried them through to the kitchen.

'Treats,' she said, placing them on the counter. She removed the lids so Rachel could see what was inside. 'And don't be shy either or Adam will beat you to it. If you're anything like me, when you get busy you forget to eat. These are to keep us going. Derek too.' She ripped off the top sheet of her notepad. 'Are you sure Derek wouldn't mind getting these things for me? I don't need them now, but by tomorrow if possible.' She held out the sheet of paper.

'I'll take it to him now,' replied Rachel. 'It's no trouble.'

While she was gone, Fran took another look around the kitchen, making sure she knew where everything was. She prided herself on always leaving things exactly as she found them, but it would help no end if she didn't have to waste time hunting for things. With the details committed to her photographic memory, Fran turned her attention to the most immediate task in front of her. She already knew what she would make for the guests; her brain had been busy sifting ideas while she had been checking provisions, but it was all extra work and the sooner she started, the sooner she could think about what came next.

By the time Rachel returned, she had already washed her hands, donned her apron and set Adam weighing out ingredients for some biscuits, while she did the same for some scones. Cut much smaller than usual and served with a thick home-made preserve and clotted cream which she'd brought with her, no one would think about how easy (and quick) they were to make. All they would think about was the taste.

'Derek says he'll go now,' said Rachel, crossing to the sink to wash her hands too. 'As long as we promise to save him some Florentines. He adores those.'

Fran smiled. 'I'm making more, so there will be plenty left for him. It occurred to me how lovely they look, like little jewel-encrusted treasures, and the afternoon isn't so warm that they'll spoil.'

'What would you like me to do?' asked Rachel, turning around.

'Can I hold you to the shortbread?' Fran replied. 'Nice and thin.'

Rachel grinned. 'Petticoats, fingers, or another shape entirely?'

Fran thought for a moment. 'Let's go with fingers. If there's any left, they'll be easier to store. We might be able to use them elsewhere – tomorrow's picnic hampers, for example. Plus, they balance better on a saucer.'

'Fingers it is.'

The next few hours passed in a blur, albeit a very systematic and ordered blur, but at the end of it, Fran was pleased. They had accomplished what they needed and at no point had she compromised on the quality or quantity of the food they had produced. Mr and Mrs Chapman's guests should be very happy with everything that had been provided for them. And if their guests were happy, Fran hoped that Mr and Mrs Chapman would be too.

Fran hadn't seen either of her clients the entire day. Aside from her ten-minute meeting with Mrs Chapman this morning, that had been it and, although she'd been informed that Mr Chapman had now arrived, he certainly hadn't graced them with his presence. Fran had catered for some very exclusive parties in her time, but never had she been ignored to this level; it simply wasn't the way she liked to do business.

They were thoughts which simultaneously irritated and pleased her in equal measure. On the one hand she thought the Chapmans' behaviour pompous and downright rude but, on the other, she had to acknowledge that their absence meant they had all been able to get on with their work uninterrupted. Given that her client's lack of communication was the reason for the extra work in the first place, it was at least some small recompense.

It was a particularly welcome thought as she laid ready the last trays of refreshments in the dining room. A message from Rachel had alerted her to the fact that the first of the guests had just arrived and, while they were unlikely to appear immediately, they'd had a long journey and would no doubt be gasping for a cup of tea at least. Now, they could wander at will through this beautiful house and find something inviting to eat and drink in each of the reception rooms.

Fran paused to take a last look around. It was certainly the perfect setting for folks to enjoy themselves. The carefully appointed room was light and airy, with double doors held open to reveal a terrace which ran the full width of the house. Even the huge mahogany dining table didn't dominate the space. It was already laid for service, with alternating candelabras and urns tumbling with flowers from the garden. Rachel had done an incredible job. Fran wasn't especially knowledgeable about such things, but she could spot solid silver cutlery when she saw it, and the finest crystal. She ran a finger lightly across a china serving platter which lay on one end of the table. Picking it up wasn't a risk she was prepared to take, but she knew without looking it would be from a world-renowned manufacturer.

She straightened a knife and, on impulse, as she walked from the room, ducked her head through the door opposite and into the study. It was almost certainly Mr Chapman's domain and she was curious to see what it looked like, whether it could give her any clues about the client she had yet to meet.

It compared just as favourably with the rest of the house, but it was slightly smaller than the other reception rooms and had a cosier feel to it. Granted a very masculine desk stood in the centre of the room, but the light here was dimmer, the fabrics heavier, and the armchair by the window was clearly a favourite spot to sit and read. Indeed, the whole wall opposite the door was filled with floor-to-ceiling bookcases either side of a rather grand fireplace, and they made Fran feel instantly at home. She could imagine a dark winter's night, reading by the light of a lamp and the glow from the flickering fire, tucked up in the chair, with a mug of hot chocolate on the small table beside her. She smiled. Who was she kidding? But it was a nice thought just the same. A picture hung above the fireplace and Fran pushed open the door a little wider so she could see it better. Riotous colour filled the frame, burnt orange and umber, bold yellow streaks and dark smudges of deep red. It certainly drew the eye. Fran remembered what Rachel had said about the artworks which Mr Chapman collected, and she had to agree with her. She had liked the one which dominated the staircase, but although this was far smaller, it was also stunning.

As she pulled the door to, voices sounded from the staircase, descending towards the hallway. Fran automatically tucked herself back inside the room. Returning to the kitchen would mean crossing the path of whoever was there and she'd rather not meet anyone just yet. This evening's reception party was the time for that.

'All I'm saying is that I want to be here, the minute he arrives. Everyone else will be waiting for Mimi's grand entrance and, knowing her, she'll be even more fashionably late than Keith is. He'll be on his own and that's an opportunity I don't want to miss.'

Fran leaned closer to the door, still open a fraction. The voices were now at the foot of the steps.

'Peter, there's such a thing as appearing *too* keen. Keith will see it as grasping, and you know how he feels about that.'

'Listen, Keith can be a contrary bastard and what he thinks changes with the wind. This weekend isn't going to have many winners and I intend to be one of them. And I need a moment to ply him with the whisky, don't forget. I'd take it to his room if I thought I could get away with it. That stuff's five hundred quid a bottle.'

'Don't I know it.'

'Now, now, Ginny, none of that. Gracious, remember.'

'Later perhaps, now I just want something to drink. And eat. I'm bloody starving, and I intend to milk Mimi's hospitality for all its worth.'

Fran pulled open the study door and cautiously peered out into the hallway. Two figures were walking towards the morning room; he, with the rolling gait of someone carrying too much weight and she, wearing a florid maxi dress which clung to her square figure. Fran gave them a few more seconds to begin investigating what the morning room had to offer before slipping from the study and, if not quite running, walking very swiftly, past the staircase and through the door on the other side. She released the breath she was holding and scuttled back to the sanctuary of the kitchen to give Adam a hand with the washing-up.

Rachel was sitting at the island, making a note on a large pad of paper.

'A request for camomile tea,' she said, looking up. 'At seven this evening, so that Mrs Dawson may sip it while she's anointing herself in the bath.'

Fran pulled a face. 'I think I've just come across them. Nice people. Is everyone tonight going to be shallow and grasping?'

'Pretty much,' she replied. 'You'll get used to it.'

Fran's eyes flicked towards the clock on the wall. 'I don't think I want to,' she replied.

5

Fran was about to continue with her account of Friday evening when Derek and DC Holmes appeared in the doorway. Nell got to her feet.

'Ah, Owen, thank you. What did you find?'

'Nothing, Boss. Everything as it should be. And all secure.'

Beside him, Derek was positively squirming, his normal genial expression replaced by an anxious frown. Fran guessed he would have been told precisely nothing about why he had just been made to tour the building with a detective in tow.

Nell smiled. A crocodile smile. It always made Fran nervous when she did that.

'Derek, is it?' she asked. 'Sorry, I don't know your last name.'

'It's Russell, Ma'am.'

'And may I call you, Derek?' She waited for his answering nod. 'Then, Derek, I expect you're wondering what's going on. I'm sorry to have to tell you that we were called to the house this morning because Mr Chapman was found dead. Is there anything you can tell me about that?' She was watching him like a hawk, Fran realised.

'Dead?' Derek swallowed, looking anxiously at Fran. 'I

could tell something was up, but... God, Mr Chapman? Are you sure? I mean— Sorry, obviously, you're sure, but he was...'

Nell's eyebrows rose. 'Was what?'

'I was going to say fit and well.'

She gave him a piercing look and then smiled briefly. 'Far from it, I'm afraid.' She let several beats of silence tick past. 'And the answer to my question?'

Derek looked blank.

'Is there anything you can tell me about his death?'

'Me?'

She smiled. 'Uh-hm.'

'Well, no, what could I tell you?' Fran could tell he wanted to look at her. This was horrible.

'Okay, just checking,' replied Nell after another deliberate pause. 'You'll understand, I have to ask. This is a murder inquiry.'

'Murder?'

This time he did stare at Fran, his Adam's apple working. 'Rachel found the body,' she said.

'Yes, didn't I say?' replied Nell. 'What time do you come on duty, Derek?'

'Um, six...'

'And what did you do first of all?'

He flashed another glance at Fran. 'I had a cup of tea, with Rachel, we always do, we—'

'And then what did you do?'

'I did a tour of the outside of the building, and then opened up the garages as normal. I have a workshop there. It's where I keep everything – a base, if you like. This morning I needed to get everything cleaned and put away from yesterday's shoot. It was—'

'Sorry, I keep interrupting you, but a shoot? God, don't tell me these people have guns as well?'

Derek nodded. 'Clay pigeon shooting. Part of the activities

yesterday, for the guests. That's what I was doing when Rachel found me.'

'So when you did this tour of the building, the one on your own, did you notice anything unusual? Anything out of place, or broken?'

'No... but then I'd checked it all the night before so I wasn't expecting anything.'

'And are you always this efficient?'

A frown furrowed Derek's brow. 'I try to be. It's my job.'

Nell nodded. 'Sorry, I'm just trying to get a feel for things here. And when you accompanied Owen just now, had anything changed from the time you first checked?'

'Only...' Derek jerked his head back a little towards the front door, towards the study.

'Quite... This is a big house, isn't it? Does it have a cellar?'

Derek nodded.

'It does, Boss,' said Owen. 'There's a coal chute, but it was bolted from the inside. There's a padlock on it too.'

'So someone couldn't have climbed in, then shot the bolt back across to make it looked like it had never been opened?'

The detective shook his head. 'Not unless they had a key.'

Nell nodded. 'Well, if they had a key, they could have had a key for any of the doors, I suppose.'

Derek cleared his throat. 'I don't see how. There's only me what has the full set. Rachel has a smaller set, the keys she needs, and the Chapmans obviously. But even they don't have any more than the front door and the kitchen door. And I keep my set on me, all the time.' He jangled his pocket to make the point.

'Good. And an attic?'

'Again, all clear, Boss. We haven't checked all the grounds, they're quite extensive, nor all the outbuildings but, as far as anywhere you could gain access to the house, they were all secure. Windows too.'

Nell's attention was caught by something over Owen's shoulder. Uniformed police officers as well as others suiting up on the steps to the house. Fran had seen enough dramas on the television to know what they would be doing.

Nell nodded. 'With me a moment please, Owen.'

The two detectives walked back towards the study, leaving Derek staring at Fran, desperate to talk but knowing he shouldn't. He'd very sensibly come to the conclusion that Nell probably had ears like a bat. He waited until she was talking to another officer before leaning in towards Fran.

'Is that where he is?' he whispered, swallowing.

'Yes, in the study,' Fran replied. 'I probably shouldn't say too much,' she added. 'Sorry.'

'No. I guess we're all suspects, are we? I certainly seem to be.'

'Don't worry about Nell, her bark's worse than her bite. Believe it or not there's a softer side to her too.'

'Hmm... I guess she's just doing her job.' He smiled. 'Are you okay? Is Rachel? I thought there was something up, she looked... scattered just now.'

'I think her head's all over the place, the same as mine. But yes, she's okay, I am too. Bit... you know...'

'Was it really horrible? Christ, poor Rachel.'

Fran drank a little more tea. 'Not the nicest way to start a day. I've been involved...' She trailed off. She wasn't entirely sure how to sum up what had happened before. 'I got to know Nell and her team last year. I catered a party for Adam's mum and someone died, murdered and... it's a long story, but his mum was implicated and me and Adam solved the case. It seems weird calling it that, but it's what it was. What it turned out to be. But there wasn't a body, not like this anyway, it was...' Fran broke off and shuddered. She was about to continue when the study door opened. Fran nodded towards it, a warning as much as anything.

Moments later, Nell came striding back down the hallway towards them, Owen hot on her heels.

'Derek, could I ask you to show DC Holmes around the grounds, please. Everything again. Gardens, outbuildings, whatever there is here, I want it checked. The CSIs are going to have enough to do in the house, it'll be a while before we can get a team outside. So, look for anything which could have been the murder weapon. Blunt force trauma. Not a clue what it is yet, but use your initiative. Oh, and one more thing: I'm thinking about the guests here, presuming we *do* still have them all here and no one's done a bunk. Only one couple arrived in their own car, I gather.'

'That's right,' answered Derek. 'Belonging to Mr and Mrs Dawson, and it's around the back. Everyone else arrived by train.'

'I see. And the Dawsons' car is still here, is it? It hasn't moved?'

'No, not that I could see.'

'Thank you.' She paused to look between the two of them, consternation making her frown. 'Right, off you go.'

'Sorry, Fran,' added Nell, sitting back down. 'Now, where had we got to?'

FRIDAY EVENING

Fran always suffered a little with her nerves before an event. It was human nature. Her business meant the world to her, and it was a matter of professional pride, if nothing else, that everything should run smoothly and importantly, that people should enjoy her food. Tonight though, even her hands were shaking. Unnecessary and completely unwarranted.

Fran had given herself several stern talkings-to. She had everything covered. Other areas of her life might be a little more... fluid, like cleaning her house for example, but when it came to her work, she was organised and methodical. The food was prepared and she knew it would meet with expectations. There wasn't anything she hadn't thought of, even her contingency plans had contingency plans should anything go awry; not that they were going to, she reminded herself. This afternoon's lack of planning hadn't been her fault, but with Rachel and Adam's help, they had more than resolved the situation. Fran could have done without all the scurrying around, replenishing tea and coffee in a seemingly never-ending round, topping up platters of scones and biscuits, but, judging by the quantity of food which had been eaten, the guests had certainly appreciated her offerings.

Now, her tray was charged with glasses and she was ready, if not entirely willing, for the evening ahead. She cleared her throat slightly as the first of the guests appeared at the top of the stairwell. She waited just beyond the bottom step, out of sight until they had stepped into the hallway when she would make herself known. She inhaled a steadying breath.

'Mr Newman, good evening. May I offer you a glass of champagne?'

The man in front of her smiled. Warm eye contact was made and then he was gone, glass in hand. Polite, but no more than he had to be. Left-handed too, Fran realised. She must remember that, it would make a difference to which side she approached him from when serving dinner. As for how to remember him, think Paul Newman, Rachel had said, although in his older, more rugged days. Blue eyes and everything. And Rachel had been right: Richard Newman wasn't an actor, neither did he make salad dressings, but he did bear an uncanny resemblance to his namesake.

The Dawsons were hot on Mr Newman's heels and Fran smothered a smile. Peter Dawson hadn't managed to be first down, after all; perhaps Ginny had taken too long in the bath.

She smiled as they walked past. 'Mr Dawson, Mrs Dawson.' Neither of them looked at her, but took a glass of champagne all the same.

Heather Walton even stopped to chat. She took a glass nervously from Fran's tray, wriggling as she did so. She was wearing a powdery-blue silk shift dress which Fran thought looked amazing, but you could tell from the way she was fiddling with the hemline that she'd rather be in jeans and a tee shirt. She grimaced at Fran.

'This didn't look as short in the shop,' she said.

'It looks stunning,' Fran whispered.

The petite redhead smiled. 'Thanks,' she said, visibly inhaling a deep breath. 'Here we go then.'

'Have a lovely evening,' Fran replied.

She watched as Heather made her way into the morning room, elegant even in barely-there flat gold sandals in which Fran would waddle like a duck. She'd been in far too many situations over the years where she'd had to drum up every ounce of courage she possessed just to walk into a room, and she felt for the young woman. Fran's job made her nervous at times, but it was nothing compared to the look of something approaching fear that had been in Heather's eyes. And yet she was a lawyer. Fran would have thought she was used to difficult situations. Curious.

Rachel was circling the morning room. Every now and again she came into view, dressed, as Fran was, in black, although far more formally, in a smart skirt and blouse. She was offering canapés, from a silver platter which Fran knew weighed a ton. As she watched, Rachel slipped through the doorway and came towards her.

'I would have thought Mr C would be down by now,' she whispered. 'Folks are chuntering through there.' Almost as soon as she spoke a door banged from above their heads. 'Aye, aye,' said Rachel, and slipped away again.

Fran turned, looking up to see not one, but two figures descending the staircase. Both wore fixed smiles. She turned her head away, shuffling her feet to stand straighter. Rachel had warned her that Mr Chapman wouldn't be as she imagined but was he really wearing *slippers*? Admittedly soft, buttery leather things, but shoes they most definitely were not. Beside him was the last of the guests, Oliver Knight, but she only had time for the briefest of impressions before they drew level with her.

'Mr Chapman, Mr Knight... Good evening.'

'You must be Francesca?' Mr Chapman smiled and took a glass of champagne. 'Thank you,' he added, glancing towards the morning room. 'I gather you've been engaged to provide for our every need this weekend?'

The man standing beside him gave a shallow wink. 'Our every need? Your hospitality just keeps getting better and better, Keith.' He gave Fran the kind of smile he thought was utterly irresistible but which Fran found repugnant. She ignored him.

'I shall certainly do my best, Mr Chapman. Everything is waiting for you in the morning room.'

'Excellent. My wife shouldn't be long.' He downed half the glass in one large gulp. 'Perhaps you could ensure that the drinks are kept flowing.'

She smiled in return. 'Certainly.'

With that, he shuffled away, the hem of his rumpled linen suit trailing on the carpet. Oliver Knight, all twinkling eyes and boyish black curls snatched a glass of champagne and strode after him.

'A word to the wise, Oliver,' said Mr Chapman as they walked away. 'Don't underestimate me. People have been doing that my entire life.'

Fran stared after them both, utterly bemused. The words had been so softly spoken and yet there was an edge to them that glinted with resolve, and something much darker.

His appearance was so at odds with what Fran had been expecting that she was thrown. Oliver Knight was dressed exactly as his smutty comment might suggest, but Keith Chapman was at least six inches shorter, with mousy, nondescript hair which didn't even look as if it had been brushed. He wore glasses with unflattering heavy black frames and had shaved badly, cutting himself at least twice in the process. Fran almost felt sorry for him. He looked as if he'd be far happier curled up in his chair with a book than mingling with a room full of people dressed to the nines. And yet, she had a feeling that quite a few people underestimated Mr Chapman.

It was hard to describe the moment when Fran became aware that Mimi Chapman was about to make her entrance. Except that it announced itself like a storm does, in the moments before it breaks. Something charged about the atmosphere, a flicker in the light. Fran might have imagined it and yet as Mimi descended the stairs, she had to remind herself to breathe.

Mimi was wearing a stunning black cocktail dress. Velvet, cinched in at the waist with a short skirt falling in a froth of glittery tulle. Tiny silver stars stitched into the fabric sparkled under the light, accented at Mimi's neck and ears by what could only be real diamonds.

Fran's greeting died on her lips, as the woman snatched up a glass from her tray and, without a word, sashayed on long legs towards the room at the far end of the hallway.

She paused as she reached the threshold of the room and Fran could only imagine the reaction from those inside. There were only eight people in there, including Rachel and Adam, so the buzz of conversation wasn't exactly loud, but the resultant silence was one in which the proverbial pin could have been heard to drop were the pile of the carpet not so thick.

Mimi laughed, throwing her head back. 'Well, hello, everyone,' she said, holding her glass of champagne high. 'Are we all ready to have a really good time?'

～

Nell groaned. 'Stop, please, because I'm beginning to hate this woman. Entirely unprofessional of me. I'm dying to know though, so did they?'

Fran looked puzzled for a second. 'Oh, what, have a good time? Well, I guess that largely depends on what your definition of that is. The Dawsons looked like they'd been sucking lemons all evening; the lovely Heather looked like she'd love someone to rescue her, in fact, I nearly did myself once or twice; Keith Chapman drank enough to fill a bath and Oliver Knight asked me more than once for Sex on the Beach – the cocktail, that is.'

Nell rolled her eyes.

'I know. He seemed to think it was highly original. So, in answer to your question, yes, they all had a lovely time.'

'What about Mr Newman? You haven't mentioned him.'

Fran wrinkled her nose. 'Hmm, odd that. He disappeared at one point, and I didn't realise he was missing until Mr Chapman called for a toast to be made. He must have gone outside because either myself or Rachel were stationed in the hallway for most of the evening and he didn't come past us. Plus, when I was relaying some plates to the kitchen for Adam to wash, I spotted him walking by the front of the house. He didn't come in the front door again though, so he must have walked on round to the terrace and come in that way. As you can see, all the rooms on this side of the house open onto it.'

'So where had he been?'

'Haven't a clue. He just reappeared. Spent most of the evening after that talking with either Mimi or Heather.'

Nell nodded. 'Anyone monopolise Mr Chapman?'

'Peter Dawson, without a doubt. Stuck to his side like glue.'

'Interesting...' replied Nell through steepled fingers. 'Very interesting. Okay, well that's given me a flavour of all the guests. Is there anything else you can remember about the evening that I should know? Any arguments? Anything unusual happen, or conversations that caught your ears?'

Fran shook her head. 'There is something I feel I should mention. I don't want you to find out about it later and it... well, you might think I've been hiding things from you, and I'm not.'

Nell's gaze was cool. 'Go on,' she said.

'Only that, as you might imagine, it was a really busy evening and, apart from conversations about food, drinks, or the course of events, I hadn't really had a chance to talk much to Adam.' She paused to check Nell's expression at the mention of Adam's name but, as usual, the detective gave nothing away. Fran wondered idly if she ever played poker. 'He's designing a new game at the moment, one involving a murder mystery in a large country house... which is obviously a complete and utter coincidence.' Nell's eyebrows rose alarmingly. 'And when we haven't been as busy, he's been working on it.'

'And?'

Fran cleared her throat. 'When we were washing up the last few things at the end of the evening, I asked him how he was getting on, if he'd had a chance to get much work done. He talked about the setting here, saying it was perfect apart from one thing... He made a joke about us not finding any dead bodies yet. It *was* just a joke, obviously. He wouldn't have meant anything by it, just Adam being Adam. The thing is, I replied. And I was tired, over-tired. It gets you like that, this job. You get really wired, and your brain does weird stuff, says things which perhaps if you'd stopped to think about them, you wouldn't have said at all. Or, said differently. My husband says I come out with real oddball statements just as I get into bed. He's learned to ignore them now, that it's simply my brain churning stuff, but—'

'Fran, are you rambling by any chance?'

She stopped and swallowed. 'Yes.' She drew in a deep breath. 'So what I said, in my reply, was that we might not have found any dead bodies yet, but that the night was still young. And, obviously, that was Friday night and not last night, but...'

Nell's eyes narrowed, ever so slightly. 'You know Munchhausen's? Actually, Munchhausen's by proxy, where parents cause their children's illness or diseases in order to gain attention. Actually, we don't call it that any more, it's straightforward abuse, but anyway, there's a case, famous in the annals of policing history, where a very high-ranking officer was actually murdering people because he got off on all the attention the case generated. He plotted the perfect murder, set up someone as the fall guy, planted all the clues and then miraculously "solved" the case.' She looked across at Fran and smiled. 'Your confession is noted.'

Fran returned her smile, although nervous twitch might be a more apt description. Nell had an incredible knack for making her feel utterly at sea.

'Right, now you've got that off your chest, I was speaking earlier with my DC, namely Clare Palmer. And I want everyone up. Now. Mrs Chapman first. Clare will be breaking the news of her husband's death to her as soon as she's down and then I'll have everyone else brought in here, sharpish. Probably best if you wait here too.'

'Okay.'

Fran's heart went out to the young detective. She knew they were incredibly well trained, but how did you tell a wife her husband had just died?

Nell looked up at the sound of footsteps in the hallway, but it was only Rachel. The housekeeper hurried towards them.

'Sorry to interrupt.' Rachel looked like she wanted to curtsey and Fran knew exactly how she was feeling – Nell had the same effect on her. 'Mrs Chapman has just asked me to prepare her water, which means she's up and about and it won't be long before she makes an appearance.'

'Thank you.' She turned to look at Fran and then back to Rachel again. 'This might sound like a stupid question, but how do you "prepare" water?'

Rachel gave a wry smile. 'Basic answer is you throw lemon, mint and cucumber in it. Mrs Chapman has a tall glass of it every morning while she's getting herself ready.'

'Of course she does. And you take this wonder concoction up to her, do you?'

Rachel nodded.

'Right, fetch it up and then come straight back here. I want to know how she seems. Not a word about Mr Chapman, mind.'

Nell watched as Rachel left the room and Fran wondered what she was thinking. Her own thoughts were in turmoil. She was very well aware that Nell was sorting through every piece of information she had been given from the moment she arrived in the house, Fran's account of Friday's events included. She was building up a picture of what had gone on over the last couple of days, because somewhere, in among Fran's comments about what people said and how they dressed, were clues. Clues which were going to help tell Nell who had killed Keith Chapman.

Fran sat back in her chair, trying to recall the details of what she had already relayed, something that had been said and that might shed light on this horrible business. Because people never notice the caterer, they talk as if they're not there, so Fran had heard no end of things she probably shouldn't over the years. The trouble was, though, that Fran knew she was practically invisible, and so often fulfilled people's expectations by switching her ears off and letting things wash over her. She could have missed something vital. Fran really wished Adam was with her – he was far better at this stuff than she was.

'Tell me, Fran,' said Nell. 'What do you know about Derek's

background? He called me Ma'am earlier. Has he ever been in the police force?'

'I don't know, I'm afraid.' Trust Nell to spot that. Fran had noticed it too. *Curious...* 'I only met him on Friday and we've not really spoken much about anything which hasn't been relevant to the weekend.'

'And your opinion?'

Fran smiled. 'He's lovely. Just a really nice, do anything for anybody type of person. He and Rachel make a great team.' She paused, pulling a face. 'I don't mean they're in cahoots or anything, but this is a big house and they do a good job. I don't imagine the Chapmans are the easiest of employers. That's all I meant.' Fran could kick herself. She didn't want to make it sound like Rachel and Derek were criminal masterminds, working together but, somehow, when Nell was beside her everything she said seemed to come out wrong.

'It's okay, Fran,' replied Nell. 'Derek and Rachel are suspects, they have to be, but they're not the most obvious ones. I imagine the death of one of their employers could have serious repercussions for both of them, given that they live here.' She dipped her head, looking up at Fran through her lashes. 'Not that I told you that, of course.'

Rachel hurried back down the stairs. 'I've taken the water up like you asked,' she said as she came into the morning room. 'And I didn't say anything.'

'Good, thank you. And Mrs Chapman, how did she appear?'

Anxiety flickered across Rachel's face. 'Same as usual.' She coloured slightly. 'She's not what you'd call a morning person.'

'By that, you mean she was ill-tempered?'

Rachel nodded. 'I think she might be a little hungover as well. She slept longer than she wanted to.'

Nell checked her watch. 'It's still quite early though. And a

Sunday morning as well. Is that normal? Particularly after yesterday's party.'

'Yes, she's usually up around eight.'

'So, right on time then. Okay, thank you, Rachel. I was just saying to Fran that we're going to bring everyone downstairs now, Mrs Chapman too, whatever state they're in. The guests will be coming in here.' She paused to look out of the window. 'If I'm going to ruin everyone's day, I might as well have a nice view while I do it.'

Fran looked at her nervously. 'Am I allowed to ask what it is you're going to do?'

Nell smiled. 'Sorry, Fran. I know this is going to affect you as well. But, if I'm right, and I think I am, then whoever killed Mr Chapman is still in the house. I'm just about to break the good news that for the foreseeable future, no one will be leaving. There's a murderer under this roof and, until we catch them, I'm afraid no one is going anywhere.'

6

Mimi Chapman's cry of anguish was loud enough to wake the whole house, had several police officers not already done so. Fran and Rachel were both standing by the door to the morning room, not exactly eavesdropping, but loitering just the same. Fran had no doubt Rachel's stomach was churning just as hers was.

'I thought for one awful minute they were going to ask me to break the news to Mrs Chapman,' said Rachel, hand over her heart. 'How do you even do such a thing, especially to someone like Mimi?'

'No, Nell wouldn't ask you to do that. In any case, there's probably some protocol or other, but she wouldn't put you through that.'

Choking sobs could now be heard coming from the drawing room and Fran winced.

'I haven't warmed to the woman,' she whispered. 'But, it's still horrible news to hear. Bad enough that your husband's died, but to be killed the way he was...' Fran was thinking about her own life, about how she would feel if anything ever happened to Jack. It was hard enough thinking that her weekend away might turn into something much longer. And she hadn't had a chance to speak to him about it yet.

'What will happen now?' asked Rachel, looking warily down the hallway. 'Are we all under arrest?'

Fran shook her head, giving Rachel a reassuring smile. 'No, nothing like that. But we will all be helping the police with their inquiries. For now, all we do is what Nell tells us to. You've nothing to worry about, Rachel, honestly. Just the small matter of an hysterical wife and her five house guests.'

Rachel's eyes widened. 'It's going to be hell, isn't it? They were bad enough when they were being wined and dined, imagine what they're going to be like when they're all told they've got to stay here.'

Overhead, a bedroom door was flung open and Peter Dawson's unmistakable tones echoed across the landing: 'What the bloody hell is going on?'

Moments later, having received no reply to his question, or not that Fran had heard, he appeared at the foot of the stairs, wearing a surprisingly tatty dressing gown. Fran was relieved to see pyjama bottoms poking out from underneath. Catching sight of her, he strode towards the morning room, where he bellowed the same question in her face.

'I'm afraid I don't have any details, Mr Dawson,' she replied as calmly as she could. 'Please, just take a seat. Is Mrs Dawson up?'

'No idea.'

Charming, thought Fran.

Oliver Knight appeared next, a short towelling robe belted around his waist. It gaped at his chest and Fran averted her gaze as he walked past her – she had no wish to make eye contact with him.

A few seconds later, Heather appeared, hair tousled, and bleary-eyed. She made directly for Fran.

'Is everything okay?' she asked.

Fran smiled, a natural one which she reserved solely for Heather. She was wearing cotton pyjamas covered in a sheep motif and this one simple detail endeared her to Fran even more.

'It's not, I'm afraid,' she replied. 'But I can't give you any details. The police will come and explain everything in a minute. Please, have a seat.'

Heather was anxious, but she still went, with the minimum of fuss, just as Fran had expected.

Ginny Dawson and Richard Newman brought up the rear, arriving together. They were whispering like children, no doubt wondering what was going on, but their voices fell silent the moment they caught sight of Nell, who now stood in the hallway just outside the morning room, warrant card in hand. They filed past Fran silently, Ginny with a deep crease down one cheek as if she'd slept in a heap. She also hadn't taken off her make-up from the night before and her eyes were smudged with mascara.

Fran had heard Heather asking if Mrs Chapman was all right but, apart from her, no one else seemed to notice that Mimi's sobs could still be heard floating through the drawing room door. How could anyone ignore such anguish? From a fellow human being? It didn't matter whether you liked them or not, suffering was suffering. Although, as Fran had learned over the last year or so, some people could not only ignore it, they could actually set out to cause it.

With everyone gathered, she and Rachel went to stand at the rear of the room. Even this early in the morning Fran could feel heat coming through the conservatory doors, the warmth of the sun on her back. It was a beautiful day out there.

Detective Chief Inspector Helen Bradley took centre stage.

'Morning, everyone. Thank you for coming down as requested. I'm sorry for rousing you from your beds, but I'm afraid I have some rather horrible news. Mr Chapman has been found dead this morning, and at this moment in time, we're treating his death as suspicious.'

Fran waited for the resultant gasp but then realised that probably only happened in films. In real life, everyone was too scared to say a word. She also realised how much she wanted to be standing at the front, simply so that she could see the expression on everyone's faces. She had no doubt that Nell's roving eye would be checking them.

'Therefore, given the nature of the crime, I'm afraid no one will be able to leave the house until such time as our initial investigations are completed. At the moment I can't tell you how long that will be, although I will give you my best estimate as we go along. I have two colleagues with me, Detective Constables Owen Holmes and Clare Palmer. They will be taking statements from each of you in turn, and you will also be required to have your fingerprints taken so that we may match these against prints we'll be collecting as part of our forensic processes. These processes are time-consuming, and I'm afraid that you will all simply have to bear with us until they are completed. You will shortly be allowed to get dressed, but this will happen under the accompaniment of one of my officers, who will also ask you for the clothes you were wearing yesterday evening. These will be taken away for forensic testing. After that you will then be asked to return to this room or the conservatory. No one is to leave these rooms without permission, and your bedrooms and your possessions will all be thoroughly searched. While we will make every attempt to make this whole process as painless as possible, may I remind you that this house is now a crime scene, everything is potential evidence, and I will take a very dim view of anyone not following my instructions. Does anyone have any questions?'

'Yeah, can we have some breakfast? I'm bloody starving.'

It was Oliver Knight who had spoken, from an armchair over by the window where he was lounging with one leg draped over the arm. An abhorrent amount of leg plus leg hair was on display, together with bare feet. Fran seriously hoped he wasn't daft enough to think that his rather short robe would in any way endear him to Nell.

Her smile was tight. 'Yes, I don't see why not. Okay, thank you, everyone, and please, just wait here until you're told otherwise.' She caught Fran's eye as she turned and with a minute nod in the direction of the hallway intimated that Fran should follow. She touched a hand to Rachel's elbow.

Once outside, Nell beckoned them both towards the doorway which led to the rear hall. 'Ladies, I'm sorry but do you think you could rustle up some breakfast for everyone? And teas and coffees, that kind of thing. It's going to be like a circus in here soon. Set everything up in the morning room. I don't want to piss people off any more than I have to, and food and drink is as good a pacifier as any. They're going to be in for a long wait; you too, I'm afraid, Fran.'

'What about all of *them*?' asked Fran. Even in the time it had taken for Nell to speak to the guests at least twenty more people seem to have arrived through the front door.

Nell thought for a moment. 'Never let it be said that I am not kindness itself. Drinks, please, and anything else if you can manage it. This is a big house, that lot are going to be in for a very long day... quite possibly several days.'

Beside her, Rachel paled. 'Is it really going to take that long?' she asked.

Nell shrugged. 'Depends on what we find. If that includes a blunt instrument in one of the guests' bedrooms with Mr Chapman's brains all over it, and a nice set of fingerprints to boot, then this may all get wrapped up quite quickly. But don't bank on it,' she added.

Rachel shivered. 'I think I'd rather be in the kitchen, away from everything else.'

Fran nodded, it was much how she was feeling herself.

Apart from Heather, she hadn't particularly liked any of the guests and had no desire to spend any more time with them than she had to. She was about to follow Rachel back to the kitchen when Nell touched her arm.

'A moment, please,' she said.

She waited until Rachel was out of earshot, time during which Fran's stomach began to severely misbehave.

'This case,' began Nell, wincing. 'How can I put it...? These things are always so damned political and it drives me mad, but this case in particular is going to attract a lot of attention. Attention that will be very unwelcome unless we get quickly to the bottom of what happened here. Attention that the district commissioner will focus on me if we don't get a result. Every life matters, Fran, but... Christ, I hate myself for saying this, but in the eyes of quite a few people, some lives matter more. And Mr Chapman's life was one of them. He was a very wealthy man. Successful, high-profile, with friends in all the right places. You do get what I'm saying, don't you?'

'Oh yes, perfectly.'

'Someone in this house murdered Mr Chapman, and that person had better not be you, Fran, because so help me, God, if it is—'

'It isn't,' she said quickly.

'Good.' She gave Fran a very forthright look. 'Because as soon as you're done in the kitchen, I'd like us to carry on working through all the events of the weekend. Would that be okay?'

Fran nodded. She knew exactly where Nell was coming from.

'One other thing,' said Nell. 'I'm aware that any calls I make on your time will mean Adam having to step up and plug the gap as far as practical arrangements go. If nothing else, you and Adam are both witnesses, so may I remind you that you're not investigating this one, Fran. We were very grateful for your and

Adam's help previously, but correct me if I'm wrong, you did keep us entirely out of the loop. Something which is never a good idea.'

Fran screwed up her face. Everything Nell said was true, but that was when Adam's mum had been in the frame for the murder of one of her friends. They'd had to investigate, for her sake.

'But this is different, isn't it?' Fran replied. 'This time we're not keeping anything from you. Adam won't get in the way, I swear. But I think better when he's around and—'

'You are not police officers.'

'No, but you have to admit that Adam has a very good mind when it comes to solving puzzles.'

There was a long pause.

'I think I might have three sugars in my tea, if that's okay? I'm beginning to feel like I need it.'

It was an utter relief to return to the kitchen. Even though it wasn't Fran's, she'd spent enough time in there over the last couple of days for it to feel totally familiar. In a world which now felt as if was freewheeling, tumbling and spinning, it was the one place where she could feel in control of something.

Rachel was leaning up against the island in the centre of the room, chatting with Adam. She looked incredibly weary and gave Fran a wan smile as she entered the room. 'Right, Boss, what do we do now?'

Fran groaned. 'Urgh, don't call me that. It makes me feel like I'm supposed to know what I'm doing when I'm not even sure I'm in charge of my bodily functions. All I want to do is follow instructions and never have to think for myself again.'

'But you've done this before,' she said, looking at Adam. 'Murder and stuff, Nell said so.'

'Not really,' replied Fran. 'It wasn't like this. Someone *was* killed but it was all so far away from me, even when we were investigating what had happened. This seems right up close and far more personal.'

Rachel nodded. 'I know what you mean.'

'But...' said Fran, drawing the word out. 'I'm certain that I'll feel better doing something as opposed to just sitting around, and breakfast is something we *can* do. Although I don't suppose that folks will have huge appetites, Oliver Knight notwithstanding.'

'So, do we do what we were going to? Before all this, I mean. It was pretty lavish.'

Fran shook her head. 'No, I think we scale it back. For one thing, I'm not sure how long folks are going to be here, and there's only so much to go round. Second, I don't think people will actually eat much, and third, someone in this house bashed Mr Chapman over the head. They don't deserve lavish.'

Rachel smiled grimly. 'Good point.'

'I think we can put out the fruit, dishes of yoghurt, toast, some of the pastries and leave it at that. I'm quite happy to make bacon sandwiches for the coppers until the cows come home, but I'm not cooking for that lot out there, not now I don't have to. I think my contract here has just become null and void.'

'Besides, it's hardly Tesco basics cereal, is it?' said Rachel, pointing at the tray of fresh figs which Fran had laid out earlier.

'*That* is very true. Kettle on first though, I think, and excuse me for a minute, I just need to make a phone call.'

Adam looked at her anxiously. 'Are you ringing Jack?' he asked. 'Only tell him this one isn't my fault.'

Poor Adam, he still harboured guilty feelings over supposedly dragging Fran into their last case. Although truth be told, Fran had walked willingly, a fact she wouldn't admit to many people, and particularly not Jack. Enjoyment wasn't exactly the right word, but if Jack thought she had found any of their last investigation thrilling, she'd never hear the last of it.

As it was, though, Jack was exactly as Fran had expected.

Worried about her, anxious, caring, and not in the least bit cross that his wife's homecoming would be delayed. That was so typically Jack – whatever she threw at him, he caught and ran with. But while it was wonderful to hear his voice, what she longed for was the solid warmth of his chest and his strong arms around her. She would have them, she knew, and hopefully soon, but for the time being his voice and warm words would have to be enough. At least while chaos reigned at her end, back at home Jack would be taking care of everything, including their daughter Martha. Admittedly, she was fast approaching the age when she would far rather have her independence than be 'fussed' over by a parent, but it was still a weight off Fran's mind.

By the time the kettle had boiled, Nell reappeared, looking to claim her cup of tea, although not with the three sugars in it she had asked for. 'I do need something sweet though,' she said, sitting down opposite Adam, who fidgeted nervously, sliding his beanie from his head.

Fran turned and collected a tray of pastries from the counter top behind her. 'Make a start on these,' she said, placing them on the table between Adam and Nell. 'I'll be back in a minute.' With a nod at Rachel, she took up another tray and together they left the room.

'I feel a little sorry for Adam,' said Rachel the moment they were outside. 'He looks as if he expects Nell to eat *him* for breakfast, let alone a croissant. What's the story there?'

'Nothing really. Simply that Nell has to disapprove of his actions, which admittedly have been borderline illegal, or actually illegal come to think of it, while simultaneously having to be grateful for his brilliant deductions. He came to my rescue once because he'd bugged my car keys and could hear everything that was going on. It's how we got the killer's confession, too. He might also have impersonated a police officer.'

Rachel laughed, pushing open the door to the main hallway.

Mimi Chapman was headed towards them and she stopped, red-rimmed eyes staring, as if neither Rachel nor Fran had any reason to be there. Rachel stepped forward.

'Mrs Chapman, I'm so sorry,' she said, keeping her voice low. 'Is there anything I can get for you?'

'What could you possibly give me that I would want?' she replied. A balled-up tissue was clutched in one hand, red all over from where she'd clenched her fist tightly.

Fran dropped her gaze. 'Perhaps some tea?' she suggested on Rachel's behalf, who looked like she'd been slapped.

'Can you get everyone out of my house?' Mimi hissed. 'All these people, fawning and bowing and scraping. Parasites, every last one of them.' She stared at Fran. 'Well, can you? Because if not, then just go away.' She gave her one last piercing look and then turned on her heel and went back to the drawing room.

Rachel swallowed. 'I know we have to make allowances. And that she's grieving, and upset and I can't begin to understand what it must be like to hear news like she's just had, but...' Fran could see her jaw clenching. 'But what I'd like to get her is a personality transplant. I don't know why I'm so surprised. She was a horrible person when she was a wife, why should she behave any better now she's a widow?' She blinked rapidly, and then bowed her head as if ashamed by her outburst. It was certainly the first time Fran had heard Rachel be openly critical of her boss.

Fran laid a hand on her arm. 'Come on, let's get this lot sorted out and then we can escape.' She nodded towards the morning room. 'I don't want to be in there any longer than I have to.' She had a feeling it was going to be an incredibly long day.

Rachel pulled a face. 'Sorry,' she said. 'I just...'

'I know,' replied Fran. 'Listen, I can deal with that lot in there, why don't you go back to the kitchen?'

But to her surprise, Rachel shook her head. 'No, go on, you

go, Nell wants to speak to you. I'll wait here and serve for a bit, then see if any of the police people want anything. I'm sure they will.'

Fran scrutinised her face but she could see Rachel's mind was made up. 'Okay,' she said, following Rachel into the morning room to set down her tray with the rest of the breakfast offerings. A minute later, she was back in the kitchen.

Adam had already eaten two croissants and was working his way through a pain au raisin when she returned. Nell, in contrast, was sitting with her hands wrapped around her mug of tea, staring into space.

'This never gets any easier,' she said, helping herself to a raspberry tartlet. She sank her teeth into it. 'I mean, it does,' she said, through a mouthful of crumbs. 'There's about eighty per cent of me that goes into automatic mode: do this, do that, look at this, think about that. But there's still twenty per cent that cannot for the life of me work out how you can hate someone enough to want to kill them.' She licked a finger. 'Actually, that's not right either. I can understand how you can hate someone that much, but to actually take a life, wilfully...' She shook her head. 'And what we had this morning was relatively civilised. Nice neat bash over the head, not much blood, little gore, no dismembered limbs, no torture, no—' She broke off abruptly as if suddenly realising what she was saying.

From across the table Adam peered at his pastry and then laid it gently on his plate.

Nell shrugged, and took another bite of her breakfast, seemingly oblivious to the custard stained red by the raspberries. 'Still, life goes on.' She blinked, rousing herself from her reverie. 'Okay, where had we got up to? Tell me what happened yesterday, Fran, you mentioned various activities.'

Fran nodded. 'Well, the day started much like this morning was supposed to. With a whopping great breakfast to soak up the remaining alcohol from the night before, pastries, fruit, smoked salmon bagels, Greek yoghurt and honey, plus a full cooked option.'

'And everybody was there, were they?' asked Nell.

'Yes. Ginny Dawson was a little later down. She looked a bit upset, actually, scarcely ate a thing, but everyone else took full advantage. After breakfast, they split into groups. The men went off with Derek, clay pigeon shooting, and the women went down to the pool area with Mimi. She had spa sessions booked for them.'

'What was up with Ginny, did you find out?'

Fran wrinkled her nose. 'Possibly... I can hazard a good guess, anyway.'

'Then start there,' said Nell. 'Tell me about Ginny.' She flashed Adam a severe look. 'You may as well stay and listen to this, save you having to ask about it later.' There was no mistaking the meaning of her words. 'But no interrupting.'

Adam looked up at her through his lashes and pressed his lips together. 'Yes, Nell.'

7

SATURDAY MORNING

Fran stared at the table and sighed. At the serving spoon for the yoghurt which had been dropped carelessly into the dish of honey, at the half-eaten slice of pineapple abandoned on top of the others, at the platter of pastries where everyone had eaten the pains au chocolat, and the cinnamon buns, but left the plain croissants and the apricot-filled turnovers. And toast... never enough white and always granary left. It was one aspect of her job which never sat easily with her: the huge amount of waste.

Give her a plated sit-down dinner any day, you knew where you were with them. She knew why buffets were popular, of course. Why have two varieties of something when you could have twelve? She loved them herself, but when faced with a pile of leftovers as she was now, her conscience still pricked. Most of what was left would go in the bin, some she would cover and store in case Derek or Rachel fancied it, but she would never be able to serve it to guests again. But, such is the life of a caterer. She put down her empty tray and began to collect the used crockery and glasses. It would take several trips to ferry everything back to the kitchen.

Not for the first time, Fran thanked whoever had made the

decision that the door leading through into the rear hallway should swing. With a fully laden tray it would have been next to impossible to open otherwise. Not without putting the tray on the ground, pulling open the door, jamming your foot in it and using your elbows to manoeuvre yourself and the tray through a space which was doing everything in its power to close. She'd catered enough dinners in houses where that had been the case.

She was returning from the kitchen for the third time when the sound of voices floating through from the main hallway caused her to stop, just short of the swing door. Ordinarily, she would have simply excused herself and carried on about her business but these were not happy voices and she held herself back.

'Why wouldn't I have told you? Don't be ridiculous. I didn't *know...*'

It was Peter Dawson, his normally strident voice lowered, but still crystal clear.

'Well, if you think I believe that, think again. You knew you were going shooting this morning, so how come you didn't know what I would be doing? That's rubbish, Peter, and you know it.'

There was a pause, and a muffled sound which Fran couldn't make out.

'Ginny, for God's sake, get over yourself. Most women would give their eye teeth for a morning of pampering. Pay a bloody fortune for it too. I don't see why you're so upset.'

'No, well you wouldn't, would you? Because you don't think. Ever. If you did, maybe we wouldn't be in the mess we're in. And now, because of it, I've got to lay about in a swimsuit all morning, next to Mimi, who doesn't have an ounce of fat on her, looks bloody gorgeous, and next to her I'm going to look like... Heather's got nothing to worry about either.'

'And whose fault is that, darling? No one makes you eat biscuits all day.'

Fran didn't hear Ginny's reply, but she could guess at it.

The sound of feet pounding on the staircase above her head was a clue.

Poor Ginny. Fran could understand exactly why she was upset and winced on her behalf. She didn't even want to think it, but Ginny was *square*. Matronly, her mum would have called it, the scourge of middle-age spread. The fact that Ginny had had this 'surprise' foisted on her would have made Fran feel sick were she in Ginny's shoes, or rather swimsuit. Let alone the comment that 'most' women would enjoy the thought of a morning at the spa. Fran couldn't think of anything worse – she clearly wasn't most women.

Fran wasn't particularly taken with Ginny Dawson but Peter Dawson had an enormous stomach of his own. Talk about double standards. Fran waited until she heard his feet on the stairs before pushing open the door.

Rachel was just coming through the conservatory doors as Fran arrived in the morning room. They had been thrown open to the morning sun and already the heat in the room was building. Mimi was lucky that the weather was being so accommodating to her plans, although Fran had a feeling that luck had nothing to do with it. The weather wouldn't have had any say in the matter.

Judging by the expression on Rachel's face, she wasn't having a great morning either, although she brightened when she saw Fran.

'Crikey, it's warm out there already,' she said. 'Or perhaps it's just the fact that I've been lugging stuff up and down the steps to the pool area. It's beautiful, but when you're carrying things, it's such a long way from the house. And now we need *more* towels, apparently.' She smiled. 'Still, rather them than me,' she added. 'Not my idea of fun, but Mimi obviously loves it.'

'You mean the spa morning?' asked Fran. She quickly and quietly relayed the conversation between the Dawsons she had overheard. 'I wouldn't enjoy it either, Ginny has my sympathy. Do you need some help?'

Rachel eyed the empty tray in Fran's hand. 'You've enough to do of your own, with all the clearing up,' she said.

Fran shook her head. 'I've done most of it. Plus, I need to know how to find the pool, I'm serving drinks there later.'

'Okay then, thanks, Fran.' Rachel picked up four jugs while she waited for Fran to reload her tray with the leftover breakfast things. 'If I go and fetch the towels, could you bring the bags of ice from the freezer? Two should do for now.'

The two women bustled back to the kitchen, regrouping moments later only to head straight back out again.

Whereas the morning room windows faced east, the conservatory at its far end opened onto the southern aspect of the house and, as such, the terraces and lawns on this side received the full glare of the hot afternoon sun. Descending from the beautifully manicured gardens which immediately surrounded the house, majestic stone steps connected two further terraces, each slightly lower than the first. The farthest one housed the pool, a shimmering oasis of blue, glittering in the sunshine.

Stone flags provided an area for sunbathing and dining amid an array of floral planting, while to one end a much larger area held a glass-fronted single-storey building.

'The cabin is where everyone changes,' said Rachel. 'There are showers in there too, plus a treatment room. Mimi has her own personal masseuse.'

Fran smiled at her knowing look.

'I see,' she replied. But what Mimi got up to was none of her business.

It was beautiful here, the setting was incredible, but the way of life the Chapmans chose was so at odds with how Fran lived, or would want to live if she had the money, that none of it felt real. It resembled a theatre set, no more.

To the front of the building, three women, all in uniform,

were busy setting up their equipment on a series of tables, which Fran imagined must have been brought down here for the purpose.

'They're from Jeunesse,' said Rachel. 'It's the spa Mimi uses in town, but she's had them here before for her little pampering parties. A series of rejuvenating body and facial treatments await Heather and Ginny, followed by a head-to-toe aromatherapy massage.'

Fran hefted one of the large bags in her hand. 'And the ice?'

Rachel grinned. 'Is for the ice buckets to keep their Evian water cooled.'

Fran rolled her eyes. 'Of course it is,' she replied.

Not buckets though, she realised, when Rachel had shown her where they were, but fully insulated wooden caskets on both sides of the pool.

'Once the picnic is ready, we'll bring it down and leave it in the cabin,' added Rachel. 'Derek has set up another couple of tables so that the food can be left in the shade, but don't let me forget the flowers, will you? Mimi does love her flowers.'

'So, the men are shooting this morning, is that right?' asked Fran, once they were walking back up to the house.

Rachel nodded. 'Clay pigeon, yes. Derek's most favourite job in the world.'

'And is it?'

'Not on your life. Four men, all trying to out-do one another, with testosterone levels reaching the point of spontaneous combustion, and all the while holding loaded guns... I think he was rather pleased to have Adam giving him a hand today. A quick learner, Derek said.'

Adam's suggestion that he help out Derek had sounded casual enough, but Fran knew better. She hadn't the heart to tell Rachel the real reason Adam wanted to help was because of an intensely curious desire to see how guns worked. Research, Adam had called it, which was fair enough except that Fran wasn't altogether sure it was only required for gaming purposes.

'Where do they shoot?'

'On the other side of the house, well away from here, I might add. We leave their hamper in Derek's workshop and he'll send Adam for it when he's ready.'

'And on that note, I had better get cracking,' said Fran. 'Or there will be nothing to put in said hampers.'

As they reached the last set of steps up to the house, they saw Mimi approaching with Heather by her side, both laughing about something or other. Ginny brought up the rear, still wearing a thunderous expression. As the group passed, Fran spotted Ginny pulling a face at Mimi's back, not realising that Fran would see it. Her response on being caught out, however, was to angle her face away, haughtiness replacing sullenness. It was a shame; Fran might have enjoyed a laugh about it with her later. It was the kind of thing she might do herself.

'You may attend to the rooms now, Rachel,' Mimi said as she drifted by. 'And I would like extra towels this time, not the single one you usually provide.'

Rachel coloured but didn't respond. There was little point; Mimi wouldn't have been interested, anyway.

'Right, extra towels it is,' said Rachel brightly as soon as they were inside. She flashed Fran a complicit look. 'Do you want to place bets on where Madam slept last night?'

~

'Madam as in Mimi?' clarified Nell.

Fran nodded. 'We didn't; place bets, that is. But there was hardly any need.'

'So where did Madam sleep? Or rather *not* sleep?'

'Put it this way, either Oliver Knight sleeps on one side of the bed for half the night, then rolls onto the other side for the remainder, or he had company. Someone who wears perfume too.'

'She doesn't seem particularly discreet, does she? If it was her, that is.'

'But that's the weird thing,' replied Fran. 'She's all over Keith when he's around. Plays the dutiful wife extremely well. It's almost as if she's two different people. Mimi obviously doesn't care if Rachel knows about her indiscretions or not. Either that, or she views Rachel as someone whose opinions don't matter, so if Rachel ever repeated what she'd seen, no one would believe her anyway. Rachel wouldn't do such a thing, but I don't imagine that Mr Chapman is oblivious to what Mimi gets up to. He has eyes and ears, he wouldn't need Rachel to tell him what goes on.'

'Perhaps Mr Chapman gets up to similar himself,' remarked Nell. 'And, he did make that comment to Oliver about being careful not to underestimate him. Maybe he does know about Mimi's wanderings and either tolerates it because it suits him, or, there's something else going on here. Perhaps he's using Mimi to gain insider knowledge of Mr Knight's secrets. Pillow talk and all that.' She sighed. 'That's the one thing I hate about this job. We see all human life laid bare. There's plenty to warm the heart, but somehow it's the darker stuff which sticks; makes cynics of us all, makes us always look for the ulterior motive, the dark secret.'

'Yes, but in this case you're right to, surely? Mimi Chapman's husband was killed. And I really don't think she's a very nice person. She treats Rachel appallingly.'

Nell toyed with a piece of pastry on her plate. 'Ah, but is she a killer? I agree though, she doesn't sound like a paragon of goodness and virtue. And there wasn't any love lost between Ginny and Mimi by the sound of things either.' She popped the pastry in her mouth. 'Which is interesting.' She chewed for a moment. 'But did it go any deeper than that? Was it just mardiness because her husband hadn't told her about the spa morning, something she was obviously uncomfortable about, or did she really not like Mimi, possibly even hate her?'

'I felt a little sorry for her to begin with,' said Fran. 'I don't think I'd be entirely comfortable wearing next to nothing in front of two women I barely know, particularly when one of them looks like Mimi does, but Ginny didn't exactly endear herself to them either. When I took some bottles of water down later, she was sitting inside the cabin, with a look on her face that could curdle milk. But thinking about it now...' Fran broke off, frowning as she recalled the scene from the day before. 'I assumed that Ginny had taken herself off to the cabin because she didn't want to join in with the others, but I could hear every word Mimi was saying, even from inside, so...'

'Go on,' prompted Nell.

'I wonder if Ginny overheard something she shouldn't have? Something directed at her, perhaps. Mimi isn't the kind of woman whose hospitality you shove back in her face. And she strikes me as the type who would be very vocal about it too.'

Nell nodded. 'It's a possibility,' she said. 'I wonder if there's any past history between the two.'

'I've no idea,' replied Fran. 'The guests are all here to do business essentially, so there must be some previous connection between them, or why would they have been invited? No one else brought partners with them though, only Peter Dawson. Oh, hang on...' She got up and crossed to the counter on the other side of the kitchen. 'Rachel made that list of the guests for you. Here...' She passed the sheet of paper across before retaking her seat. 'Rachel would probably know a bit more about their backgrounds.'

Nell nodded. 'Thanks, yes, I'll ask her.' She studied the guest list for a moment before looking up. 'I'll get my team to start making inquiries, because it strikes me that if you found out that a person was having an affair, someone you really didn't like and wanted to get back at, then the easiest thing to do would be to tell the husband. We need a motive for murder and the Dawsons have already caught my eye, so we'll start with them. Excuse me for a moment.'

The second Nell left the room, Adam's eyes lit up.

'This is so cool,' he said. 'Our second case. Incredible. A house full of people and one of them's the murderer.'

Fran stared at him. 'Adam, someone's been killed. It's not incredible at all. Nell is never going to let us investigate this, you heard what she said. And it most certainly is not cool.'

'Not even a little bit?'

He was looking up at her with such an endearing expression of hope that Fran couldn't help but smile.

'Okay, it is the teeniest bit cool, but only the investigating bit. I saw him, Adam, the owner of the house with his head bashed in, and that wasn't cool at all. Far from it. It's different from our last case; we investigated a murder then but the person was poisoned and died in hospital. There wasn't blood and... other stuff. It wasn't quite so...' She was struggling to find the right word.

'Close?' suggested Adam.

'Yes, exactly that. And I'm serious. Nell won't let us get involved, we're both suspects, Adam, you as well as me. If she treats us differently from anyone else it's only because this is going to be a very high-profile case and she has one eye on her career.'

'Fair enough,' replied Adam. 'But what she doesn't know won't hurt her. I've been here all weekend too, don't forget. And maybe I've seen something or heard something which has a bearing on things. I haven't had a chance to think about it all yet, but I will. Plus, while everyone is being kept in the house, there'll be plenty of opportunities to mingle with people. It's amazing what you hear when you're loitering in the background.'

'Adam, are you seriously asking to be among people? This from the man who by his own admission avoids people like the plague.'

'I'm maturing,' he said, a cheeky gleam in his eye. 'Also... I'm discovering that some people are okay. I still mostly think they're weird, but if they can give me some clues, I'm prepared to overlook it.'

'You crack me up,' she said solemnly. 'But, okay, keep your ears and eyes open.'

By the time Nell returned to the room, Adam was busy eating yet another cinnamon bun and was the picture of innocence.

'Right,' said Nell in business-like fashion, sitting back down. 'My people are going to get some background checks running. I want to know what relationship the guests all have with Mr Chapman – the facts, mind, not the version of it they choose to tell me. There's something else too. I checked in with the team working in the study and when you were there earlier, you might have noticed one of the picture frames. It was lying face down on the floor, but the frame was broken as if it had been smashed down on something. Well, the picture it contained is missing. It's been very carefully cut from the frame. So we're now looking at theft as well as murder.'

8

Fran gasped. 'Are you talking about the painting that was over the fireplace?'

Nell nodded.

'It's worth a lot of money. Sorry, I can't remember the artist's name but there are several of his paintings in the house. There's a huge one hanging halfway up the stairs. Rachel would know, or Mrs Chapman, obviously.' Her eyes widened as a sudden thought came to her. 'Oh...'

Nell leaned forward.

'I've just remembered a conversation I overheard.' She tucked her hair behind her ears. 'Oh God, I wonder if that's it?' She stared at Nell. 'After lunch I went down to fetch the hamper from the pool area. There was stuff strewn everywhere. It annoyed me actually and... never mind, but it took me a lot longer to clear up than it should have done. And while I was collecting everything together, I heard two people talking... and giggling. They were inside the cabin. There are showers in there, a changing room, and the treatment room that Rachel told me about. I don't know which room the voices were coming from, but it was definitely a man and a woman.'

'What did they say?' urged Nell.

'I don't know, it was all a bit indistinct and—'

'Hold on, a moment ago you said you overheard a conversation?'

'I'm just getting to that.' Fran paused as Rachel came into the kitchen, carrying a tray of glasses.

'Sorry,' she whispered, crossing to the sink.

'This is just my opinion,' continued Fran. 'And I don't actually know who the people were in the cabin but, at the time, I assumed it was Mimi and Oliver.' She held up a hand. 'Perhaps I shouldn't say that, jumping to conclusions probably, but it was what I thought. It made me nervous; I didn't want to get caught and be accused of eavesdropping so I just gathered everything up as quickly and quietly as I could, bunged it all in the picnic hamper and hurried back up to the house.'

'When was this?' It was Rachel who spoke, a puzzled expression on her face.

'Early afternoon,' answered Fran. 'When everyone had finished with lunch and dispersed.'

Rachel nodded. 'Then it can't have been Mimi and Oliver, because after lunch I brought them tea in the drawing room.' She smirked. 'He was reading her poetry, would you believe. They looked pretty cosy, actually. I'd say they'd been there for a little while.'

'Oh... so who was in the cabin then?' asked Fran. 'It wasn't the Dawsons because that's what I was just coming to, they were in the garden, on the terrace outside the conservatory.'

'And it couldn't have been Richard Newman,' added Rachel. 'Because he was sitting reading on the morning room terrace, where it's shaded.'

'So, by a process of elimination,' said Adam, 'the two people in the cabin must have been Keith Chapman and Heather Walton.'

Nell looked at him sharply. 'Yes, thank you, Adam,' she said, but then gave him a wry smile. 'But that is interesting. I wonder what they'd got to talk about? And in such a secretive manner too.' She let her words sit for a moment and then shook her head. 'But that wasn't the conversation you wanted to tell me about.'

'No, it was the Dawsons,' said Fran. 'By the time I got to them I was feeling a bit hot and bothered, awkward about the whole thing. Like I said, I assumed the two people in the cabin were Mimi and Oliver and I'm not used to those kind of shenanigans, especially not under the same roof as her husband. Anyway... I was musing on people's behaviour when I heard more voices talking as I walked up to the house. I was taking a slightly circuitous route, um, taking a bit of a breather actually, so I'd stopped to sit on a bench on the second terrace. The planting screens it from the one above and, as I sat there, I heard the Dawsons talking above me.'

'And?'

'Peter Dawson was not happy. You know I mentioned hearing how he'd bought a really expensive bottle of whisky for Keith Chapman? Well, after they'd finished their shoot, Mr Chapman gave it to Derek as a thank you for his services that morning. You can imagine Peter's reaction.'

'Ouch...'

Adam nodded. 'He was livid. Up until then he'd been pretending to be Mr Joviality.'

'Exactly,' said Fran. 'Plus, after they'd had lunch, Keith Chapman apparently walked back to the house with Peter, leaving Oliver and Richard chatting and Keith made several references about only wanting the best on this new project, saying there was no room for losers. Peter took it that Keith was referring to him; that he was the loser. Rachel, maybe you know more about this than I do, but Peter reckoned it meant he wasn't going to be in on this latest deal?'

Three heads swivelled in Rachel's direction.

She nodded, joining them at the table. 'I don't know a great deal, but Mr Chapman's latest project is the size of a small village. You saw the ice sculpture at the party, Fran, and that was just a tiny part of it. Houses, a village green, shops... At first I thought it was a lovely idea – you know, a bit like Rowntree or Bournville – villages built by Quaker employers for their workforce, a proper community. Now I realise it's just another opportunity to make vast amounts of money. Investment from third parties is high, but so are the returns.'

'Peter Dawson must care a great deal about this new venture of Keith's,' said Nell. 'Things like that make me wonder why. The lure of money is always strong, but is there some other reason why the investment was so important to the Dawsons?'

'Well, they're broke,' said Adam. 'I would imagine that's the reason.'

Nell looked up sharply. 'They can't be that broke if they can afford bottles of whisky that cost five hundred pounds.'

'Yes, but don't forget what Ginny said when she was bickering with Peter about the spa morning,' said Fran. 'She said that Peter didn't think, and that if he had done, they wouldn't be in the mess they were in. A financial mess maybe?'

Nell wriggled forward in her seat. 'Adam, just now you said that Peter Dawson had been *pretending* to be Mr Joviality. What do you mean by that? Do you *know* the Dawsons are broke or are you just surmising?'

'No, they're broke. This weekend is Peter Dawson's last-ditch attempt to recoup some of the money he lost on an investment that went wrong. People are so weird. None of them really like Keith Chapman at all, yet they act like the sun shines out his—'

'Don't say it,' warned Fran.

'Did something happen at the shoot?' asked Nell. 'I think you'd better explain...'

SATURDAY LUNCHTIME

Adam had never held a real live gun before. He'd spent a lot of time firing imaginary ones, in imaginary places, fighting imaginary wars, but computer games were no substitute for the real thing.

'Not that I want to kill anything,' he said, as he and Derek walked out to his workshop. 'Well, maybe an alien if they ever do invade, but actually...' He squinted into the sun, shivering suddenly. 'I'm a complete wuss. I'd be sick, I think. I don't understand why people want to shoot stuff for real. Animals and things, I mean.' He paused. He wasn't sure he was explaining himself at all well, and Derek was probably kicking himself for accepting his offer of help. Thankfully, Derek smiled.

'Aye, I know what you mean. I don't like guns myself. I can appreciate them – the mechanics of them, the craftmanship that goes into making them – but not what they represent. Shooting clays isn't a bad sport, but the people that shoot them can be a bit—' Derek broke off, smiling. 'My mum used to say to me: "the only difference between men and boys is the size of their toys," and I reckon she was right. The blokes act like children sometimes – over-competitive, acting the big *I am* and then sulk when things don't go their way. Our job today is to try to make sure that everyone gets a little bit of something going their way. You don't want tempers flaring when there's guns around.'

Adam swallowed. 'No one's going to get shot, are they?'

Derek grinned. 'Well, I've not lost anyone yet,' he said, not altogether helpfully. 'Don't worry,' he added as they reached the workshop. 'There're a few rules to abide by, and as long as we do, everything will be fine. Besides, Mr Chapman might be many things, but he's not cavalier when it comes to safety.'

He led Adam inside and crossed to a cabinet on the far side of the room. Hitching a bunch of keys from the waistband of his trousers, he selected a small silver one. 'Ammunition first,' he said, opening the metal door. 'And then we'll get the shotguns.'

It surprised Adam how many bullets there were; cartridges, Derek called them. Boxes of them. And as he held out his arms to receive them he began to wonder if he'd been just a little too hasty in his decision to help out. He'd thought knowing how the guns looked and felt up close would be good research, and help satisfy his continual thirst for knowledge. Now, he wasn't so sure. Each one of these innocuous-looking cartridges in their bright red shells was capable of killing someone and he was carrying hundreds of them. He was very pleased when a few minutes later they walked back out into the sunshine.

Once the shooting was underway, Adam and Derek's job was to reload the guns. The clay pigeon 'trap', as Adam had learned to call it, was automatic, the tray loaded with the clay discs set to fire at regular intervals. All four men stood in a line away to its left – Keith Chapman and Richard Newman furthest away from him and next to Derek, leaving Oliver Knight and Peter Dawson closest to Adam. Two men each to look after. It was pretty simple, but you had to be quick, darting between them once they'd fired with another set of cartridges.

Adam wasn't at all surprised to discover that Keith Chapman was a crack shot. After all, he'd be highly unlikely to choose a sport for his guests to enjoy that didn't make him look good. And, as Derek had already informed him, Keith practised for hours whenever he was at home. What was a revelation, however, was just how good everyone else was too. Particularly, Peter Dawson.

Richard Newman had a casual stance and an almost lack-adaisical approach to firing his gun, but it was surprisingly effec-tive. Oliver took more time, his gun barrel pointed in the air the whole time, tracking the flight of the clay as it soared overhead. Peter, however, only raised his gun to fire seemingly at the last instant, but with a surety of movement that made Adam a little nervous. He was glad when it was all over.

Except it wasn't all over at all, because what Adam hadn't realised was that while the shooting had been nerve-wracking and tedious and exceedingly hot and sweaty, what it hadn't been was full of conversation. Everyone had been wearing ear defenders, a fact which didn't allow for much in the way of chit-chat. But once the men had had their sport, Adam was sent to fetch the picnic hamper containing lunch from Derek's work-shop and, as the wine began to flow, the real business of the day began. And it was infinitely worse.

The picnic was being served beside a large wooden summerhouse which sat in a shaded area of garden on the opposite side from where the pool was bathed in sunshine. Derek had already set up some chairs earlier in the morning, and all Adam had to do was lay everything ready on tables. He'd barely finished when two of the men appeared, Oliver and Peter, both smoking, their eyes roving over the contents of the tables as if they couldn't remember when they'd had their last meal.

Peter picked up a glass of wine and swallowed half of it in one gulp. 'Good shots this morning, Ollie,' he said, drawing on his cigarette. 'I can see you've been practising. So much less embarrassing when you can miss the clays *deliberately*.'

Oliver's answer was a snide sneer out of the corner of his mouth. 'Oh, Peter, Peter... don't be so holier than thou. Pretending to miss shots isn't the only charade going on from what I hear.' He stubbed out his cigarette on a plate and claimed a glass.

Beside him, Adam could see Peter stiffen, his bulk towering above Oliver. 'And what's that supposed to mean?' he demanded, throwing a furtive glance behind him.

'Only that I heard you lost big, Peter,' added Oliver, his voice soft. 'Bad investment, was it? A little bird told me that you need to score this weekend or you might be out of the game for good.'

'Well, your little bird told you wrong,' hissed Peter. 'I'm good for the cash.'

'Really? Even when the little bird in question happened to be your wife? Ginny's none too pleased with you, Peter. She really does wax quite lyrical when you pay her the right kind of attention. Told me the whole story last night – how you didn't do your homework properly – how you blew almost everything on the Rackham development and lost the lot. I'm a little surprised by that, actually, I thought everyone knew Simon Rackham was a crook. Not you though, apparently. But then again, maybe Ginny got it wrong – she had had rather a lot to drink.' Oliver raised his glass with a slow smile.

Peter's eyes blazed. 'At least I'm in this for an honest day's work. You wouldn't know what one of those was. Too busy trying to romance your way into the money.'

'Ah... the lovely Mimi,' drawled Oliver. 'I can't lie, she's quite a catch, don't you think? And absolutely besotted with me, fortunately.'

Adam swiftly removed the dirty plate and replaced it with a clean one, wrinkling his nose at the still-smouldering cigarette. He kept his head down, but there was really no need. Neither man had given even the slightest acknowledgement that he was there.

'You know, you really are a piece of work, Ollie. Flaunting your little romance under Keith's nose. You're a fool if you underestimate him. He'll make it his life's mission to break you if he finds out.'

'Yes, but he's not going to find out, is he?' retorted Oliver, smiling. *Like a shark*, thought Adam. 'Who's going to tell him? Not you. You wouldn't want to run the risk of your little secret getting out. Once Keith learns of your financial embarrassment, he'll drop you quicker than the proverbial hot potato.'

'You bastard!'

'Now, now, Peter, don't get so hot under the collar. I'm not going to tell Keith a thing. Just like you're not going to mention my little dalliance with Mimi. I think we can both see the merit in minding our tongues.' He raised his glass. 'And here comes Keith now. May the best man win, Peter.'

Ollie stepped to one side so he could see clear past Peter's shoulder. 'Ah, here he is, the man of the hour. Excellent sport, Keith. On top form as usual.'

Peter spun around. 'Let me get you a drink, Keith. Super morning. And what a gorgeous spread. I've worked up quite an appetite.'

~

'Good God,' said Nell. 'You weren't kidding, were you? So the Dawsons *are* broke. And there's no love lost between any of them. Interesting that Oliver and Peter have what amounts to a pact going on though, each promising to keep the other's secret. I wonder what will happen if that changes?' She stared at Adam, who fidgeted under her gaze. 'They're really not a nice bunch of people, are they?'

'It sickened me,' said Fran. 'Listening to the Dawsons talk in the garden. As if everything could be bought, and what couldn't, could be taken in other ways. And that's not all,' she added. 'Peter Dawson was of the opinion that if Keith wouldn't accept his investment this weekend, then there were other ways to recoup some of their losses. He openly said to Ginny that they were sitting in a house full of eye-wateringly expensive things, far too many things for a person to need, or keep track off. Peter said it was lovely of Mimi to leave a note in their rooms saying they were welcome to keep the bathrobes that had been laid out for them, but that he was planning on taking home a damn sight more than that. He told Ginny to keep her eyes open.'

'Bloody hell,' said Rachel. 'He's nothing but a common thief. I might not necessarily approve of the way the Chapmans live, but that doesn't mean their belongings are open season for anyone else.'

'Okay, so now we might be getting somewhere with motive,' put in Nell. 'A theft gone wrong, perhaps? They attempt to steal the painting, are interrupted by Keith and in the ensuing struggle, he gets bashed over the head. It's a possibility.'

'But a painting isn't the easiest thing to steal, is it?' said Fran. 'If you just wanted to pinch something that was worth a lot of money, why not pocket some silver or something else relatively small?'

Nell blew out her cheeks. 'True. I wonder how much the painting was worth though?' She pulled out her phone and quickly made herself a note. 'I'll get someone to check with Mrs Chapman.' She looked up from her phone and stared into space. 'We also need to know what Heather and Keith were doing down in the cabin. Am I right in thinking that the guests essentially had free time during yesterday afternoon?'

Rachel nodded. 'They finished up from lunch about two-ish, the men were slightly later than the women, and Fran didn't serve dinner until seven. Most of the guests went back up to their rooms about half past four, to either get ready, or have a siesta.'

'That's quite a lot of time when people could have been doing anything, anywhere,' answered Nell, clearly thinking. 'And what about Richard Newman? The man about whom we seem to know relatively nothing except that he disappears at odd intervals for reasons unknown. Adam, did you learn anything about him yesterday?'

Adam shook his head. 'Compared with the others he said very little.'

'So when he and Oliver were left talking after the shoot – when Peter and Keith walked back to the house – you didn't hear what they were saying?'

'No... I'd gone to clear up. The field they used for the shoot was full of empty cartridge shells. Derek took the shotguns back to his workshop to put them away, and I was left picking up all the damned things.' His mouth was a thin line. 'Took me hours.'

'So neither you nor Derek were with the men at the end of lunch?'

'No, sorry.'

Nell nodded. 'Okay. And I have a feeling that once we start taking statements the sequence of events is going to become a little confused, even contradictory.' She sighed. 'Going back to what Peter Dawson said about his potential investment for a minute, which is, after all, the point of the whole weekend – what happened about that? Did Keith make a formal announcement about who he'd chosen to invest with him, or is it a little more low-key than that?'

Rachel gave a wry smile. 'It's tantamount to cloak and dagger. Business is never openly discussed, but people are incredibly foolish if they think the weekend is just a jolly show of hospitality. It isn't, it's one long interview. Keith would have been weighing up every action and every conversation the entire time folks have been here. Mimi will have too. Which is why poor Ginny truly dropped herself and Peter in it by not enjoying what was on offer. Mimi and Keith may not have the best marriage in the world, but when it comes to business and the making of money they're both as ruthless as each other.' She frowned. 'What I don't know is if Keith had made any decision. As far as I know, nothing was said last night, so it's possible he'd been planning to say something this morning, only...' She trailed off. 'Excuse me for a bit, won't you?' she added, getting up from the table. 'I promised I'd make your team a drink. Bacon sandwiches were mentioned as well, so I'd better go and gather a list of what everyone would like.'

Nell nodded. 'Thank you. I know they'll appreciate that.'

'Adam, you couldn't give Rachel a hand, could you?' asked Fran. 'There are a lot of people out there.'

Adam stared at her as if she'd asked him to push a pea up Vesuvius with his nose, but then he suddenly caught on to the reason for her suggestion. It was the perfect opportunity to loiter in the background. He scrambled from the table in such haste he almost knocked his stool over.

'Right,' said Nell with a smile, looking expectantly at Fran. 'I've noted all that. So, let's get back to the sequence of events on Saturday. What happened after lunch through into the evening?'

9

SATURDAY AFTERNOON

Fran was making her way to the front door when the view into the dining room stopped her in her tracks.

'Oh, Rachel...'

Two faces looked up at her.

'She does a grand job, doesn't she?' said Derek from where he was sitting beside Rachel, like her, a polishing cloth in his hand.

'She really does,' Fran agreed.

While Fran had been busy turning a set of raw ingredients into five courses of exquisite food, Rachel had utterly transformed the dining room.

Pistachio-coloured raw silk had been wrapped around each of the chairs at the table, tied in a large bow at the back, and a matching table runner laid along the impressive mahogany table. Napkins had been crafted into the shape of water lilies and each place setting had been laid with the finest crystal and china. A candelabra entwined with ivy and roses had been placed in the centre of the table and an enormous bowl of flowers sat either end, tumbling with peonies, lisianthus, roses, sage and stocks. It both looked and smelled amazing.

Derek and Rachel were in the process of polishing a mountain of silver: platters, charging plates, cutlery and serving spoons. Derek had the smile on his face of someone who probably didn't mind what he was doing, as long as he was doing it beside Rachel. And it was, Fran realised, the exact same way that Rachel looked at Derek. A reminder that even among such excess and greed, something simple could still be far more beautiful than anything else the house contained. Fran gave them both another smile and ducked back out of the room, just as the front door bell clanged.

Fran's heart was in her mouth as she opened the door. She'd only ever ordered an ice sculpture for clients once before, and that was far more simplistic than today's design would be. It had to be perfect. She knew it would make the most incredible centrepiece, but the details she'd been able to give the company who made it had been few and far between. She just prayed it had been enough.

The man standing on the step was a burly individual, biceps bulging through the thin material of his tee shirt. He also had one of the finest beards Fran had ever seen: fox-red and dense as they come.

'You must be Mac?' she said, although the large black liveried van behind him was something of a giveaway.

'I am indeed... Fran, right?'

She nodded, but he missed it, his attention captivated by the setting.

'I reckon I'm in the right place anyway,' he said, staring up at the imposing building he had found himself in front of. Gaze shifting slightly, he peered over her shoulder and into the hallway. 'It's going in there, is it?'

'Yes, will that be all right? The steps, I hadn't thought, sorry.'

Mac grinned. 'Not a problem, she's on wheels, and I

brought my ramp,' he said, throwing open the rear doors of the van.

Fran focused her attention on a large trolley in the centre of the van, or rather the bulky object which sat atop it, covered by a sheet. She really didn't know what she was going to do if Mac had misled her about his skill in any way. But from the very first glimpse she could see she needn't have worried. The object beneath the sheet glittered and sparkled even in the minimal light coming in through the van's doors, and with a flourish, Mac revealed the rest of his sculpture. Fran beamed in reply.

Derek and Rachel were duly summoned and ten minutes after that, Mac had not only shown them how to set up the hoses which connected to the plinth where the ice sculpture sat, draining away the meltwater, but he had also rigged up a little battery pack which would make real lights shine from deep within the sculpture. He left in a shower of grateful thanks.

Fran grinned at her colleagues, colleagues who were rapidly becoming friends. 'Well, if that doesn't blow the Chapmans' socks off, I don't know what will,' she said.

'It's stunning,' said Derek simply, and Fran knew he meant it. He was a man who could turn his hand to pretty much anything of a practical nature and he would absolutely appreciate the skill involved in producing such a captivating work of art.

Having decided to leave the sculpture in the dining room until it was needed, Fran returned to the kitchen with a far lighter heart than when she had left it.

The remainder of the afternoon progressed at a rapid pace and, fortified by strong cups of coffee and several chocolate digestives, Fran and Adam gave everything one last push. Whenever she catered for a large event, there was always a moment when it seemed that nothing would be finished in time, and despair would begin to eat its way into her. But, from experience, Fran also knew that this moment was followed very soon after by the sudden coming together of everything as if by magic. And today had been no exception. They had done all they could, and with only the last-minute preparations to make, it was time to change into their formal clothes.

It seemed an extraordinarily long time since Fran had left her room that morning, and it would be many more hours yet until she could return to it. But, as she sat on the bed and breathed deeply, a quiet and calm sense of achievement stole over her. She was good at her job and, barring accident or emergency, she would soon be serving everyone with the results of her labours.

Busy with her mascara wand, it took a little time for the sound of a slamming door to register. Most of the guests were busy getting ready and there had been sounds of movement for a while, but it was only when Fran's brain reminded her that the room next to hers was vacant that she realised how out of place the noise had been. And now voices were drifting in through her open bedroom window. Voices that were raised in anger.

'We had a deal, Mimi, we've always had a deal. So why you think you can simply change the terms is beyond me.'

A pause and a muffled comment...

'I keep up my end of the bargain, Keith, don't you dare accuse me of doing otherwise. I've entertained those dreary women for you all morning – for God's sake, the Dawson woman wouldn't crack a smile if her life depended on it. And when do you ever hear me moaning? I have supported you in all the ways you've asked.'

'Except for the most important perhaps. I thought we both knew where we stood – I turn a blind eye to your dalliances, after all there's not much I can do about them when I'm stuck in London, so all I ask is that when I'm here, you at least try to behave like my wife. And yet you've been draped over Oliver all afternoon, there's no need to be quite so obvious about it.'

'Oh, Keith, darling, you are funny. Ollie's good for a bit of fun, but the man is a total arse. For heaven's sake, he thinks I enjoy listening to him read poetry. Fortunately, his ego is as big as his bank balance and if it wasn't for me, he wouldn't even be in the running for your latest project. I've been keeping him sweet, that's all, and for a man like that, my so-called interest in him is made all the sweeter because he assumes you know about it. So, the fact that he thinks he's getting one over on you is almost as good as getting his leg over me. We're all playing games, Keith, you included.'

'There's one thing carrying on behind my back, Mimi, but—'

'Me? And what do you do when you're in London, Keith? Don't tell me you live like a monk, not when Georgia Mackenzie tells me all your secrets, darling.'

Another pause, this time accompanied by sounds of movement and a sudden intake of breath.

'Get your hands off me!' yelled Mimi.

'Don't flatter yourself, darling, I'm acting too, or hadn't you realised? Christ, I even pretend I enjoy your attention, I could win awards for my acting skills.'

'You bastard! You can't have it both ways.'

'Neither can you. As soon as this weekend is over, you'll be hearing from my solicitor. And you know what that means.'

Fran had drifted towards the window to hear the conversation better and a sudden loud crash made her jump. It was followed immediately by the sound of a door closing. If she had to hazard a guess, she'd say that Mimi had thrown something. Well, that *was* interesting. Keith very obviously knew about Mimi's relationship with Oliver, and whatever he was threatening her with, one thing was certain – Mimi Chapman would now be in a foul mood. And that didn't bode well, for any of them.

. . .

When Mimi Chapman descended the stairs a little while later, however, it was as if the argument with her husband earlier had never even happened. Maybe that's what it was like when your whole life appeared to be nothing more than putting on a show, waiting in the wings for the scenery to change before walking out to act another scene. From the pause at the top of the stair-case, to the slight shake of the head, the placement of one foot in front of the other to maximise her pose, Mimi Chapman was waiting for her audience's attention. She only had one chance to nail her entrance and she wanted to be sure to get it right.

She was dressed in a gold lamé sheath which skimmed her body, barely touching her hips and breasts as she walked. Even so, it left nothing to the imagination and Fran was certain Mimi wasn't wearing any underwear. She wouldn't want anything to spoil the line of the dress. It fell straight to the floor, held in place by a simple clip, fixed to one shoulder. Much like the dress, Mimi's skin shimmered as she walked, toned, lithe and a perfect accompaniment to the golden sun of the evening. At her throat was an elaborate choker and, as she passed Fran without even the merest hint of acknowledgement, she could see at its centre a leopard's head, glittering with diamonds. Mimi Chapman could stop traffic.

Fran watched as she walked into the morning room in an almost repeat performance of the evening before, except that this evening there was an air of fevered anticipation. All the guests had taken the greatest care over their appearance; even Ginny Dawson, who had chosen a structured blue-black taffeta mid-length gown, looked transformed. Beside her, Keith wore the same regulation tuxedo that all the men had chosen, but his hair was slicked down, a neater pair of glasses framed his face, and his casual slouchy manner of before had entirely gone. Tonight, he was all business.

Now that Mimi had arrived, Fran returned her silver tray swiftly to the kitchen, so that Adam could reload it with another set of glasses filled with champagne. She slipped out into the hallway and along to the dining room, where Derek was already waiting for her. It wouldn't take long to move the sculpture, but first she needed to dress it with the hors d'oeuvres which Mimi had requested. The base of the structure was filled with crushed ice and it was the perfect place to nestle oysters. Caviar would also be served from small dishes with tiny silver spoons, the only other accompaniment to these being blinis and sour cream. Taking inspiration from the beautiful flowers with which Rachel had filled the house, Fran had also tucked flower heads in between some of the serving dishes and, as she stood back to check the presentation, Derek gave a low whistle.

'Very nice,' he said. 'Now doesn't that look good? I can't stand caviar, oysters neither, but it's perfect. You've done a blinding job, Fran.'

She smiled at him, looking very dapper in a dark suit. 'We all have,' she replied. With yet another glance to check the time, she nodded. 'Best get this thing moving then before my heart actually comes out of my chest. Is yours going like the clappers too?'

'It used to. Over the years, my anxiety levels have receded a little, but I know exactly how you feel. When I first came here, Mimi's parties used to make me feel physically sick. Now, it's not so bad, but I know better than to relax.' He gave her a twinkly smile. 'Soon be over, though,' he said. 'Come on.'

Mimi was waiting for them in the hallway.

'It's not going to melt everywhere, is it?' she asked, eyes narrowing.

'Well, it will melt,' replied Derek, 'but the sculpture itself is set into a shallow trough. The trough collects the water and funnels it to the rear, where a pipe draws it away into a bucket. It's all hidden by the skirt around the base, no one will even be aware it's happening.'

'Just so long as we don't have water dripping everywhere. The carpet could be ruined.'

'I assure you that won't happen, Mrs Chapman,' said Fran.

Mimi's eyes flicked up and down the structure, still hidden beneath the cloth, but when it was evident she couldn't think of anything else to find fault with, she gave an impatient tut.

'Well, let's have a look then.'

Derek dipped his head. 'If I could ask you please to step out of the way for a moment, Mrs Chapman, just while we move it. The sculpture's solid and very heavy, it could do you a nasty damage if it fell on you.'

It took only a moment to have everything perfectly positioned. Fran was very conscious however that the sculpture should only be revealed in full at the appropriate moment, but she lifted the cloth so that Mrs Chapman could take an advance peek. She could hardly refuse.

Mimi was silent a moment but, eventually, the corners of her mouth moved upward a fraction. 'Yes, excellent.' She turned to Derek. 'Now if I could inspect the dining room, please, provided Rachel is around...?'

'I'll go and fetch her,' replied Fran, cheeks burning. She let out the breath she had been holding for goodness knows how long and tried to breathe evenly. It was all going to be okay. She'd been warned that Mrs Chapman wasn't overly generous with her praise, but an 'excellent' surely merited an inward whoop of relief if nothing else.

Reaching the morning room door, she gave Rachel a nod and, taking the platter she was carrying, smoothly took her place in the room, circulating among the guests. Heather was standing alone by the fireplace and Fran crossed over to greet her.

'Ms Walton? May I offer you something?'

She was wearing a blush-pink evening gown, Grecian in style, thin gold bands tied to accentuate her waist and breasts but, despite the warmth of the evening, her face looked pinched, almost as if she was cold.

She shook her head, eyes dropping from Fran's almost immediately and Fran was surprised to see a hollow look in them. For some reason, Heather's lightly bronzed shoulders seemed to be carrying the weight of the world on them.

'I'm fine, thanks. They're too tempting, and I'm not sure I'll manage a five-course dinner as it is. My meals tend to be smaller and nothing like as grand.'

Fran smiled. 'Beans on toast, with a little black pepper and cheese on top is my absolute favourite,' she said. 'But don't tell anyone I said that.'

Heather's face relaxed a little. 'Oh yes, or boiled egg and soldiers. I work late,' she added by way of explanation.

'You're a lawyer, I believe?'

'At the moment, yes.'

It was an odd reply, thought Fran, and made all the more so by the slight but significant pause before Heather started to speak. Becoming a lawyer was a lengthy process and the kind of career you worked towards for a good part of your life and then, once achieved, something you stuck with. It didn't seem at all the kind of job that you would simply try on for size and then take off and opt for something else instead. She would have asked another question but Heather's gaze had sunk back to the floor and Fran got the feeling she wasn't in the mood for conversation at all.

'Enjoy your evening,' she said and moved away.

Adam had everything ready to go and, in a carefully orchestrated sequence, they each took up their places. As Keith Chapman walked forward to give his speech, the doors into the hallway were closed and Fran dimmed the lights which glowed above them from the upper floor. The evening sun would be shining for a while yet and the idea was not to completely darken the hallway where the ice sculpture stood, but to provide some contrast so that its lighting effect could be properly appreciated.

'I was going to talk about Summershill,' began Keith. 'About the vision I saw for its future. A future which, thanks to all of you, now stands a very good chance of becoming a reality. It's a vision which has been a long time in the making and, I believe, will spawn a new way of living, integrating business spaces with social and residential ones, providing communities which will thrive and grow over time. Communities which everyone will want to be a part of.' He paused for effect. 'Instead, I think I should simply show it to you, and let you imagine the possibilities for yourselves.'

With that, Keith drew off the white silk sheet which covered the ice sculpture and let it drop to the floor. And, just as he had anticipated, murmured surprise and expressions of delight filled the hallway. A spontaneous round of applause broke out, picking up strength until the sound echoed around them in the confining space.

Fran felt a surge of pride, happy that her idea had paid off in such a brilliant way. Plus, whatever else happened this evening, she felt as if she had just earned herself a get-out-of-jail-free card, and that felt good.

The dining room hadn't been in use until this evening and now it was Rachel's turn to take a bow. The table looked stunning, the room filled with a heady scent of roses and, as the guests began to scoop up oysters or load up the tiny blinis with caviar, she flashed Fran a wide smile. It was time to get everyone seated and bring out the fish course.

Crab, smoked salmon and quails' eggs, oyster mushrooms, basil and rocket, oak-smoked duck, plum puree and caramelised figs, elderflower sorbet, raspberry tuiles and dark chocolate... They each took their turn, and in turn were each admired until, hours later, and with many more miles under the feet, dinner had been served.

It was at this point in the evening that Fran usually felt invincible, but there were still hours to go before they would be finished for the night and she couldn't relax just yet.

Back in the kitchen, she smiled at Adam, who had his arms elbow-deep in washing-up water. 'How are you holding up?' she asked.

'Why is it my nose only itches when my hands are in no position to scratch it?'

She pulled another stack of plates closer to the sink. 'Come on, I'll take a turn now. Why don't you get yourself some pudding?' she suggested. 'It's in the fridge in the utility.' Fran had never seen someone peel off a set of Marigolds so fast.

She had just thrust her hands in them when Rachel came back into the kitchen carrying another tray loaded with dishes.

'I should stay in here if I were you,' she remarked. 'The fireworks are about to start.'

Fran looked up, frowning. 'I didn't know...' She broke off as the penny dropped. 'Oh, you don't mean actual fireworks, do you? As in pyrotechnics?'

Rachel gave her a wry smile. 'No, I might be keen to watch those. But Mimi has a face like thunder, Heather looks about to dissolve into tears any moment, and Richard's gone walkabout again. I have no idea whether any of those things are connected but...' She blew out a puff of air. 'A word to the wise.'

Fran could feel her relief that the meal was over going into freefall. 'But they all seemed fine during dinner.'

Rachel quite accurately guessed the reason for her anxiety and gave her a warm smile. 'Because they were all eating such amazing food,' she said. 'This has nothing to do with anything you have or haven't done, don't worry, but rather everything to do with the weekend's business.'

Fran nodded. 'Heather seemed pretty morose earlier. No, that's not quite the right word.' Fran thought for a moment. 'She did seem down, but also... hard to describe, but almost as if she was waiting for the axe to fall.'

'Maybe it is,' replied Rachel. 'People are willing to invest a lot in Keith's projects, not just in terms of money, but also the proverbial blood, sweat and tears. They will have jumped through a huge number of hoops just to get an invite here this weekend, so if they leave tomorrow without a deal, for some of them it could meaning losing everything.'

'Well, I've found Richard,' said Adam, reappearing from the utility room, a large bowl in his hand. He nodded towards the window, where Richard could be seen walking around the side of the building and into the rear courtyard. He was engaged in the circular wander which people often adopt while on the phone, stopping every now and again to kick at something with his foot, leaving gouges in the gravel which Derek had spent hours raking smooth.

And it was evident that Richard didn't like what he was hearing. His hands began to gesticulate wildly, in movements which became more and more exaggerated as time went by. At one point he turned around and Fran was shocked to see what she could only describe as a snarl on his face. Whoever he was talking to was getting it with both barrels.

Fran looked at Rachel's anxious face as they both stared at him through the window. 'It's shit really, isn't it?' she said. 'You know, the more I'm around these people, the more grateful I am that I live the way I do. I might not have pots of money, but no one here seems particularly happy, do they? The kind of wealth these people have, and the power that goes with it, just seems to destroy things.'

Rachel's expression was grim. 'Doesn't it just.' She held Fran's look for a moment and then brightened her face with a smile. 'But, on the plus side, everyone is now stuffed full of food and drink and won't be wanting anything for a while. Time for us to have a breather and something to eat.' She grinned at Adam. 'I see you're starting with dessert.'

As she spoke, Fran caught movement out of the corner of her eye. Richard Newman had just hurled his no doubt very expensive phone at the courtyard wall. A large piece of something detached itself and dropped to the floor, before the phone bounced once more and landed beside it. Richard didn't even stop to check what damage he'd done, or even inflict further, he simply stalked off, back the way he'd come.

'I think we'll all be keeping out of his way for the rest of the evening,' she said, rolling her eyes. 'Although I wonder if whatever's eating him is the same thing that upset Mimi?'

'I doubt it,' replied Rachel. 'I think that has more to do with a certain Mr Knight, judging by the daggers she was throwing at him. If looks could kill...'

~

'Well, well, well,' said Nell, 'that is interesting. So, we have the Dawsons who will be in a spot of bother if they haven't secured a deal with Keith, and are clearly on the take. We have the wife, obviously having an affair, and threatened too. With what? Divorce?'

'It certainly sounded that way,' answered Fran. 'And it was odd that the Chapmans chose to have their argument in what's essentially a spare room. Although, of course, it did mean that they were well away from Oliver Knight's bedroom. No chance of him or any of the other guests overhearing something they shouldn't.'

Nell's eyes narrowed. 'Hmm... Mimi might be playing games but they all seem to revolve around Oliver Knight. Then there's Heather Walton, who had been heard giggling with Keith in the cabin by the pool earlier yesterday afternoon, but then suddenly lost her sense of humour, and lastly, we have the often-disappearing Richard Newman, who now that he's been told he's got to stay in the house for the time being may well be regretting hurling his phone at a wall. But he's disappeared once too often for my liking, and I want to know why. Who was he talking with on the phone? And where does he keep wandering off to? In any case, he's someone who was very angry at the end of the evening.' She looked at Fran, eyebrows raised. 'You'd probably need to be angry to bash someone over the head, wouldn't you?'

Fran gave her a tight smile. 'That's why you'll always find me in the kitchen at parties,' she said. 'Aren't people supposed to enjoy themselves?' She'd never really thought about it before but, by nature, Fran wasn't especially gregarious. Parties, particularly when she'd been younger, had always been viewed with trepidation. Was that why she decided ultimately to become a caterer? So that she *could* always be a part of the background and never in the limelight.

Nell reached for another pastry and then stopped herself. 'So who did get the green light from Keith then?' she asked.

'I really don't know,' replied Fran. 'If I had to guess, I'd say no one. There were certainly no announcements made that I'm aware of, and none of them looked particularly happy as the evening ended. But it's like Rachel said, no one usually mentions the reason why they're all here, not directly anyway. And, apart from Keith's little speech when the ice sculpture was unveiled, that was it. Keith was in a really funny mood though at the end of the night. He was drunk admittedly, he'd been drinking steadily all evening, and quite possibly a large part of the day as well, but even when you're maudlin you often speak the truth, don't you? Or some shade of it at least.'

'Why?' asked Nell. 'What did he say?'

'That he wondered whether it was all worth it.' Fran paused a second. 'Sorry, I should explain. We'd just finished clearing up. The guests had all retired to bed, and we were about to turn in ourselves when I remembered that I hadn't checked the bucket underneath the ice sculpture – the one that collected melted water. Can you imagine Mimi's reaction if it overflowed in the night and ruined her carpet? I'd already sent Adam up to bed, and said goodnight to Rachel, so I walked back down the hallway and realised there was a light under the study door. I thought it had been left on by mistake, but when I opened the door to turn it off, Keith was sitting in his chair by the window, a glass in his hand. I nearly wet myself. Honestly, these are not people you walk in on uninvited or unannounced. But, like I said, fortunately for me, he was so far gone he didn't realise how annoyed he should be.' She broke off to pull a face.

'That sounds horrible, doesn't it? And I can't even say that he'd been rude to me during the weekend, he hadn't, but neither had he made any acknowledgement of the contribution I'd made, the food, the sculpture, nothing. Sometimes it's what people *don't* say which has as much impact as what they do.' She chewed at her lip. 'Anyway, that's what I thought when I first went in there, but then he started talking. He asked me if I was married, if I had a happy life. When I told him that I did, he said that he thought *he* did too, once upon a time, but not any more. He said that all his life he had worked hard, believing that he would only ever be successful if he closed the next deal and then the next one. Always something more, always something better. And now, after years of following what he thought was his dream, he'd realised he's just a middle-aged man with a whole load of utterly meaningless stuff. At that point he wafted his glass around as if he wanted me to look at the room and acknowledge he was right.'

'Sounds like the whisky talking to me.'

'Yes, I thought that. But then I wondered whether he'd had some sort of an epiphany. That he'd realised some deeper truths. Mid-life crisis very possibly – I guess you can have those even if you seemingly have it all. But that's what I wondered;

whether he'd become sick and tired of people fawning over him? False relationships, fickle friends. Everything being about money.' She held up her hand as Nell opened her mouth to interrupt. 'I'm not saying he didn't bring it all on himself, because clearly over the years he has. But take the example of Peter Dawson's bottle of whisky. It cost them a lot of money, and Keith just gave it away, in front of him. On the one hand his action looks callous in the extreme, but if you look at it another way, perhaps he was making the point that he couldn't be bought, that he was regretting his materialistic ways.'

Nell smiled, a wry expression on her face. 'Be lovely to think so, wouldn't it? But I'm not sure a leopard can change its spots so easily. What did he say after that?'

Fran wrinkled her nose. 'He got a bit more personal. Lurched to his feet and said that we hadn't had much time to talk over the weekend. Thanked me profusely for everything I'd done and asked me what I thought of him. Him and his house.'

'And what did you say?'

'I'm not daft. I started heading back towards the door. Told him I thought his house was beautiful. Thanked him for allowing me to cater for them all this weekend, said I was glad he was happy with everything, and that I was sorry for interrupting him.'

'Do you really think he was going to make a pass at you?'

Fran shrugged. 'It's possible, but I think he was making suggestions his body wouldn't have been able to deliver. He was wavering on his feet, I doubt he could have stood up for much longer. Besides, he wouldn't be the first client who got a little over-familiar. I can take care of myself. I felt a bit sorry for him, actually.' She shook her head. 'I must be getting soft in my old age.'

She would have added more but at that moment there was a soft knock on the kitchen door, followed by the appearance of a head. It was Clare Palmer.

'Boss?'

Nell immediately got to her feet.

Fran didn't know the young detective constable, hadn't even been formally introduced to her, but there was still no mistaking the *I've come with important news* tone to her voice.

Annoyingly, Nell closed the door on her way out, but Fran had hardly time to wonder what they were discussing when she reappeared.

'Right, we've had the preliminary time of death,' she said, sitting back down again. 'But go on, what were you about to say?'

Fran frowned, her train of thought interrupted and now it would seem, permanently derailed. 'Nothing really,' she said. 'That was it.'

Nell nodded. 'So, what happened then?'

Fran smiled. 'I said goodnight pretty sharpish. Mr Chapman might have been in the mood for talking, but I wasn't. I didn't want to be rude, but by then it had been an incredibly long day and I just wanted to get to bed.'

'So that's what you did? Did you see anyone else?'

'No. I checked the ice sculpture... almost forgot that's what I'd set out to do originally.' She rolled her eyes. 'Switched the buckets over and emptied the water out of the first in the kitchen, there wasn't much. Then I replaced it, and went up to my room. Everything was quiet on the landing.'

'Okay, and this would have been what time?'

'Gone one in the morning, probably nearer half past actually.'

Nell was silent for a moment, her eyes on Fran, with an intensity of gaze which Fran had seen a few times in the past. And on every occasion it had sent her pulse racing. Nell looked as if she was about to say something, even opened her mouth to do so, but then closed it again, leaving Fran feeling very uncomfortable.

'What?' she asked, when she couldn't bear it any longer.

And still Nell took a moment to respond, and when she did, a smile came first. An odd smile, thought Fran. An attempt at warmth, a little regret, even perhaps an apology...

Fran's heart began to beat even faster.

'See, the thing is, Fran,' said Nell eventually, 'the pathologist has put the preliminary cause of death somewhere between 2.00 and 5.00 a.m. this morning. And that being the case, it very much looks as if you were the last person to see Keith Chapman alive.' She dropped her head slightly. 'I probably don't need to tell you what that means,' she added softly. 'But at the moment, Fran, I'm sorry, you've just become our prime suspect.'

10

'I won't let them arrest you,' said Adam quietly.

'I should hope not,' replied Fran, her face pale. 'I haven't done anything wrong.' She attempted a smile. 'But I appreciate the sentiment.'

Adam watched her as she stared out of the kitchen window. God in heaven, how had things come to this? She wasn't someone who got involved in stuff like this, she was at Claremont House as a caterer, nothing more. Okay, so they'd dabbled in a little mystery solving once upon a time, but that didn't mean anything, it had been a one-off. She'd been in the wrong place at the wrong time, or, as he liked to put it, in the *right* place at the *right* time, but murder and mayhem wasn't supposed to happen again. It was like lightening striking twice in the same place and what were the odds of that? He sighed. Perhaps it was all his fault. Maybe he attracted chaos to him like iron filings to a magnet...

The irony was that if Nell made any allowances for Fran at all, she had done so *because* of their past involvement. Otherwise Fran would probably already have been arrested and thrown into a damp cell with her leg in chains, or whatever they did nowadays.

She'd also been really looking forward to this weekend. Saying it was an opportunity to work with some very high-profile clients and hopefully gain a testimonial which would look incredibly impressive on her website. Cupcakes were all very well, Fran had told him, but she didn't want to settle for making those until the end of time, she said she wanted to stretch herself too. Personally, Adam thought that was a real shame. He'd eaten a lot of her cupcakes and didn't want her to ever stop making them. He hadn't told her that though. It was the kind of thing which would have earned him one of her looks. The special kind she reserved just for him.

'I never really thought how your mum must have felt,' she said, turning back to Adam. 'When it looked as if the finger of suspicion was pointing at her. I knew it wouldn't have been nice, but I didn't account for the feelings of sheer panic she must have experienced. It's ridiculous, but I'm terrified the police are going to find something incriminating.'

'Like what?'

She sought for an example. 'I don't know, a blood-encrusted dagger or something.'

Adam gave her his own special look, the one Fran said that despite his being twenty-four, still reminded her of the look her teenage daughter had perfected. 'Fran, may I remind you that Keith has had his head bashed in, he wasn't stabbed.'

'I know! But see what I mean, I can't think straight.'

'The police aren't going to find anything because there's nothing to find.'

'Yes, but someone could plant something on me. They do that in films all the time. Someone gets framed for murder and the police are all bungling idiots and—'

'Do you want to say that a little louder, Fran, I don't think everyone heard you.'

She flashed him a helpless look. 'Sorry,' she said, lowering her voice. 'But you know what I mean. People get, what's the phrase? Fitted up? And their life is never the same again. They lose their jobs, their homes, their marriage falls apart, they're left destitute and...' She trailed off at the look on Adam's face. 'So I might be being a little melodramatic, but you get the idea.'

He gave her a warm smile. 'Meanwhile, back in non-TV land, none of those things are going to happen for the simple reason that you aren't guilty and the police will find no evidence that you are. More to the point, they will also find evidence that someone else *is*. Besides, I'm not going to sit back and let you be accused of anything.' He really meant that, he hoped Fran knew.

'Not being funny, Adam, but how are you going to do that? Nell is hardly going to share details of her investigation with us, is she?'

'Probably not,' he admitted. 'In which case we'll just have to conduct our own.'

'Adam, no. You heard what Nell said. If we do this again, we're going to get into heaps of trouble.'

'An hour ago, I'd have agreed with you. I'd have been perfectly willing to let the police solve this one. Aside from the normal human response that killing someone is very wrong indeed, I didn't particularly like Mr Chapman. I didn't like Mrs Chapman either, or any of their guests and, no offence, Fran, but why would I care what happens to a bunch of rich—'

'Don't say it!'

Adam grimaced. 'A bunch of wealthy individuals with the morals of alley cats. I don't give a stuff what they've done, or what happens to them, so I'd have been perfectly happy to let the police do their thing, but not now, this is different. This is personal.'

Fran sighed. 'Adam... I really appreciate this, but how are

you going to help when you won't have access to anything the police find out?'

'I haven't entirely worked that out but there's heaps we already know.'

'Heaps?'

Adam nodded. 'Yes! Come on, Fran, think about it. What did we do the last time we were trying to catch a killer? Motive, means and opportunity, that's what it's all about. And we have... some of the answers to some of those things.'

'How reassuring.'

'Sarcasm will get you nowhere,' he replied, smiling indulgently at her as he waggled a finger in her face. He withdrew it swiftly when Fran looked as if she wanted to bite it. 'It's better than nothing,' he added. 'And all we have to do is fill in the blanks. Let's go through the list of what we know, starting with opportunity, because that's easiest.'

'Yes, it is,' said Fran pointedly. 'Answer, everyone had opportunity.'

'I wasn't going to put it quite like that, but okay, yes, it's theoretically possible that anyone could have snuck down in the middle of the night. But means, what about that?'

'Blunt force trauma, that's what Nell said had happened,' replied Fran. 'But I guess that just tells us Keith was hit over the head. It doesn't tell us what the murder weapon was.'

'No, it doesn't. But it sounds very much as if Keith died when he interrupted a robbery in progress, in which case the murder weapon would have been something to hand, so something already in the study. Can you think of anything which was obviously missing?'

Fran shook her head immediately. 'I was only in there for about five minutes last night, and even less than that this morning. I've no idea what's usually in the room; besides, I wasn't really looking around me.'

'So then we need to ask Rachel if she's aware of anything. I know she wasn't in the study for long either, but it's possible she noticed something. It would have been big and heavy so... a lamp? A crystal decanter maybe, you said he'd been drinking. As yet, I don't think there's any sign a weapon has been found. I'm sure we would have got wind if it had.'

Fran thought for a moment. 'Would that make a difference to who could have done it? I'm usually the first to stick up for women's equality, but I think it's fairly true to say that generally men are stronger than women. So, are we looking for a man? That narrows the list of suspects down considerably.'

'I think we have to keep an open mind,' replied Adam. 'Keith Chapman wasn't a big man and he—'

Fran waggled her fingers. 'I've just thought of something. You're right, Keith wasn't especially well-built, but he was also very drunk. I'm not sure how much of a fight he'd be capable of putting up. Does that widen the field of suspects?'

'I think it has to.'

'I'm also wondering whether he even left the room at all. It was very late and he looked as if he was settled in for the night.'

'Maybe he didn't. That could put a whole different slant on things.'

Adam's mind was racing, filling with all manner of scenarios. How on earth would they get to the bottom of it? 'Okay, so means... We have no idea what the murder weapon was, but there are one or two things we can check. Anyone could have wielded it, man or woman we now think, but the bigger question is, where is it? If it was a biggish item, possibly taken from the study, where is it now? There are only so many ways to dispose of something, or even destroy it, depending on what it was made from.' He stared at Fran, feeling his heart sink. 'Police forensics are going to turn that up and we'll never be privy to the information. We'll never find out what it was.'

'Never say never,' said Fran matter-of-factly.

'So, opportunity, means... Now it gets more interesting...

Motive. Who do you reckon is in the frame?' He gave her a smile that was more of a wince. 'Apart from you, that is.'

'My money's on Peter Dawson,' said Fran. 'He was overheard suggesting he or Ginny should steal something, and you found out they were in financial trouble. I did think it might have been Mimi...' She pulled a face. 'But maybe that's just because I'd like it to be her. She's been up to all sorts of tricks this weekend, I'd like to see her get her comeuppance.'

'But she wouldn't steal her own painting.'

Fran sighed. 'No, of course not... so I guess that effectively rules Mimi out, doesn't it?'

'Or...' replied Adam, thinking. 'Maybe it doesn't.' He pursed his lips. 'If Mimi did murder Keith, what better way to turn suspicion away from herself than by making it look like a robbery gone wrong? We've just almost discounted her for exactly that reason.' He cocked his head. 'I wonder if Nell's team have spoken to her about the painting yet, I'd love to know what her reaction was.'

'Right,' said Fran, nodding. 'So we rule her back in. I heard Mimi and Keith arguing, and he threatened her with divorce, don't forget. He clearly knows she's having an affair.'

'We need to ask ourselves what's the benefit to Mimi if Keith dies,' said Adam. 'I'm guessing the usual – money. Either from a life insurance policy or an inheritance perhaps? We have no idea whether Mimi has any money of her own, but I think we need to find out somehow.' He looked around the kitchen. 'Has all this; the house, the lifestyle, been funded by Keith? Or did Mimi come to the marriage with money of her own? Family money, perhaps.'

'That should be easier to check,' said Fran. 'We definitely need to find out what we can about her.' She took a deep breath. 'So, that leaves us with Heather, Richard and Oliver Knight. They're all potential investors so they must have a fair amount of money otherwise Keith wouldn't have even invited them here this weekend. And if that's the case, why would they need to steal a painting?'

'Unless one of them is hiding something,' said Adam. 'And actually needs money quite badly. The Dawsons seem to have had everything riding on this deal; maybe one of the others did too, and so, on finding out they weren't successful, decided to help themselves. It's the only thing I can think of.'

Fran wrinkled her nose. 'Me too,' she said. 'So all we can do is try to uncover a bit more about their backgrounds and hope that gives us some kind of clue. Plus, Heather was hidden away in the cabin with Keith for a while. I want to know what that was all about.'

'And who Richard was on the phone with that made him so angry,' added Adam. He had an idea about how he could find that out, but he'd keep it to himself for now. He didn't want to get Fran's hopes up if nothing came of it.

'The really odd thing though is that it doesn't sound as if anyone got the contract,' said Fran. 'None of the guests are exactly cock-a-hoop, are they? So did Keith simply not have time to let the successful person know?'

'Or, maybe, none of the guests were chosen. It would be easy enough to check, and I would imagine they'd all be keen to share with us if they had been successful. After all, if you were on the point of signing a lucrative deal, you'd hardly be in the market for stealing a painting, would you?'

'Indeed...' Fran absently flicked a bit of fluff from her sleeve. 'So, that's it then. We've covered opportunity, means and motive and, apart from a few things to check, I'm not sure we're any further forward. But at least—'

'My God, I've just thought: where's the painting?'

Fran stared at him, open-mouthed.

'If you'd just lost a contract, were angry, possibly desperate and had stolen a painting, wouldn't you have done a bunk? Fled under cover of darkness… But everyone is still here, so where *is* the painting?'

Fran's shoulders slumped. 'That's quite probably why my room is being turned over as we speak,' she said. 'I suspect it's only a matter of time before everyone else's is too.'

'Shall we have another cup of tea?' asked Adam kindly.

'I feel like a bloody teapot,' replied Fran. 'I'm not sure I can stomach another, but you have one if you want.'

'I wasn't actually thinking about me,' replied Adam. 'I was thinking that I might have a stroll out there.' He pointed a finger in the direction of the main hallway. 'See if I can get the gist of what's going on. And taking everyone tea is as good a way of doing it as anything.'

Fran smiled. 'I'll put the kettle on,' she said.

While she was fiddling with mugs, Adam began to pace the floor. 'I've been thinking too… I haven't been asked to give a statement yet, and I bet Nell will leave me until last. Partly because I don't have any connection to this at all, but also because she's so adamant that we're not to investigate this case, that she doesn't want to give me the opportunity to say anything. It's professional pride, which I can understand, particularly as this is such a high-profile case, but it's also something I can use to my own advantage. And if she's not careful, it's going to go against her.'

'Why?' asked Fran warily.

Adam gave her a bright smile. He'd been keeping this to himself for a while but under the circumstances now was probably the time to share it. 'Because I may have seen some things which might help us. Things which Nell doesn't know about yet.'

Fran groaned. 'Go on…'

'It was very late when we all got to bed last night, and I don't generally sleep very well anyway. Too many cogs whirring around.' He made a circular motion against the side of his head.

'So, after about an hour or two I woke up and I was hot, thirsty too. I got a drink from the tap in the bathroom and went to stand by the window for a bit to cool down. My room overlooks the garden,' he added pointedly.

Fran's eyes widened. 'What did you see?'

'Someone slipping back into the house in the wee small hours. And I'm pretty sure it was Mimi Chapman. Not only that, but she was naked.'

'Naked?'

'Yes, you know...' He paused. 'Rhetorical question?'

Fran nodded. 'Rhetorical question. Never mind, go on.'

'Well, that was it really. She walked up the terraces from the bottom of the garden.'

'And you're sure it was her?'

'It was dark,' said Adam, suddenly blushing. He hadn't come across many women like Mimi Chapman before. 'So I can't be sure, but there was enough moonlight to see a little and no one else looks like that, do they? All...' He broke off. He had been about to mime a series a curves with his hands, but he wasn't sure Fran would appreciate it. 'Another odd thing though – whoever it was, I could have sworn their hair was wet.'

'Maybe they'd been for a swim?' suggested Fran. 'Although with a houseful of other people, would you really do that naked? No, scratch that – if it was Mimi Chapman, she'd definitely swim naked.'

'Maybe she had, but what if she hadn't?'

Fran narrowed her eyes. 'What are you thinking?'

Adam shrugged. 'I've absolutely no idea. Yet. But it'll come to me.' He grinned at her. 'Right, let's get tea sorted for everyone and I'll see what I can find out.'

Ten minutes later, he left Fran restlessly fidgeting in the kitchen while he delivered drinks. It felt horribly like time was running out. Which was ridiculous really, there was no indication whatsoever that it was. Nell had been almost apologetic when she'd asked Fran to wait in the kitchen while she had a chat with a few people. She clearly didn't think that Fran deserved to be top of their suspect list, and that it really had been a case of being in the wrong place at the wrong time, but Nell had a job to do and she'd also made that very clear. One thing was certain, though: Adam was very glad he was around. If this was his fault then at least he was here to do something about it.

He could hear Nell at the far end of the hallway, talking with two of her police officers. He hung back, trying to look like he was moving slowly for fear of spilling the mugs of tea. Adam wasn't the most graceful of people, or the most agile. Falling over his feet and ruining Mimi's expensive carpet was just the kind of thing he *would* do. On this occasion, however, it was all about buying him some time.

'And I want their backgrounds checked as soon as possible, please,' said Nell, walking towards the dining room door. 'Specifically find out whether he's ever been in the police force. She's been here for years too, but I'd be interested to find out what she did before coming here. Richard Newman too, I don't know nearly enough about him yet either.' There was a pause and then Nell spoke again. 'Right, so as soon as Clare appears, let's have Oliver in. I'm keen to see how he fits into all this.'

The next second, Nell strode back out of the doorway at such speed that Adam nearly did drop the tray. She had a habit of doing that, appearing unannounced.

She narrowed her eyes at him suspiciously. 'What are you doing?'

He looked down at the tray and then back up.

'Yes, all right,' Nell retorted. 'I can see what you're doing. Give me that.' She took the tray from him before he could even open his mouth to reply. 'Now, go away, shoo...' She flapped a hand at him, holding the tray in her other hand as if it were no more than a piece of paper. How did she *do* that?

Adam had almost reached the rear hallway door before her voice floated back at him. 'Oh, and thank you for the tea...'

He scurried back to the kitchen, and hurriedly took a seat next to Fran. There was a plan forming in the back of his mind and he leaned closer. 'So, any minute now they're going to start interviewing Oliver,' he said. 'Nell told another of the police people that Clare and she were going to have him in.' He drew quote marks around his last words. 'So I need to get myself somewhere I can listen to what's going on.'

'Adam, you can't do that.' Fran shook her head. 'No, I won't let you. If you get caught, Nell will...' She trailed off. 'I'm not sure what she'll do, but it won't be pleasant.'

'I don't intend to get caught. Besides, how else am I going to find out what's going on?' He looked at her pointedly. 'So, if anyone asks, you haven't seen me. Say you don't know where I went, or you think I might be somewhere else. I'll leave the choice up to you. The important thing is that no one notices I'm missing and, if they do, doesn't think I'm up to no good.' He checked his watch.

Fran put a hand on his arm as if to detain him. 'I've been thinking too,' she said. 'About something Heather said to Ginny earlier. I was in the morning room and Heather was saying to Ginny that it was odd because she hadn't heard a thing in the night, and she's usually a light sleeper. And I've just realised that her room is around the corner from mine, which puts her right above the dining room, opposite the study. So, if there was noise in the night, shouting, the sound of furniture being over-turned, that kind of thing, surely she would have heard something?'

'Maybe she's not so light a sleeper as she thinks she is. They'd all had a lot to drink, don't forget.'

'True. But then I realised that my room *is* directly over the study. And I didn't hear anything at all.'

Adam stared at her. 'Which is odd.'

She nodded. 'It's a very old house though, well built, with stone walls. Perhaps the sound doesn't travel well? Not like it would in a more modern house anyway.'

Adam shrugged. It was possible, but unlikely, he thought.

'*And*, I noticed this morning that one of Mimi Chapman's hands is very red. What do you think to that?'

'Yes, I noticed that too. But she had a tissue balled up in her hand. It looked like she'd been squeezing it and I just assumed that was the cause.'

Adam was crestfallen. 'Oh... I didn't think of that. It looked to me like she'd scalded herself. But how could that have happened?' He thought for a moment. 'Scalded... or burnt? There's a wood oven down by the pool. You know, those things people cook pizzas in. I wonder if Mimi had been trying to set fire to something, as in trying to get rid of something... Like a *murder* weapon...' His eyes lit up. 'Maybe that's what she was doing when I saw her in the night. If it was her I saw.'

'What, naked and with wet hair?' Fran frowned. 'I think you might have read one too many detective stories.' She paused. 'But check anyway.'

He nodded several times. 'I must go,' he said, jumping to his feet. 'Wish me luck.'

'Adam, where are you going? What are you going to do?'

He turned back from the doorway. 'You don't want to know,' he said.

11

The plan was really very simple. It was a stifling hot day, sultry, and the windows of the dining room, like a lot of the others in the house, were open to the garden and the chance of fresh air. All Adam had to do was position himself in the right place and he'd be able to hear everything that was being said inside, namely the interview with Oliver Knight. What Adam had forgotten, however, was that the dining room windows stretched almost from floor to ceiling, and the only way to remain hidden would be to crouch directly beneath the window, where he would be shielded from view by an array of shrubbery which grew there. In a space that was only about half a metre high.

It had already taken him far too long to sneak around the edge of the building. He couldn't go past the morning room or the conservatory because the double doors in both rooms were also open and he'd have been spotted in an instant. That kind of invisible sneaking about only happened in films. Therefore, he'd had to go the other way – out of the utility room door – around to the front of the house – past the study window, or rather underneath it almost on all fours – then finally, past the front

door, and all of it on gravel which wanted to announce his presence every step of the way. He must have looked extremely odd,
placing each foot down as if worried he was stepping on a land-
mine, waiting for the gravel to give under it, silently with any
luck, before placing his other foot down and repeating the
process all over again.

Eventually, he reached the corner of the house and could
step onto the solid terrace which stretched around two sides.
The dining room windows beckoned enticingly.

It was the perfect place to interview everyone. Being opposite the study, it was contained within the part of the house
which had been sectioned off, and so, since early morning, none
of the guests had been allowed near it and the police had set up
camp there. The drawing room, in between the dining room
and the morning room, was also empty and provided a buffer,
ensuring that the sound wouldn't travel where it shouldn't.
These were big rooms with thick walls, as Fran had already
noted.

Adam paused a moment, his heart jumping uncomfortably
in his chest. He was hot and his tee shirt was sticking to him, the
hairs on the back of his neck already saturated with sweat. He
took a steadying breath and then, without dwelling too much on
what he was about to do, dropped soundlessly to a crouch and
then carefully onto all fours. Some kind of creeper grew around
the corner of the house, its roots emerging from a flower bed
which ran directly under the dining room window. Being the
middle of summer, its leaves were big and glossy and would
provide the perfect cover for anyone wishing to hide
themselves.

He crept closer, ears pricking up at the sound of voices from
within the room. They weren't loud, but he could make out
enough to decipher what was going on. Almost level with the
window now, Adam realised that the pose he had adopted was

still not sufficiently low to enable him to sneak beneath the window unseen, so he ditched all fours in favour of a weird and very uncomfortable belly shuffle. Gluing himself as close to the wall as he could, he pushed deeper into the undergrowth, and began to listen.

'...your relationship with Keith Chapman.'

It was Nell speaking, her voice calm, with a ring of authority.

'I've known Keith for years, we're friends.' Oliver Knight sounded equally calm, almost nonchalant.

'Friends?'

'Friends... and business colleagues.'

'I see, and how many years would that be, Mr Knight?'

'Um, five or six.'

'That long? Excellent. So you knew Keith Chapman well, then?'

'I wouldn't say well exactly... but—'

'And which came first – the friendship or the business relationship?'

'The business, yes. Definitely the business.'

'I see. So you became business colleagues about five or six years ago and that relationship deepened into friendship over time. So are you quite familiar with Claremont House in that case?'

'This place? No, not really. Not at all.'

'How many times have you been here before?'

Adam was momentarily distracted by a flicker of movement out the corner of one eye. An ant was making its way purpose-fully across the ground in front of him. He rubbed a hand across his head and changed his position slightly. It was almost unbear-ably hot down here.

'A few... How many is a few, Mr Knight? Three? Four?'

There was a pause. 'About that, yes.'

'Okay, we'll say three then, shall we? And those occasions, would they have been weekends like this?'

'A couple were, I can't really remember.'

'So maybe you do know the house quite well after all, if you've spent what's probably three weekends here in total?'

'Well, I know where the rooms are if that's what you mean. But... actually I think this is only the second weekend I've spent here.'

'Two weekends... okay.' Nell fell silent. 'But yet you'd been friends with Keith Chapman for years. He and his wife seem like very generous people. I would have thought you'd have been here more often than that.'

'Well, I haven't.'

A shiver rippled up Adam's arm. He was lying in the flower bed, propped up on his elbows and something was tickling him. He wiggled his arm slightly.

'Okay. We have your address in London, Mr Knight. Is that the only property you own?'

'No, I have several investment properties as well.'

'But you don't live in those?'

'No, they're tenanted.'

'I see, and how about personal property?'

Another tickle.

'Yes, I have a house in the country too.'

'Which is where?'

'In Wentnor.'

'Oh, that's not far from here, is it?'

'About half an hour away.'

Another pause. Another tickle.

'So you know the local area quite well?'

'I guess so, yes.'

'Okay... Just going back to this weekend for a moment...'

Adam glanced down as another shiver twitched his arm. Ants. Lots of them, all crawling... He jerked his head back so he could see the sleeve of his tee shirt, realising with horror that it was covered with the little creatures, and as soon as he realised that, he saw where he'd wriggled his elbow... deeper into the undergrowth and directly onto an ant's nest, which was swarming over the foot of the wall. He swallowed, feeling one begin to climb his neck.

'... You were here as a potential investor in Keith Chapman's latest project, is that right?'

Adam blew out of the corner of his mouth, wriggling his shoulders frantically.

'Yes.'

'And what isn't clear to us is whether Mr Chapman had made any decisions over who he wished to—'

The ant was making for his nose now and he dashed a hand at his face. A hand that was also creeping with them – he could see their little antennae waving, seeking... He screwed up his face, feeling a wave of panic begin to build. Teeth clenched, he tried to refocus his attention.

'I see, so he didn't give you any indication that—'

An ant crawled across his lip. And without thinking, Adam shot to his feet, frantically brushing his face and arms. 'Get off,' he shouted. 'Get off!'

There was a moment during his mad dance when everything stood still, when he turned slightly, facing the window. And, as he glanced up, everything else disappeared from view save for Nell's astonished face through the window, her eyes locked on his. *Shit.*

He moved before she did, trying to stay calm, trying to look as if he had every right to be out on the terrace and not at all engaged in eavesdropping. Every fibre of his being was telling him to run, but he knew he couldn't, and it was only a matter of seconds before Nell's strident voice rang in his ears.

'Adam Smith, don't you dare move! What on earth do you think you're doing?' She was slightly out of puff from having legged it out of the dining room, through the front door and around the corner of the house.

He tried to answer but he was still brushing maddened ants from his body and all that emerged was a strangled noise which bore no relation to any words he knew.

But Nell wasn't daft. And he could see the thought processes marching through her head, as if she was reading a script. *Nell Bradley looks at the flower bed. Nell Bradley looks at Adam Smith. Nell Bradley looks back at the flower bed and notices the crushed leaves. Nell Bradley realises that Adam Smith has been up to no good...*

'Have you been listening to us?' she demanded.

There was little point in trying to evade her question. The eyes boring into his were better than any lie detector test.

'I was only trying to help.'

Nell stared at him for several long seconds. 'Help? Adam, this is not your investigation. How many times do I have to make that clear? The last murder you got involved with was... I'm tempted to say a fluke, if only so that you get the idea out of your head that this current situation has anything to do with you. It does not. Do you understand me? You are a designer of computer games and the sooner you remember that and stop being such a... such a pain in the arse, the happier I'll be.'

'But, Fran?'

'Fran what?'

'It's her I'm trying to help. I don't give a fig about any of the others.'

'Well, fortunately for them, I have to. And for goodness' sake, Adam, I'm not about to arrest Fran for murder, not yet anyway.'

'But you've had her fingerprinted... you're searching her room.'

Nell clicked her tongue. 'Yes, it's a little thing we do when we're trying to eliminate someone from our inquiries. I doubt

Fran had anything to do with this, but I have a job to do, Adam, and there's a right and a wrong way to do it. It's not enough for me to believe Fran is innocent, I have to categorically prove that she is, and that means documenting evidence, and checking details so that it's indisputable. That's how the law works.'

Adam dropped his head.

'Oh, Adam...' Nell sighed, letting out a breath which seemed to go on forever. 'I know you're only trying to help, but please, if you really want to help Fran, you'll let us do our jobs.'

Adam nodded, scarcely able to meet Nell's eyes.

'So, do you think I can get back to my interview now...? *Excellent.*' Her face softened as she touched his arm. 'Come on, I'll take you back inside.'

She led the way along the terrace and into the drawing room, holding the French doors open in a solicitous manner so that he could step inside. 'It will be okay, Adam. I'm sure Fran is feeling all kinds of horrible just now, but the sooner we get on and finish our inquiries with her, the sooner I can tell her not to worry. She just needs to sit tight, and you can repeat that to her if you like.'

He nodded. 'Okay.'

Nell held open the kitchen door too, ushering Adam inside to where Fran was still sitting pretty much where he'd left her. She looked up in surprise.

'I should bloody arrest you for obstruction,' said Nell from the doorway. 'But... I must be mad. Just sit here, until I tell you otherwise, okay?' And with that, she disappeared again, closing the door firmly behind her.

Fran got to her feet. 'Adam, what have you done?' Her voice was low. The special kind of low she reserved for people who had done something wrong. She was almost as scary as Nell at times.

He swallowed. 'Listening to an interview. But look, it's all okay.' He swiftly crossed to the island, pulling out a stool and sitting down. He fished his phone from one pocket and a pair of headphones from the other. 'Quick,' he said. 'Sit down.'

'Uh-uh, not until you tell me what's going on.'

Adam was deeply aware of precious seconds ticking past. He didn't want to miss anything. Sighing, he ran a hand through his damp hair. 'I was lying under the dining room window. I told you, the police are interviewing Oliver.'

'*Adam...*'

'Nell caught me, okay? I put my arm down in a bloody ant's nest and they were crawling all over me.' He shivered. 'But it's okay because Nell doesn't really believe you killed Keith, and I did what I set out to do. Come on, sit down.'

But Fran appeared to be rooted to a spot in the centre of the kitchen. 'What did you do, Adam?'

He ignored her for a moment, tapping his phone to open the app he needed. He screwed one of the headphones in his ear and held out the other to Fran. 'Stuck a bug on the windowsill.'

Fran's mouth dropped open. 'I told you to leave those at home. You promised!'

He gave her a sheepish look. 'Okay, so I might have had my fingers crossed, but you'll be really glad I did. They're about to start again. Shh... come and listen.'

With one final, very hard stare, Fran came to sit beside him. 'Okay, but we are *so* talking about this later.'

She took the proffered headphone, and he could see the sides of her mouth twitching. Fran could never stay mad at him for long.

'That's Nell,' he said. 'She's the one asking the questions.'

Fran nodded, leaning in towards him, and together they started to listen.

'Right, where were we?' said Nell. 'I'm sorry about the interruption, Mr Knight. You were telling us about your involvement with Mr Chapman's latest project, and what isn't clear to us is whether any of the guests here have been successful in securing the investment opportunity. Could you tell us what you know about that, please?'

There was a bitter laugh. 'Well, it wasn't me. Wasn't Dawson either, he and his wife both looked like they'd been sucking on lemons. As for the others, I wouldn't know, but I don't think either of them got it.'

'But you don't know for certain? Was there no announcement?'

'No. Keith was a mischievous bastard, he liked to keep everyone hanging on.'

'But I thought you were friends? Didn't you expect him to give you the opportunity, that being the case?'

'Not really, no. That isn't how it works.'

'Even so, I would have thought you might have expected it. Been irritated that he hadn't?'

'Again, not really.'

'Okay, Mr Knight. So how would you describe your relationship with Keith Chapman?'

'Well, I didn't bloody kill him.'

'That wasn't quite what I asked.'

'I told you, we were friends.'

'And that friendship, was it strong? Warm? How would you describe it?'

'I dunno, we were just friends, that's all.'

There was a long pause.

'And how about your relationship with Mrs Chapman, Mimi? How did you get on with her?'

'Okay. As much as anyone did.'

Fran turned to stare at Adam.

'So would you describe her as a friend too?'

'Not really, not in the same way as Keith. I mean, you don't with the wives, do you? They're just people you have to get along with when you're in business.'

'So you weren't having a sexual relationship with her?'

'No!' Oliver's reply was instant. 'Of course I wasn't. I told you, Keith Chapman was a friend.'

'So what would you say if I told you that several people have suggested that you and Mimi Chapman are having an affair?'

'Well, they're wrong! That's ridiculous.'

'So when we search your room for forensic evidence we won't find anything which will tell us she's spent time in your bed?'

There was a long pause. 'No, I told you...'

'Okay, Mr Knight, could you tell us what you were doing between the time when the party finished last night and when you got up this morning?'

'Like what? I went to bed.'

'Like did you go straight there? Did you get up at all in the night?'

'Yes, I went straight to bed. No, I didn't get up.'

'And what time would that have been?'

'I don't know, I didn't check.'

'Your best estimation then.'

'About one o'clock.'

'And did you see anyone as you were going to your room?'

'I said goodnight to the Dawsons. Their room is opposite mine and we walked up the stairs together.'

'I see. And did you shower first or read for a while? Anything like that?'

'No, I said, I went straight to bed.'

Another pause. 'Did you sleep alone, Mr Knight?'

'Yes.'

'You're certain about that. And you didn't get up again for any reason?'

'No... and yes, I'm certain.'

There was a long pause, and the sound of paper rustling.

'Hmm,' said Nell, a few moments later. 'I'm a little confused. We're talking about last night, yes? Saturday night.'

Oliver didn't answer but Adam could imagine the look on his face.

'It's just that when we spoke to Mrs Chapman about last night, she mentioned that she'd spent it in your room.'

'Damn, she's good,' said Fran.

'Shhh...'

Oliver made a strangled noise followed by a loud expletive. 'Okay... For God's sake! Yes, we slept together. Happy now? But have you looked at the woman? I mean, who wouldn't...? It doesn't mean I murdered anyone. Having sex isn't a crime.'

'No, you're right, it isn't. But we're trying to establish who might have had reason to steal from Mr Chapman, who might have killed him. And lying to me when I put a straightforward question to you doesn't suggest you're entirely trustworthy, does it? So, I'll ask you again, Mr Knight. What can you tell me about your relationship with Mimi Chapman?'

There was a very audible sigh.

'Okay... we're in love if you must know. Planning to marry. And no, I'm not particularly proud of going behind Keith's back, but it was just one of those things. The attraction was instant between us and we tried to fight it for a while, but... I guess in the end nothing could keep us apart.'

'Oh, please...' murmured Fran. 'Pass me a bucket.'

Adam gave her an exasperated look. 'Shh...'

'So you didn't kill Keith?' asked Nell. 'Kill him so that you and Mimi could live happily ever after, enjoying the money that she stands to inherit after his death?'

'But why would I want to kill Keith when I have money enough of my own, as does Mimi?'

'He still stood to come between you and your love for Mimi. He could have made things very awkward for you.'

'Well, I guess now we'll never know, will we? But, like I

said, I didn't kill him. Keith didn't know about me and Mimi and when the time came for her to ask him for a divorce she would have done so, calmly and appropriately. We're all adults. There would have been no need for melodrama, would there?'

Adam couldn't hear what Nell said next, but he could guess. There was a long pause and then her voice came again, strident and clear.

'Okay, Mr Knight. So, returning to the night in question. The night you spent with Mimi Chapman. Didn't you think that was a little risky? Sleeping together under the same roof as her husband.'

'Perhaps. But they haven't slept together for months. They have separate rooms, so he wouldn't know. Besides, he'd had that much to drink I doubt he knew what day of the week it was.'

'And you're certain that you and Mrs Chapman spent the night together, in your room?' asked Nell.

'Yes, I am.' A defiant note had crept into Oliver's voice.

'And yet, when everyone was roused this morning, including Mrs Chapman, you were each in your own rooms.'

'Well yes, of course we were. Mimi slipped back to her own room around six thirty. Appearances, you know. I'm afraid I fell back asleep.'

Adam could picture Nell nodding.

'I see... well, that explains it. Just one final question then, Mr Knight. Did you hear anything at all during the time you were in your room? Anything unusual?'

'No... slept like a baby, in fact.'

There was a long pause. 'Okay. Now before I ask you to return to the morning room, is there anything else you'd like to tell me? Anything which might have a bearing on what's happened here. Either the theft of the painting or Mr Chapman's death?'

Oliver's reply was instantaneous. 'No, why would there be?'

'No reason,' replied Nell smoothly. 'But you and the other guests have all been here a while, since Friday afternoon, in fact. I wondered if you could have seen anything out of the ordinary, or heard something which didn't seem right. Even if at the time it didn't strike you as odd.'

'I honestly can't think of anything.'

'Well, perhaps if you do, however trivial it may seem, you could either tell me or one of my officers. I think that's all we need to ask you for now.'

There was a pause during which a door could clearly be heard closing and then a voice came again, not Nell's this time, so presumably that of Clare Palmer.

'What do you reckon, Boss?'

Nell's words were much quieter this time. 'Lying through his teeth,' she said.

Adam pulled the headphone from his ear and placed it gently on the table. He blew a soft whistle. 'So Mimi and Oliver were definitely having an affair then,' he said.

'Well, I don't think there was ever much doubt about that. But what it also means is that Mimi and Oliver both have an alibi, one which would be hard to disprove.' Fran's eyes narrowed. 'Urgh, this is all far too confusing.'

Adam thought for a moment. 'So what else did we learn?'

'Not much,' replied Fran. 'Although I'm with Nell, I think Oliver was lying about something. He seemed far too cagey for my liking.'

He picked up the headphone again, but Fran stilled his hand.

'Don't,' she said.

He gave her a quizzical look. 'Why not?'

'Because I don't think you should. Nell has already caught you once, and if she finds out you've planted another bug, she will do all kinds of unmentionable things to you. But worst of all, she'll send you home.'

Adam was taken aback by the look in her eyes.

'I'm scared, Adam. I know what Nell said about me. I trust her and I know if she can cut me some slack, she will. But this is a big case. She's got her bosses breathing down her neck and she needs to make a quick arrest. I don't want that person to be me.'

Adam held the look in her anxious eyes. Last year he had sat in front of Fran and practically begged for her help. And he needed that help because he was almost certain that his mum was going to be accused of murder. And while most people would have told him that his fears were unfounded, or to stop being over-dramatic, Fran hadn't. She had listened and she had thought about what he'd told her. And then she had put her life on hold to help him out, to help his mum out. For no other reason than because she could see that her help was needed. If ever there was a time to repay her kindness, it was now.

'It won't be you, Fran, I promise. Not if I have anything to do with it.' He picked up his headphones and shoved them back in his pocket. Fran was right, Nell would send him home without any qualms at all, never mind his ability to solve problems. She had a whole team here, why would she need him?

A heavy rumble filled the kitchen and Adam shot another glance out of the window at the rapidly darkening sky outside. 'Sorry,' he said. 'You're right, we need to think for ourselves, not rely on what scraps of information we can glean from the police. We can work this out, Fran, I know we can. Besides, once it starts raining, my little bug friend will die a rather alarming death anyway and bang will go that source of information.'

Fran smiled. 'Thank you,' she said, and Adam knew it was for far more than just putting his headphones away.

He was about to ask her something else when an alert fired in his brain. A sudden connection made between something he'd mused upon earlier and the imminent storm.

He jumped up from his stool, staring at Fran in excitement as his brain lurched into life. He'd been so stupid, it was one of the first things he should have checked. He just had to hope he wasn't too late.

'I've just had a thought,' he said, registering the astonished look on Fran's face. 'Wait here, there's something I need to check!'

12

The first raindrops hit as Adam's feet pounded across the lawn of the second terrace. Big fat things which would very soon become a solid wall of water. The sky had been shifting uneasily for the last couple of hours, the morning's heat trapped beneath heavy cloud and now about to be released.

He jumped off the top step of the last terrace, not quite making it to the bottom in one leap, but the pool was ahead of him and, as yet, the storm hadn't broken. A minute or two later and any chance of finding what he was looking for would be quashed.

For a moment he stopped dead, taking in the opulence of his surroundings. Water rippled against the tiles at the pool's edge, whipped up by the increasing wind, but all else was still. And perfect. He wasn't sure what he expected.

The wood oven was tucked to one side of the cabin and, eyes scouring the ground, he moved towards it. The rain was heavier now, icy drips finding their way down the back of his neck. Ignoring them, he pulled out his phone. If he was right, then he'd need to take a photograph as evidence. Once the rain hit in earnest, things would be very different.

But he could see straight away that he was wrong. The surface of the wood oven was smooth, pale clay, both inside and out, and looked as if it had scarcely been used. Adam didn't imagine that was the case for a minute; more likely, as with everything else at Claremont House, it had been extremely well cared for. There were no ashes inside the oven, in fact, nothing at all. The whole thing had been swept clean. He laid a hand on the base but it was cold, as was the roof.

He'd been so certain he would find something here. The charred remains of whatever Mimi Chapman had been wearing when she'd clubbed her husband to death. Perhaps even the murder weapon itself. But, whatever she'd burned her hand on, it certainly hadn't been the wood oven. These things kept their heat and it hadn't been used in a while. More than that, there were no traces of it having been recently cleaned. Of ashes having been swept out and perhaps some fallen to the ground.

He thought a moment. Supposing you'd just killed your husband, were desperate to dispose of incriminating evidence, and in the dark too. You'd be in a hurry, careless, maybe not as thorough as you would like, but the area around the cabin and poolside was so clean it was almost clinical.

A gust of wind blew a line of rain into Adam's face. The squall was really getting up now. He was about to leg it back to the house when a thought came to him.

The cabin was built for the summer. An acreage of glass poured in light and a series of huge ceiling fans assured that whoever was in there wouldn't feel too much of the heat the light brought with it. The soft furnishings were lightweight and floaty, pale colours and sumptuous finishes that were designed to aid peaceful relaxation.

There wasn't much at all inside the cabin and Adam guessed that was the point of it. He imagined that for people who had more possessions than they knew what to do with, quite possibly the only way they could fully relax was in an environment that was minimalist. In this case, absence was soothing. But this kind of interior also left very little in the way of hiding places, not like in the main house. Even Adam's cursory inspection was enough to tell him there was nothing to be found here.

He wandered to the far end, where two shower rooms also provided an area for changing and, again, both were beautifully but very simply furnished. It was only as he entered the second room, however, that he spotted something. He might not have seen it at all had a sudden flash of lightening not lit up the room for a second. A soft sheen of water lay on the tiles closest to the drain. Retracing his steps, he checked the shower in the first room, but it was dry. He drew a finger underneath the shower head. Also dry.

He wasn't sure if what he'd seen was in any way significant, but the pool area had been in use by Mimi and the female guests the whole of yesterday morning. It was quite conceivable that one of them had had a shower during that time, or even at some later point in the afternoon if they'd been for a swim. It was, after all, their purpose. Confirming for himself that there was nothing else to be found inside the cabin, Adam ducked out into the rain, which was now hurling itself to the ground with quite unnecessary ferocity. The whole area had that sad look of a holiday resort out of season. Unwelcoming and cold. He ran the whole way back to the house.

Fran met him at the back door, holding up a hand towel as he entered.

'Here,' she said. 'I saw you running around the side of the house. God, you're soaked.'

He stood on the mat, his hair dripping water down the back of his neck where it slid in icy trails. He was both hot and out of breath from running and completely frozen at the same time. 'Thanks,' he said, grimacing as he rubbed at his hair and face.

'Where on earth have you been?'

He heaved in a lungful of air. 'Down to the pool,' he replied, sniffing. 'I wanted to check something before the rain came down.'

'And did you?'

He smiled. 'Just. Although the rain wouldn't have made any difference, there was nothing there.' He peeled off his shoes and socks and stepped into the room. His jeans were wet through.

'You need to go and get changed,' said Fran, 'or you'll get cold. Go on, I'll make you a drink and then you can tell me what you've been doing. And for goodness' sake, go up the back way and don't let Nell see you. She'll only want to know where you've been.' She wafted him away. 'And bring your wet stuff back down with you, I'll see if I can get it dry.'

There were voices as Adam reached the top of the stairs and he hung back, out of sight.

'There's nothing here, as expected.'

It was Owen Holmes, moving away from Adam towards the doorway which would take him around to the main landing and the principal bedrooms.

'Okay, Oliver Knight's room next.' A new voice this time. Clare Palmer. 'Oh, and preliminary's just in on the murder weapon. We're looking for something with what could have a triangular end to it. Solid though, metal rather than wood, she suspects.'

'Triangular? What, like the corner of something square? Lamp base? Candlestick, that kind of thing?'

'I think so, yeah.'

The voices faded away as they disappeared through the door and Adam hurried up the rest of the stairs, his bare feet virtually soundless on the treads.

Stripping quickly, he pulled another pair of jeans and a tee shirt from the bag he hadn't even bothered unpacking and got changed as quickly as he could. His jeans stuck uncomfortably to his damp legs as he tried to pull them on. Grabbing another pair of socks, he wrestled his feet into them and, bundling his wet clothing in his arms, he hurried back downstairs. He shut the kitchen door firmly behind him.

'Fran?'

Her face appeared in the pantry doorway. She was holding a large plastic box.

He motioned through into the utility rooms. 'Is anyone through there?' he whispered.

She shook her head. 'Why?'

'I know what the murder weapon is,' he replied, his voice still low, although he could barely keep the excitement out of it. 'I heard the two detectives talking about it upstairs. I think your room is clear, by the way.'

Fran placed the box on the table and held out her arms for his clothes. 'I should bloody well hope so, seeing as I haven't killed anyone.'

Adam gave her a sheepish look. That hadn't come out quite the way he had intended. 'Whoever did for Keith used something heavy, but which also had a triangular shape to it. Owen suggested it could be the corner of something square, like a lamp base.'

'That shouldn't be too hard to find, should it?'

'I wouldn't have thought so. We must remember to check with Rachel if she noticed anything missing from the study.'

Fran nodded. 'So where have you been exactly?' she asked, eyeing his hair, which was still wet.

'Looking for something which would incriminate Mimi. I had a sudden thought that she might have tried to dispose of any evidence by burning it in the wood oven by the pool.'

Fran's face lit up. 'Did you find something?'

'No.' He pulled a face. 'More's the pity. It was a bit of a long shot anyway, but when I saw the storm coming, I was terrified the evidence was going to get washed away. But there was nothing there. The wood oven hasn't even been used for a while, there were no ashes, and it isn't that it's been recently cleaned either – the whole area is spotless. Besides, the oven was stone cold.'

Fran stared down at the bundle of clothes in her arms. 'I'll put these on to wash,' she said, turning to look out of the window, where the rain was still lashing the courtyard. 'It was a good hunch. You never know, you might have got lucky, and one thing's for sure – if there's anything out there now in the way of evidence, it'll have been washed away.' She sighed and went through to the utility room.

Adam watched her leave, thinking about her words. Was there anything out there? They weren't just looking for the weapon that killed Keith, but the painting too. So where would you hide that? It was pretty big, not something you could conceal all that easily.

'Do you think whoever did this could have had an accomplice?' he asked as Fran returned.

'Two people working together, you mean?'

'I was thinking more of someone outside of the house,' he replied. 'Only, the set-up of this feels odd to me. On the face of it, what happened looks straightforward. Someone tried to pinch the painting, got caught in the attempt and Keith was killed in the resulting struggle. But what's the one thing you'd do if you'd stolen something, or killed someone for that matter?'

Fran shrugged. 'Run away?' she suggested.

'Precisely,' said Adam. 'You wouldn't hang around, would you? You'd get yourself as far away from the scene of the crime as possible, taking the painting and whatever you'd used to kill Keith with you. So why is everybody still here?'

'Well, I guess because if you left, it would immediately make you look guilty.'

This was why he liked talking to Fran. She had a knack for making everything seem simple, whereas he usually went straight for the most unlikely, most imaginative scenario. Great when you're designing computer games intending to fox players, but not so helpful in real life.

'There's also the fact that we're in the middle of nowhere,' she added. 'And most of the guests arrived by train. Derek picked them up from the station. Only the Dawsons came under their own steam so, aside from them, no one would have been able to leave even if they wanted to.'

'Which means...'

'That it's far safer to sit things out if you can. If you'd done a midnight flit, I would imagine the police would catch up with you very quickly.'

'Which also means...'

Fran smiled. 'That both the weapon used to kill Keith and the painting are still here.'

'Or... whoever did this had an accomplice. Someone from outside.'

'My God, you're right.'

Adam shook his head, cross with himself. He hated it when he thought he was right and then realised immediately that he wasn't.

'I'm not though, am I?' he said. 'Because we *are* in the middle of nowhere, which means that someone would need a vehicle of some sort to get here and Derek would have noticed straight away if the gravel on the drive had been disturbed. He even raked it smooth again after we'd arrived. Plus, there's something all a bit spur of the moment about what happened. To have someone on the outside receiving a stolen painting means you'd planned the whole thing in advance, maybe even had a buyer ready and waiting on the black market. So you'd need to have done your research beforehand and...' He shook his head again. 'No, it just doesn't feel as if that's what's happened here. More like someone taking revenge on Keith, or at least someone desperate for money and, finding out they weren't going to be in on his latest project, seeking to level the score.'

'I agree, which makes everything much simpler, doesn't it? The answers are all in this house. They have to be.'

Something still wasn't sitting right for Adam. It had been bugging him right from the start, he realised. Maybe it was just him, but people weren't reacting the way he thought they would.

'What?' said Fran, studying his face. 'The answers aren't in the house?'

'No, they are, it's just... I don't think most people are that clever.' He wrinkled his nose. 'Supposing you'd just tried to pinch a painting; in itself, unless you're an international art thief, something that would make you pretty jumpy. Particularly if it was something you did out of desperation because you'd just lost out on a last-hope business deal. Then, it all goes horribly wrong. You get caught in the act, and in the process, end up killing Keith Chapman.

'Again, unless you've killed someone before and are an old hand at it, wouldn't you panic? Fall apart and be utterly unable to think straight? I know I would. That being the case, you'd probably do one of two things. You'd either call the police and fess up on the spot, or you'd do something to try to cover up your dirty deeds, because you knew you couldn't leave the house. And that's where I have the problem, Fran. Because most people, when faced with that kind of situation, would be like me, they'd make mistakes. They'd put their arm in the ants' nest, they'd shove the painting down the back of the sofa, and throw whatever weapon they'd used out of the window or in the bin, somewhere stupid at any rate. And all the while leaving a trail of forensic evidence behind them. But that isn't what we've got here. Granted, you might go back at a later time to try to rectify your mistakes, but when we all woke up this morning, nothing was out of place, except for in the study. All the guests were present, and all acting perfectly normally apart from the odd grumble about being asked to get out of bed earlier than they would have liked. It doesn't make sense to me.'

Fran was staring at him open-mouthed. 'You know, that actually *does* make sense.'

Adam nodded. 'So it's a spur-of-the-moment irrational act on the one hand, but also very clever and calculating on the other. Two things which aren't naturally compatible. This should be a straightforward case for the police. They have a house, in the middle of nowhere, no one's come in, no one's gone out, and somewhere inside or immediately outside of it, both a painting and a weapon have been hidden. So why do I get the feeling there's nothing straightforward about this at all?'

He shivered again, feeling excitement bubble up inside of him. 'You've got to admit it's intriguing,' he added.

Fran gave him a knowing look. 'I know what you're doing, Adam Smith. Trying to get me to admit I'm excited about the possibility of solving this case too.'

'And are you?'

'I couldn't possibly answer that question,' she replied. 'But come on then, what do we do now? We know that Oliver and Mimi were having an affair, but not much else. We need to think what the police will be doing.'

Adam was about to answer when the kitchen door was flung open and Nell appeared, looking harried.

'Fran, I'm really sorry, but we're about to start interviewing Mrs Chapman and she's decided that she feels incredibly faint and couldn't possibly. Would you mind making her something to eat? Just toast and jam, it doesn't have to be anything fancy. Seriously, I'm not hanging about while she has poached eggs and avocado, or whatever people like her eat.'

Fran nodded. 'Toast and jam it is. I'll bring it through when it's ready, if you like.'

'Thank you.' Nell turned back for the door. 'Oh, and just to let you know, your room's clear. That doesn't mean you're off the hook, but I wanted to tell you.' She paused. 'I know this is hard.'

'Thanks, Nell, I appreciate that.' Fran flashed Adam a look. 'Would I be able to get my laptop then?' she asked. 'Only I've got work I could be getting on with.'

'I don't see why not.' Nell dipped her head, narrowing her eyes at Adam before ducking back out of the door.

Adam grinned. 'Francesca Eve, you wouldn't be about to start fishing for information, would you?'

Fran merely pointed at the loaf of bread still sitting on the side. 'You heard what the Boss said. Two slices of toast and jam. Back in a minute.'

13

How did we ever find out about people before the internet,
thought Fran. Good old-fashioned legwork or countless tele-
phone calls, she imagined. And, after only ten minutes of
searching, Fran had discovered more about Mimi Chapman
than she ever wanted to know. Because when you looked like
Mimi, you were always good for a story and people were fasci-
nated by her. Or rather what she wore and what she looked like.
Nothing Fran uncovered told her what Mimi was like as a
person. Did anyone even know? Maybe not even Mimi herself.

Fran had found countless articles, all detailing events that
Mimi had attended. For the most part these were charity
fundraisers or other society parties where the great and the good
congregated. But once you'd read one, you hardly needed to
read the others, they all said much the same thing. The only
details which varied were the colour of the dress Mimi wore, or
the name of the organisation she'd been supporting. It was trivia
and Fran needed to go much deeper than that.

Thinking for a moment, she tried another tack. What she
wanted to know was the kind of background Mimi came from.
She had obviously adopted her husband's name on their

marriage, but what was her maiden name? And who were her family? And there was one place Fran could get all that information and more: Facebook.

Love it, or loathe it, it was a treasure trove of information and who hadn't looked up someone's details just because they were being nosey? If their privacy settings were lax, you could find out all manner of things and Mimi, it would appear, was an open book. Within moments of logging on, Fran uncovered her profile, and as everything about Mimi was for show, everything about her was *on* show.

In a flurry of activity, probably when the account was a new plaything, Mimi had carefully filled in details of what TV shows she loved, what restaurants she favoured, and a whole host of other trivia. By looking at her liked pages, Fran could also see which hairdressers she rated, nail bars, masseurs, gyms, anything and everything to keep Mimi looking at her best. What was also very obvious, however, was that Mimi didn't want to admit she existed beyond a certain age. There were no schools listed, no universities or colleges attended, no family members given, and no home town either. She could, of course, be being protective, but Fran was more of the opinion that life for Mimi started when she became Mrs Chapman. But there was more than one way of finding out about her past.

Clicking on Mimi's photos first of all, Fran checked whether she had created any albums beyond the ones which Facebook automatically allocated. And there were loads. Parties mostly. Fundraising events. But not the kind of album Fran was looking for at all, nothing personal. She could look through them all and see if anyone had been tagged, but, instead, she started to look at Mimi's list of friends. And settled down for a very boring stint of name checking.

From his seat opposite, Adam tutted in frustration. 'Well, Keith Chapman's company website is a waste of time. Locked down tighter than a—'

'Don't say it,' Fran warned.

He grinned at her over the lid of his laptop. 'He doesn't want anyone to know anything, it's just page after page of marketing speak; meaningless rubbish. There's a "Portfolio" page but all that's on there are half a dozen projects from the last couple of years, with a paragraph written about each. And that's it. If he has a team to meet, we're not about to be given the pleasure. How are you getting on?'

'Similar. Google searches bring up loads of stuff about Mimi, but all that really tells me is how extensive her wardrobe is. I'm on Facebook now, trawling friends, or more importantly, their surnames.'

'What for?'

'I want Mimi's maiden name. And somewhere among all the friends are hopefully a few family members, or rather male family members who will have the same surname Mimi was born with. So I'm looking for duplicates, which is going to take a while...' She let out a groan.

'You know, that's actually really clever.'

Fran rolled her eyes. 'I know. Sometimes I amaze myself.'

'I think I might start with someone else,' replied Adam. 'Something tells me that Keith Chapman is very careful what information gets out about him. In fact, I'm almost certain he'll have some kind of press person who manages these things. If he's the kind of property developer I think he is, he's probably crossed quite a few people in the past, but I very much doubt any of it has been reported on. What do you think? Who shall I start with?'

Fran thought for a moment. 'Heather Walton,' she replied. 'She's the only guest who seems in any way likeable, but there's also something about her which doesn't quite add up. Plus, she was in the cabin with Keith yesterday afternoon, and I'd like to know what that was all about.'

'Heather it is.'

Adam's hand reached forward to claim another biscuit from the plate in front of them and Fran smiled. Fuel to the fire.

It took her nearly two hours. Writing down names, crossing them out, cross-referencing them against their owners' own Facebook accounts, following link after link until, at times, she was so far down the rabbit hole she hadn't a clue where she was and had to go back to the beginning, but eventually Fran had a name.

'Hastings,' she announced triumphantly. 'Two brothers, Ryan and Steven, two sisters-in-law, Louise and Michelle, and countless nieces and nephews, but it's definitely her. Mimi Chapman was born one Miriam Hastings. And if she went to the same school her brothers did then she grew up in a not particularly nice suburb of Birmingham. I might be wrong but I don't think it's Mimi's money which funded the Chapmans' lavish lifestyle.'

For a moment, she wondered if Adam had heard her. The whole time she'd been trawling through names she'd scarcely been aware of him, save for the sound of regular munching, but now she could see he was lost in his own research, peering at the screen with ferocious concentration. And, judging by the expression on his face, he too had hunted down his own particular rabbit.

She waited until he sat back slightly, his facial features relaxing before waving a hand gently in his direction.

'Found something?' she asked.

'Hmmm, not sure yet, but very possibly. Heather Walton is a bit of a shining star.'

Fran frowned. 'You're making it sound as if that's a bad thing.'

'I'm not sure yet, except that I can't help thinking of the old adage, the higher you are the further you have to fall... and, unlike Keith Chapman, the firm Heather works for have a website which is very touchy-feely. Potted biographies of all

their staff, right down to the admin team and, as a senior part-
ner, Heather's is full of glowing accolades. Not only that, but in
the course of my research I'm happy to report I now know the
difference between a solicitor and a barrister, as well as all the
different fields in which they work. As far as we're concerned
though what we need to focus on is that Heather specialises in
corporate work, which could rather change the reasons why
she's here this weekend.'

'Could it?'

'Yes, because I'd assumed she was here for the same reason
as the other guests, as a potential investor in Keith's latest
project, but I don't think she can be. She and Keith obviously
have a connection – she wouldn't be here otherwise – but if
that's because he's her client, she couldn't be an investor, it
would be a conflict of interest.'

Fran wriggled forward on her stool. 'So what kind of thing
would Heather be advising him on?'

'Mergers and acquisitions... joint ventures, that kind of
thing. If I'm right, she could be the person who oils the wheels
of Keith's deals. Which would make her a very important
person indeed.'

Fran snaffled a chocolate digestive, but then paused, trying
to decide whether she should eat it or not. 'She could have even
been here to advise him on the other potential investors.'

Adam grinned. 'That's exactly what I was thinking. Dishing
the dirt on the other guests. As yet, I haven't found any
definitive proof that Keith was her client, but I'll keep looking.
There will be something somewhere.'

'Interesting,' said Fran, breaking the biscuit in half. Who
was she kidding? Of course she was going to eat the whole
thing. 'So, did she bring news about one of the other guests, I
wonder? And if so, who? Maybe all of them... Plus, why was she
looking so upset yesterday? One minute giggling with Keith in
the cabin by the pool, and the next looking like she was about to

burst into tears.' Fran paused. 'No, that's not right, not close to tears, upset yes, but more fearful than anything, as if she was scared about something which could happen.'

Adam stared at her. 'Then I really think we need to find out what that could be,' he said. 'I need to keep looking. I think I've been asking Mr Google the wrong questions, but perhaps changing them slightly might turn up some new information.'

'Never mind Google,' Fran replied, 'I'll go and ask her.'

'What?'

'Everyone is still sitting in the morning room, or the conservatory. I'll go and ask her. Bugger sitting about for hours trying to get lucky with an internet search. Although...' She narrowed her eyes. 'While I go and talk to Heather, there is something you can be checking out, or rather some*one*, namely Mimi Chapman, who was born into the world as Miriam Hastings, somewhere around Balsall Heath in Birmingham.'

Adam's eyes lit up. 'Oh, well done, that's brilliant!' He pulled his laptop closer. 'Leave it to me.'

Fran stuffed the last of her biscuit into her mouth and slid off her stool. Strictly speaking, she was supposed to stay in the kitchen, but if Nell was busy... what she didn't know wouldn't hurt her.

Fran eventually found Heather sitting inside the conservatory. She was tucked into a corner beside a huge palm, which had the added benefit of partially screening her slight figure from the room, a move which Fran suspected was her intention all along. She thought at first that Heather might be reading but she wasn't, instead she was simply sitting, staring out of the window.

Everyone else was in the morning room, loosely gathered around the table where the remains of breakfast still lay. Ginny Dawson was huddled with her husband on a two-seater sofa, a cup of tea on a low table beside them. Even from a distance, Fran could see it was stone-cold, a film of milk on the surface. Oliver sat opposite, his head bent reading a newspaper, although Fran suspected his nonchalant pose was anything but. Richard Newman was nowhere to be seen. Ginny looked up as Fran passed by; the two men completely ignored her.

Heather stared blankly as Fran sat down beside her. It wasn't that she looked unfriendly, more that she scarcely even recognised her. And Fran had seen that look before, last year, on the face of a man whose wife had just died under very tragic circumstances.

'Sorry, do you mind?' Fran asked, indicating her chair. 'Just that everyone else is busy talking and I didn't want to interrupt them.' She gave a nervous smile. 'It's horrible this, isn't it? Have the police spoken to you yet?'

There was momentary pause, as if Fran's words were taking a while to reach Heather, like the lag on an international phone call. Eventually, her eyes focused on Fran's.

'No... er, Mimi is in with them at the moment. Sorry, I'm... I can't be sitting in there with everyone else. Don't these people realise how serious it is?' She leaned forward, dipping her head towards Fran, her bright red hair glinting in the light. 'It's one of us,' she said. 'Someone here killed Keith.'

'Yes, and at the moment I'm worried they think it's me,' said Fran, wringing her hands. 'I'm the last person to see him alive apparently.' She put a hand to her mouth. 'I'm not, obviously, because that would be the person who killed him, but...'

Heather gave her a sympathetic look. 'Don't worry,' she said. 'There are plenty of people here who have far more reason to bash Keith over the head and nick one of his paintings than I suspect you do. The police are just doing their jobs.'

Fran smiled. 'You're a lawyer, aren't you?' she whispered. 'You know about these things.'

'I know about the law,' she replied. 'Not police procedure,

that's rather different. And I'm afraid I don't specialise in criminal law either. But don't worry, I'm sure everything is going to be okay.'

Fran let out a slow breath as if she'd been holding it. She was relieved to hear Heather's words but she wasn't as anxious as she'd been making out.

'Thank you. That makes me feel a bit better at least. I've never had any dealings with the police before,' she lied. 'And I don't really know much about the law either. What do you do then if you don't do the criminal stuff? What else is there?'

Heather smiled, but it wasn't at all patronising. Another tick in Fran's good book. 'It's complex, complicated. But basically, you can either be a solicitor, or a barrister, and they usually deal with court cases – they're the people who wear the silly wigs and are often in TV shows. Solicitors work on all aspects of the law, from criminal, to family, that's divorces and so on, employment and corporate law, which is what I do. I specialise in advising clients about company acquisitions.'

'Is that what you do for Mr Chapman then? Sorry, *did* do for Mr Chapman?'

'What makes you ask that?'

Fran dropped her gaze. 'Sorry, I just assumed...' She pulled a face. 'I don't really understand why everyone's here this weekend. I just cook the food, it's much simpler.'

'I doubt that.' Heather sighed. 'But yes, you're right, that is what I was here for. And I suppose with all the questioning going on, it isn't going to be long before everyone finds out anyway.'

'Don't they know?' asked Fran, pretending astonishment.

Heather pressed her lips together. 'Hardly, and most of them aren't going to be very happy when they find out. Some more than others. Not that it matters now, of course. I don't suppose any of them are going to be doing business with Keith's company, even those who had the money.' Her brows creased as an anxious look crossed her face.

Fran's eyes were round as an owl's. 'Who didn't have the money then?' she whispered, looking over her shoulder. 'I bet it was the Dawsons... sorry, but I don't much like them. Ginny Dawson looks at me as if I'm something she can't shake off her shoe.'

Heather smiled. 'Actually no, Peter was good for the investment, just about. Although he's had to pull a lot of rabbits out of a lot of hats to find it.' She smiled at Fran's bemused expression. 'Liquidating assets,' she explained. 'He hasn't had much luck recently. No, it's the loveable Ollie Knight who's been trying to pull a fast one,' she whispered. 'Everyone thinks he's loaded, but his money isn't real at all, it's just a series of ever more risky loans, one piled on top of the other. And the whole lot is about to come tumbling down.'

Fran leaned closer. 'Really?' She thought quickly. 'Does he know? That *you* know, I mean?'

'Who? Oliver? No, I don't think so.'

'But Keith knew?'

'Oh yes, he knew all right. I told him yesterday. I'd had my suspicions for a little while, but have only just had it confirmed. I did suggest to Keith that he'd be better off inviting someone other than Oliver here this weekend, in case my suspicions were founded, but he wouldn't listen, too busy playing one of his little games. He was good at that.' She turned her head to stare out the window, her face desolate.

Fran watched her for a moment. 'I didn't know him, obviously, but I get the feeling that neither of the Chapmans could hold their scruples up for rigorous inspection. Even so, to die like that, no one—'

'I'm glad he's dead,' said Heather bluntly. She held Fran's look. 'I'm sorry, I didn't want him dead, but I can't pretend I'm not glad he is. Keith Chapman was the kind of person who had no loyalty to anything or anyone, but yet he expected absolute loyalty from those around him. He had one set of rules for him and one for everyone else. I despised him, actually. I wish I'd never got involved with him in the first place.'

'Involved?'

'I mean as my client,' she replied, eyes darting away for a second. 'That's all. That was more than enough.'

'Had you worked with him long?'

'Ten years or so. I was a relative junior at the time we met, handed his enquiry by one of the partners in the firm I work for, and... I guess you could say I've grown with him. I was young and ambitious, and...' She took a deep breath. 'Anyway, that's all in the past now.'

Fran's head was reeling. The implications of what Heather had told her could be massive, and they stretched in several directions at once. It was another reminder of how extraordinarily complex other people's lives were compared with her own. Although that was getting more and more complicated by the minute.

'If you don't mind me asking,' she said. 'Why are you here this weekend? Couldn't your business with Keith be conducted by email or phone?'

'It could, but it was partly Keith's attempt at a thank you, for services rendered, that kind of thing. Come and enjoy a weekend of hospitality at my expense.' She paused. 'But I think what it actually was, was a reminder of the power he wielded. I almost didn't come, I haven't in the past, but I thought this time...' She inhaled a deep breath. 'God, I've been so stupid. We had unfinished business, which in my naivety I thought we could bring to a conclusion. Keith certainly alluded to that fact. But I should have known better. A leopard never changes its spots.'

Up until now, Fran had been content to let Heather talk and direct the conversation, she clearly had things she needed to offload. But there was one thing Fran really needed the answer to. She flashed a quick look over her shoulder and inched closer to Heather.

'Is that why you were in the cabin with Keith yesterday afternoon?' She winced at the sudden look of horror which crossed the solicitor's face. 'Listen, I'm not about to tell anyone, don't worry. But I happened to be there, clearing up after lunch. I didn't hear what was being said... It's just that it had to be you, everyone else was back up at the house.'

Heather shook her head. 'It's pathetic,' she replied. 'You know, when I was younger I swore I'd never let a man make a fool of me. I thought I was young enough, and clever enough, independent enough and had money enough that I'd never need to be taken in by anyone. I'd make relationships on my terms. But stupidly, I think I only ever considered personal relationships, not business ones, so I let my guard down. I let myself be used, and now the time has come to get myself out of the mess I'm in, what do I do? Resort to the most feeble means at my disposal, my so-called womanly wiles. So, I battered my eyelids at Keith, and I flattered and I flirted, but in the end it got me nowhere. I let myself down, and for nothing.'

Heather's fingers plucked at the hem of her tee shirt, rolling it over and over between her fingers. The action tugged at Fran's heart strings, or at least those which played the tune of sisterhood. 'I'm sure whatever you did couldn't have been that bad,' she said gently.

To Fran's horror, Heather's eyes began to fill with tears. 'It was. It happened years ago, and I knew it was wrong, but I was ambitious and I didn't think it would matter. I didn't know where it would lead.'

'What did you do?' Fran whispered, eyes wide.

'I gave information to someone I shouldn't have done. Confidential information. And he used that information to buy shares in a company whose merger was about to be announced.

When the share price of that company went up, he made a fortune.'

'And that person was Keith Chapman?'

Heather nodded, a tear spilling down her cheek. 'We hadn't been together long. He wasn't a client of mine then, just someone I'd met at a party of a friend. She was a lawyer too. But he was very suave and very attentive and *very* persuasive. He was just starting out in the property game, a small player, but the money he made allowed him to finance the deal that he essentially built his fortune on. We split up not long after that, and I... I bought my first house,' she added bitterly. 'Naively, I thought that would be the end of it.'

'Why? What happened then?'

'Several years later, when Keith had made it big, he appeared at my firm's door. And I had no choice but to take him on as my client.' She lowered her head. 'What I did was insider trading. If anyone found out, I could go to prison.'

'Yes, but so could he?'

Heather shook her head. 'People like him always end up above the law somehow. I knew what my chances would be. But I never intended to use that information against Keith, I just wanted him to find another lawyer, but he wouldn't. He liked the power he held over me.'

'And that's what you were talking about down in the cabin yesterday?'

Heather nodded. 'And now Keith's dead. I know how it looks.'

Fran stared at her, a slow realisation dawning.

'But I didn't kill him,' said Heather. 'I swear. Except that now the whole sorry story is going to come tumbling out, I know it is. I don't think I can bear it.'

Fran was torn. She knew what Heather had done was wrong, but was she a criminal, or simply a victim? She pursed her lips. She couldn't openly tell Heather to lie but...

'Whatever hold Keith had over you has gone now he's dead. If no one else knows then maybe it is all over.'

Heather looked up, her green eyes brimming with tears. 'Oh, it isn't. It isn't over by a long stretch.'

Adam's eyes were wide by the time Fran finished relaying what Heather had told her.

'Don't you find it weird?' she asked. 'That people's lives are so complicated? Maybe mine is too, to someone else looking at it, but it struck me last time we got caught up in murder, and now I'm thinking about it all over again. Secrets, lies, deception, everywhere you turn. People who you think are quite ordinary but who turn out to be anything but. And Heather's a solicitor, she's the last person you'd think would be involved in... shenanigans. I can't think of a better word for it.'

'But she's human too,' put in Adam, a sympathetic look on his face. 'So subject to the same impulses, the same irrational behaviour as everyone else and just as likely to be lured by the smell of money and success.'

Fran stared at him. That made it worse. 'Is that why *I'm* here?' she asked. 'It is, isn't it? I took this job because I thought it would look good on my website. "Look at me with my swanky list of clients." Ergo, I want more clients like that, more money, more success.' She shivered. 'No thank you. After this I'm going back to making cupcakes for christening parties in the village hall.'

Adam smiled. 'Fran, you are not like that.'

'I am... There's no difference.'

'You're not, simply because we're having this conversation. You have more insight than most people I know.'

'Adam, you don't know anybody. May I remind you that when we met, you were hiding in an under-stairs cupboard, precisely so that you wouldn't have to meet "most" people.'

'As were you...'

Fran was about to fire back another retort when she suddenly stopped and, rolling her eyes, met Adam's with a sheepish look. 'Okay, point taken. But if you ever notice me becoming shallow, grasping and having a very inflated opinion of myself then—'

'I shall certainly inform you and beat you about the head until you stop.' He smiled. 'Feeling better now?'

Fran wriggled her shoulders. 'I'm just scared in case whatever is in the air in this house sticks to me. You too for that matter. But poor Heather, she did look absolutely distraught. I can't condone what she did but I can understand why. A young girl, seduced by Keith, lured with promises of love and riches and...' She shook her head. 'It's still wrong, but I can't help but feel sorry for her. She made one mistake and she's been paying for it ever since.'

Adam nodded. 'Do my bidding or I expose what you did. It would certainly keep her in line, wouldn't it?'

'She'd be struck off, apart from anything else,' exclaimed Fran. 'Remember what she said to me on Friday evening, when I asked her if she was a lawyer? She said, "At the moment, yes." It struck me as an odd thing to say at the time, but if she was scared her past deeds were about to catch up with her, not so very odd at all.'

'No wonder she's glad Keith's dead.'

Fran drew in a sharp breath. 'But all of this is also a probable motive for killing him.'

'It is. But it doesn't explain why she would pinch the painting.'

'No, it doesn't. Not unless it's a kind of insurance policy. What if she was trying to untangle herself from Keith and his affairs, and he refused, threatening to share what he knew about her. If she knew her career was about to go pear-shaped, maybe she thought she could at least go out with something she could cash in for a pretty penny. Something to tide her over.'

'Possibly...' said Adam, but Fran could tell he wasn't convinced. 'But Heather wouldn't just lose her job if the truth came out, she'd be going to prison. Somehow I don't think a priceless painting would be of much use to her in there.'

'Poor Heather,' replied Fran, pulling a sad face at Adam. 'She may well be guilty, but I can't think of her in the same way as the Chapmans. I'd put the blame for anything she did squarely at Keith's door.'

'Sadly, I don't think the police will view it the same way. A crime is a crime.'

Adam looked at her, resignation written all over his face. She knew he was probably right.

'There's something else too,' he said.

Fran wasn't sure she wanted to hear any more.

'What Heather told you about Oliver makes a real difference to things, especially if you put it together with what we heard from Oliver's interview with Nell. I haven't had a chance to look into Mimi's background much yet but, according to what Oliver told the police, he and Mimi were planning to marry. Call me cynical but would she really marry someone who had no money of his own?'

'But she didn't know he was broke, did she?'

'Unless someone told her...' Adam left his words hanging for a moment. 'And that person could have been Keith... And it could also have been Heather. To our knowledge, they're the only two people who knew.'

'When I overheard Keith and Mimi arguing he told her she'd be hearing from his solicitor and she knew what that meant. I assumed he meant divorce, but I got the feeling there was more to the threat than just the end of a marriage. Maybe Keith threatened Mimi that if they divorced she wouldn't get a penny. Or maybe it related to his will. I've no idea what Mimi stands to inherit now that Keith's dead, but I'd love to find out, wouldn't you? If Mimi did go waltzing off with Oliver, perhaps Keith would have changed his will so that in the event of his death she got nothing.' Fran swallowed. 'Both of which reasons would give her motive enough to kill him. I don't think Mimi would like life with no money in it.'

Adam nodded. 'And it would also give Oliver motive to kill Keith too. If he has no money then shacking up with Mimi would be a very good move on his part. He certainly wouldn't want her finding out his finances are as shaky as a house of cards. If Keith had warned Oliver off Mimi, perhaps threatened to tell Mimi his secrets if he didn't, then Oliver might want him silenced?'

Fran stared at him. 'I need a cup of tea,' she said. 'Two hours ago it looked like I was the prime suspect, now we have three people who had clear motive to kill Keith.'

Adam tapped his chin. 'So which one was it?'

14

———————

'This is interesting,' said Adam the next morning.

Fran came over from the cooker, where she was frying a large quantity of eggs and bacon. The smell was making her unbelievably hungry. She peered at his laptop.

'What is?'

'I was checking into Mimi's background, seeing if I could find out anything about her marriage to Keith, and there's a very old piece in a society magazine about the wedding itself. It's full of the usual fluff – the dress, the cake, the extravagant setting in a first-class hotel, that kind of thing – but I also found an opinion piece claiming that neither family were enchanted about the union. Keith's folks didn't like *her* because she was a gold-digging wannabe with no money of her own who came from the wrong side of the tracks, and Mimi's family didn't like *him* because from the minute Keith came on the scene, Mimi turned her back on her family. None of them were even invited to the wedding. Her mum gave a quote saying how heartbroken they were, and how they blamed Keith for turning Mimi against them.'

Fran raised her eyebrows. 'Well, that *is* interesting. Sounds as if Mimi saw an opportunity and took it. Keith was obviously her ticket out of there.'

'Very much so. It's no wonder she doesn't want to lose what she's got. Unless there's been a reconciliation over past years, she doesn't even have a family to fall back on.'

'Who's this?' asked Nell, coming into the kitchen. She looked strained.

'Mimi Chapman,' Fran replied. 'We were just...' Fran broke off. She didn't want to reveal what they'd been talking about, but she could hardly ignore Nell's question. She pulled a sheepish face. 'Gossiping,' she finished. 'Sorry.' She turned back to the cooker to flip the slices of bacon.

'Don't apologise to me,' said Nell. 'I really don't like the woman. I know I shouldn't say it, unprofessional and all that, but I can't warm to her at all. My bark is worse than my bite, you know that, and I usually feel for any victim of a crime, but not her though. She's currently holding court in the morning room, having decided to be magnanimous now that she's heir to Keith's fortune and consequently handing out favours like they're sweeties.'

'She did inherit then?' asked Fran.

'Oh yes, Mimi Chapman just became a very wealthy woman and, as that wealth now includes Keith's company, she's declared it would be awful if nothing good comes of the weekend and so she's promised all the guests a share in the investment they came here for. She's sure it was what Keith would have wanted.'

Fran caught Adam's eye and grimaced. She could imagine exactly how Mimi was behaving. 'And this from the woman who not long ago asked Rachel and me if we could get those "parasites" out of her house.'

'Yes, well, that just about sums her up, I'm afraid. Two-faced...' She gave Fran a direct look. 'I didn't say that. Have you been paid for this weekend yet? Because make sure you are.'

'No, and I'm beginning to worry I never will be,' Fran replied, taking the pan off the heat. 'There's been a whole load of extras to provide which weren't in my original quote, simply because I wasn't told about them. Rachel said I should add everything to my bill, assuring me it will be paid. That was fine before, but given what's happened, I'm not sure Mimi will be in any hurry to settle her debts.'

Nell was watching her closely, Fran realised. 'Does Rachel have authority to say that?'

Fran frowned. 'Well...'

'Only, it's not really her place to be free with her employer's money, is it?'

'Oh...' Fran flashed a look at Adam. 'I don't think she meant it like that, more that Mimi doesn't normally quibble about paying her bills. Either that or she doesn't check them. Rachel wasn't suggesting anything untoward.'

'Okay,' said Nell lightly, gesturing at the frying pan. 'Who's that for?'

'Your lot probably. I can't see Mimi eating this, can you? I didn't know what to do, so I thought I'd make a start anyway; I'm not sure who else is up.'

'Well, in light of Madam's behaviour I was going to say forget the toast and jam, let's roll out the avocados, caviar and smoked salmon. But my team never usually get any opportunity to eat on the job, so you'll earn their undying gratitude if no one else's.'

'Will you have something?' asked Fran. She could see the tussle on the chief inspector's face.

Nell sat down with a grin. 'A bacon and egg sarnie wouldn't go amiss.'

Adam got to his feet, closing the lid of his laptop. 'Do you like your bread buttered, Boss?' he asked. Fran had him well trained.

'Of course... and ketchup if you've got it.' She raised an

eyebrow, just the one. It was a move Fran wondered if Nell practised in the mirror. Try as she might, she could never get her eyebrows to move independently.

'You wouldn't be trying to get into my good books, would you?' Nell added, the eyebrow rising even higher.

'Why would I want to do that?' Adam replied, turning away to butter two slices of bread.

Fran smiled, catching Nell's eye as she did so. Adam's response would have carried a lot more weight had he not blushed furiously as he replied.

'Can I ask how things are going,' said Fran. 'And if you've got a chief suspect yet? Apart from Keith's loving wife, that is.'

'Who now has an alibi,' replied Nell, pulling a face. 'How fortuitous.' The eyebrow raised once more. 'Apparently, she and love's young dream spent the whole night together. So, if you believe that, you believe anything. Unfortunately, until I get proof to the contrary, I may have to. Although, of course, she'd still also like us to believe that she's a grief-stricken widow. Covering all her options.'

Fran picked up the tongs and neatly slid three rashers of bacon onto Adam's carefully buttered bread. 'So, who's your money on, him or her?' she asked.

Nell gave her an amused look. 'You wouldn't be fishing for information now, would you?'

'Shamelessly,' replied Fran, sliding an egg on top of the bacon.

'Well, between these walls, my money's on the wife. It always is, or the husband, of course, depending on who has been killed. Just have to hope we can prove it. Although in this case I'm damned if I know what she hit him over the head with. Plus, bizarrely, she seemed genuinely surprised when we told her about the theft of the painting and that makes no sense at all. My money's still on her though, although outside these walls... it's an open book, obviously.'

She took her sandwich from Adam with a smile, no doubt in acknowledgement of its precise diagonal cut.

The first mouthful elicited a groan of pleasure but the second was cut off by a quick rap on the kitchen door. Nell lowered her breakfast as Clare Palmer's head appeared in the doorway.

'Sorry to interrupt, Boss, but Heather Walton hasn't appeared as yet. Would you like her roused, seeing as we want to carry on with her this morning?'

Nell stared at her sandwich, perhaps in recognition that whatever she was doing, she was never far away from being on duty. Or never far *enough* away from being on duty. 'Can you give me five? And then yes, please. I know we all had a late night last night, but I rather like it when people have their feathers ruffled before they speak to us, makes it so much easier to spot anything they're trying to hide.'

'Boss, you're all heart.'

'Aren't I just,' Nell replied, sinking her teeth back into her sandwich. A drip of egg escaped from the bottom, which she immediately scooped up from the plate with her finger. 'Haven't had one of these in far too long,' she said, licking her lips.

'I could go if you like?' offered Fran. 'Take her up a cup of tea, if that isn't smoothing the ruffled feathers too much?'

Nell smiled. 'Yes, all right, I like her too, Fran. Point taken.' She looked back at Clare, still standing in the doorway. 'Let's leave her a wee while. I'll give you a shout when we're ready. Have you shared the good news yet to Derek about the shot-guns?' she asked.

'I did, yes. About ten minutes ago. He was very relieved to hear they were all clean.'

'Yes, I bet he was.' A small smile flickered around Nell's lips. 'Okay, thank you, Clare.' She switched her focus to Fran.

'Good call about Heather,' she said. 'No need for the tea just yet, I'll have my breakfast first.'

Fran paused for a moment, unsure. 'Am I allowed to ask how things are going?'

'No, but seeing as so far we haven't got anywhere, there's not much I can tell you anyway.' She smirked at Fran from under her lashes.

'So yesterday's searches didn't turn up anything?'

Nell flashed a glance at Adam, who was busy looking nonchalant. 'Not a thing,' she replied. 'Which is a bit of a bugger, actually. I was hoping for a nice quick turnaround on this one, but the lack of a murder weapon isn't helping one little bit. Damned frustrating, actually.'

'You mentioned shotguns just now. Would those be the guns that were used at the shoot on Saturday?'

Nell picked up her sandwich, bit into it and chewed reflectively. 'They would, as it happens. The butt of which just happened to fit the shape of the murder weapon. Did you know that Derek used to be a police officer?'

'No...' The question came so out of the blue that Fran's stammered reply stuck in her throat.

'I mentioned before that he called me Ma'am the first time we met. Well, it turns out that Derek served for five years. Exemplary record, left because, in his words, he was fed up with dealing with scumbags. But it made me nervous, a past like that. He *knows* things... And it made me particularly nervous when I found out that Rachel, a woman he works with very closely, has quite a past too. I wondered if that's who you were talking about when I came in – Rachel, I mean. When you said that she didn't have a family to fall back on.'

Fran shook her head slowly. 'I'm sorry, I don't know what you mean.'

'So you don't know anything about Keith Chapman being more or less responsible for the death of Rachel's mother?'

'No! Was he...? God, that's awful.' Nell's gaze was intense and Fran could feel a wave of heat prickling the nape of her neck as the implication of Nell's words hit her. 'I swear I don't know anything about it. What happened?'

'I mean it should be easy, shouldn't it?' added Nell, ignoring her question. 'We have a group of people, none of whom have left the house since the painting was taken and Keith Chapman was killed. There's no evidence that anyone from outside was involved, so somewhere, someone has not only hidden the weapon used to kill Mr Chapman, but the spoils of their ill-gotten gains as well. And, so far, we've drawn a big fat blank on both. It's a large house, but not that large, it should be relatively easy to find either or both those things.' She waved her sandwich and swallowed. 'Because when we do, I'm quite convinced it'll be curtains for whoever did this.'

'How so?' Adam retook his seat, opposite Nell.

'Because forensics will be all over it,' she replied. 'I'm convinced we're not dealing with a criminal mastermind here, and most people are daft buggers, they have no clue how much evidence they leave behind them. Except people like Derek, of course,' she muttered darkly. 'It should be just a matter of time once we find what we're looking for.'

Fran got up and began to fill the kettle without saying a word. Her head was still reeling from the sudden realisation that either Rachel or Derek could be responsible for Keith Chapman's death. Given what Nell had just told her, Rachel certainly had motive to kill him. She may even have had Derek's help...

She gathered mugs together, savagely throwing teabags into them. No, she couldn't believe that. Rachel wouldn't do something like that, she... Fran turned the unwelcome thought aside, deliberately focusing on something else. The location of the painting was something she hadn't given nearly enough time to yet. Something had been hidden under their very noses, but where? The painting wasn't small, but neither was it something which would stand being manhandled. It hadn't been 'stuffed' anywhere, it had been carefully secreted and that smacked of forethought. Which was perhaps the most interesting thing about it. If Fran had pinched it, where would she choose to hide such a thing? Out of sight *and* imagination, but where could that be?

She reached for the pot of sugar, just one spoonful for Heather. None for Nell, Ginny, Rachel, Richard, and Mimi (obviously). Heather, Oliver and Clare all took one, as had Keith when he was alive, which left a requirement of two sugars for Owen, Derek, and Peter. She fished out the teabag absently. It was just one of the ways her memory worked, some things ridiculously easy to retain while others eluded her absolutely. And try as she might, she couldn't get rid of the feeling that she had seen something or heard something which would solve the puzzle of Keith's death and where the painting had been hidden. But whatever it was, it was hiding just as elusively.

'Shall I take this up to Heather now?' she asked, adding milk to the tea. Nell had finished her sandwich.

'Yes, go on then. Time we were getting on.'

Fran hesitated a moment. Her conversation with Heather had been quite a few hours ago now, and she should probably share with Nell what she'd learned. But from what Nell said they had obviously made a start interviewing Heather yesterday and, given what she'd also said about Mimi covering all her options, she could guess the direction of Nell's questions. No doubt Heather had already told them about Oliver's financial affairs. But had she come clean about her own situation yet, that was the question.

'Back in a minute,' she said, smiling at Nell, who was still chasing breadcrumbs around her plate.

It had been late by the time everyone had been allowed back to their rooms last night and, despite the day's events, Fran had descended into sleep almost instantly. Defence perhaps against the emotional battering which had taken place since the morning. The guests were obviously feeling it too. Only Ginny and Peter Dawson had appeared so far today and Fran didn't blame the others for staying in bed, she'd certainly been tempted.

It wasn't a surprise, therefore, when her knock on Heather's door brought no reply. And if it wasn't for the fact that the police were waiting to talk to her, Fran would have left it right there, cup of tea or no cup of tea.

The second unanswered knock brought indecision – Fran never enjoyed having to wake people, even her own daughter – but the third, much louder than the others, brought concern.

Fran's first reaction was to dismiss it. In all likelihood, Heather wasn't even in her room. She had probably taken the other staircase, coming down while Fran had been going up. Her second reaction was embarrassment. She tentatively pushed open the door, praying that Heather wasn't in the bathroom and hadn't heard Fran knocking. Her third reaction however, on seeing Heather prostrate on the bed, bedclothes rumpled and stained with vomit, was a violent shake of her hand, which threatened to spill tea all over the floor. And it was this response which dragged her eyes downward, allowing her to take in the syringe, positioned a little distance from the bed.

'Ms Walton... Heather?'

Fran swallowed and crept closer, but she didn't need the confirmation of her eyes to know that Heather was dead. The massive absence within the room had hit her the moment she'd entered. She turned her head away. If she could spare poor Heather anything it would be the indignity of her death.

Fran's breath came in a violent shudder, a reminder of her own ability to breathe and keep on breathing. But it was hard, standing there, assailed by loss. She backed away, staring at the door, at her hand. She should close the door. No, she should leave it. But if she didn't close it, someone could see in, see poor Heather. But if she closed it, then she would have to touch it. And she mustn't touch anything. Should she?

She held the mug with Heather's tea in both hands, hooking her elbow into the handle as she tried to bring the door towards the jamb. She couldn't leave Heather like that. On display. It wasn't right.

Nell was exactly where Fran had left her, staring into space while Adam washed up at the sink. It seemed such a mundane contrast with what Fran had seen upstairs that she almost shouted with hysterical laughter. She must have made some kind of noise, however, because next thing she knew, Nell was beside her, a hand steadying the mug in her shaking hands. The knuckles around it were white.

'Fran, it's okay, you can let go now, I've got it. It's okay...'

But Fran didn't want to let go. For some reason it was suddenly very important to her that none of the tea should spill.

'Adam?'

Fran heard his name being called, but she couldn't understand why. Couldn't understand why his arm was suddenly around her, where Nell was going in such a hurry, or why she was being asked to sit down when she really didn't want to. And then, blinking, she remembered.

The house sprang to life, the opposite of poor Heather. There were shouts and ordered instructions. Heavy feet on the stairs. She heard Nell's voice, strident and staccato, and much closer, Adam's, soft and warm. It was happening all over again. Another death. Another puzzle.

It went quiet after that, or perhaps it was just that Fran blocked out the noise. She knew she put down the mug of tea that was Heather's and accepted another. That she drank the sweet and soothing liquid it contained and that Adam had held her hand in between for a short while. Poor Adam. He would have been embarrassed by that. And then Rachel and Derek appeared and eventually, Nell, at which point her world came back into sharp focus.

'Bloody hell, Fran, you're not making my life any easier, are you?' she said. 'What is it with you and dead bodies? People are going to talk.'

Fran stared at her, feeling her alarm subside as she recognised the soft look in Nell's eyes, the compassion which, given her often acerbic manner, others failed to see.

'How are you doing?' she added, with a complicit look at Adam.

'I'm okay,' Fran replied. 'Sorry, I was a bit... shaken, I suppose.'

'I thought you were going to snap the handle off that mug for a moment, but don't ever apologise. The day a death stops doing that to you is the day you know you're beaten. And you're not, not by a long chalk. Me neither. I'm going to catch the bastard that did this, Fran, and you're going to help me.'

Fran must be feeling better because her head worked out what Nell had said in a heartbeat. 'Someone killed her?'

'I think so, yes. It was a clumsy attempt at making it look like suicide. Of course, it could just be a clumsy suicide, or an even clumsier attempt at oblivion on Heather's part, but we'll know more in a bit.'

Fran nodded. 'I saw the needle.'

'Hmm... Can't be certain yet, but my money's on a drug overdose. Seen it before. Unfortunately.'

'Drugs?' queried Fran. *Dear God, what next?* 'You mean like heroin or something? But Heather didn't—' She broke off. She didn't know what Heather did. Not for certain. She didn't know anything about any of the guests in the house.

'That was my impression too,' agreed Nell. 'And on first glance there was nothing else in the room to suggest she was a user. My bet's on cocaine, incidentally. People like the Chapmans and their guests... Gross stereotyping, I know, but they like to party, you know what I'm saying. But if you're at the stage where you're injecting, that's not recreational, that's abuse, and nothing about Heather has suggested that to me.' She paused for a moment, looking at the others in the room. 'I need to ask you some questions, Fran. Is that okay?'

Fran nodded, looking at Adam.

'He can stay,' replied Nell. 'But Rachel and Derek, sorry, could I ask you to wait in the morning room again. It's a bit like Groundhog Day in there. My team are just waking everyone else up, or should I say rounding everyone up, and, for the moment, no one's to go anywhere.'

Rachel nodded. 'And if people want tea, coffee, or anything to eat, they can damn well wait.'

Nell raised an eyebrow but didn't reply, waiting until they had gone before speaking.

'Tell me about Heather,' she said to Fran.

Fran chewed at her lip. 'She didn't answer her door,' she said. 'That was why I went in, I didn't really want to. If she'd been that deeply asleep, I would have left her if I hadn't known you wanted to speak to her. So then I thought maybe she was in the bathroom... I called out, and opened the door. She was just lying there.'

'So did you go into the room?'

'A couple of steps maybe. No more than that. I didn't need to, I could see she was... dead.'

'And you didn't check?'

'Oh God, no, I didn't... should I have? I might have been able to—'

'Fran,' interrupted Nell gently, 'there's nothing you could have done. I was more interested in whether you'd moved anything.'

Fran shook her head, several times. 'No... I realised I mustn't touch anything. And I knew she was gone. Maybe that's why I didn't check to make sure. I didn't want to touch her, but mainly it was because I knew there was something missing in the room when I went in, and I can only think it was Heather herself.'

'What did you do then?'

'I backed out. Stupid... I think I retraced my steps, literally, and all I could think about was not spilling her tea. I could feel my hands shaking. It was weird, almost as if I sensed that if I didn't hang on tight, the cup would leap from my hand and I knew I had to keep hold of it. I don't really know why.'

'Shock, I expect,' said Nell. 'It takes us all in different ways.' She smiled as if to reassure Fran she didn't think her weird at all. 'And did you notice anything? Anything which struck you as odd? Or hear anything? Smell anything?'

Fran thought for a moment but there was nothing she could bring to mind. 'I don't think I noticed anything much. I could see she'd been thrashing about, and had thrown off her bedcovers. She'd been sick too. But everything else looked quite tidy.' A sudden thought came to her. 'Just now you said you thought it was a clumsy suicide, or had been made to look like one. There was something odd if that's the case.'

'Go on...'

'Heather had one of those carafes by her bed – you know, the kind with a glass which sits over it. And the carafe was full. Why would you put water by your bed ready to drink in the night if... you know?' Fran couldn't bring herself to say it. 'And she'd hung some clothes on the wardrobe door, but they weren't the clothes she had on yesterday, so could they have been what she was planning to wear today?'

Nell nodded. 'Yes, I rather think they were. I spotted those too. And who puts clothes out for the next day if they're not planning on living to wear them? It doesn't add up. There was a note too, half tucked under her pillow. All it said was "sorry", but it was a scrawl, no more than that. And where was the pen or the paper she'd used? None that I could see. No, either

Heather was a total neat freak, and you'd have to be borderline OCD to clear the place up before taking your own life, or—'

'Someone came in and did that to her,' finished Fran. Her thoughts were skipping ahead. 'But I didn't hear anything last night,' she added. 'Surely you'd shout out if someone came into your room in the middle of the night. Admittedly I didn't get to bed until very late but... Oh, do you think she might have already been dead?'

'It's possible.' But the look on Nell's face told Fran that it was almost certainly probable. She shuddered.

'Right, so after you retraced your footsteps, what then?' asked Nell.

'Nothing. I just came back down here.'

'But the door to Heather's room was almost closed when I got there.'

Fran dropped her head. 'Sorry, yes, that *was* me. I didn't touch it, I...' She made the action with her arm to illustrate. 'I tried to hook my elbow in the handle and pull the door to. I knew I shouldn't touch it, I just didn't want anyone to see her like that. It didn't seem right. Sorry, I probably shouldn't have.'

'It was a kind thing to do,' replied Nell. 'I don't think you did any harm.' She smiled. 'You stuck up for her earlier as well, when I asked Clare to go and rouse her and you offered to go instead. You liked her, didn't you?'

'I did.' Fran thought a moment. 'I don't really know why, I hardly knew her. And I certainly hadn't spent much time talking to her either, but we chatted for a bit yesterday and there was something about her. She seemed vulnerable, and...'

Nell leaned forward.

'It's hard to know how to describe it without hindsight putting words in my mouth,' continued Fran. 'But if I didn't know better, I'd say she was scared.'

15

Nell's eyes widened. 'That's an interesting observation...' She let her sentence run off and Fran knew she wanted her to fill in the resulting silence. She'd never been very good at holding her ground during such moments. Her daughter used to dare her sometimes (in her teenage all-knowing, all-powerful ways) to a game of 'stare', where the loser is the first to blink or look away. It was always Fran. Always.

'Maybe scared isn't quite the right word... Fatalistic? Doomed? I don't know. That sounds horribly melodramatic but I got this sense that Heather knew something was coming and there was nothing she could do to change that, or its outcome.'

'Funnily enough, that was my impression too,' replied Nell with an anxious look. 'It was something I wanted to pick up with her today, because we didn't get nearly enough time with her yesterday. When we broke for the day we'd only just moved on to her relationship with Keith Chapman, but I had the feeling it was going to prove far more useful than any of the other things we discussed. Perhaps that's something you might have touched on.'

Fran could feel Nell's gaze intensifying. Very soon Fran

would be caught in its tractor beam and there would be nothing she could do to evade it. She would be compelled to tell the truth about every single misdemeanour she had ever committed. Like the occasional times – very occasionally, she might add – when she used the same knife she buttered her bread with to get jam out the pot. It was exactly this level of honesty which Nell's gaze required, and Fran had never been able to work out whether it was a police thing, or a Nell thing. Either way, it unnerved her.

Trouble was, she could also feel Adam looking at her too, anxious that she didn't give away everything they had learned, both about, and from, Heather. But the woman was dead, how could Fran hold anything back now? She swallowed.

'We *had* been talking about why Heather was here, yes. She didn't strike me as the type of person who would be investing in Keith's project, so I asked her about it. I knew she was a lawyer, but turns out Keith was her client, which makes sense if you think about it.'

Nell nodded. 'Yes, we got that far. But when I asked her how long she'd known Keith, she went off on a tangent talking about another client altogether. Call me cynical, but I don't like tangents, and in Heather Walton's case, a woman well used to speaking concisely and directly, it wasn't the product of a rambling mind, but instead an attempt at shifting the conversation away from something she didn't want to talk about.' Nell glanced over at Adam, or more precisely his laptop, which lay closed on the table. 'So I wondered what you'd managed to find out about her. Which one of you wants to tell me?'

Now Adam was caught in Nell's tractor beam too, and he very wisely smiled like the proverbial eager beaver he most definitely wasn't. He'd be gutted at having to give up the information Fran had found out, but they had no choice but to come clean.

'Okay...' replied Fran. 'Not that we know much of the

detail, but it seems that Heather and Keith had a bit of a fling once, a long time ago, and well before Mimi came on the scene. Heather was a young lawyer looking to shine, and Keith was only a fledgling property developer, but at some point, Heather gave him some information, insider information. I don't really understand how all this works but Keith bought some shares in a company, the price of which then went through the roof and he made a huge amount of money from them. Money which effectively started his career big time. He and Heather split up, but years later, he sought out her professional services, using the knowledge he had over her as leverage and she's worked with him ever since.'

Nell leaned forward. 'No wonder she didn't want to tell me about their relationship. But go on – it's sounding to me like she might have had an equal hold over Keith. Are you telling me you think they were threatening one another? Blackmail even, something like that?'

Fran shook her head. 'I don't think so. Heather had been trying to get Keith to release her from her obligations to him, but he wasn't having any of it though. And with his death, she was terrified her secret was going to come out.'

'So killing Keith might have solved her problem rather neatly. Unless anyone else knew about the insider dealing, of course.'

'She knew that. She told me that everyone would think she was the murderer.'

Nell's eyes narrowed. 'Yet even if she didn't kill Keith, she would still have been afraid that her crime was going to come to light as a result of our investigations. It would have had serious consequences for her, prison most likely.'

'Exactly. She knew that too...' Fran held Nell's look for a moment, gratified to see sympathy in her eyes. Whatever the circumstances, Heather's was still another life taken too soon.

'Do you think she was scared enough of the consequences to kill herself?'

Fran shook her head almost immediately. 'No...' she replied. 'But I think we're being manipulated to believe that.'

Nell's look was grim. 'Yes, I'm beginning to think that too. Unfortunately, however, Heather isn't here to tell us what actually happened, and neither is Keith, which makes me think there might be some coincidence about their deaths. Or have I just got a suspicious mind?'

Nell gave them both one last long look and then got to her feet. 'I'm sorry you had to discover Heather's body this morning, Fran, but thank you for doing what you have. I'm off to be a police officer now and bark some orders, read the riot act to the guests who, once again, will be confined to the downstairs rooms for the foreseeable. Although I'm very interested to see how everyone takes the news. Sit tight, you two.'

Adam growled the moment Nell was through the door. 'You can't get anything past her, can you?'

'Probably just as well,' replied Fran. 'Given that she's a detective inspector.' She gave him a pointed look. 'I know you want to solve this, Adam, but we can't keep things from Nell, we'll be in all kinds of trouble.'

'She didn't mention Oliver Knight's lack of cash though. Do you think she knows about that?'

'Possibly. She doesn't think Heather's death was an accident. She doesn't think it was by suicide either. So, if it wasn't either of those things, and someone murdered her, who do you suppose the most likely culprit could be?'

Adam didn't reply. He didn't need to.

Nell's disappearance from the kitchen lasted about twenty minutes and, by the time she arrived back with an apologetic request to provide breakfast and drinks for everyone, Fran, in an attempt to keep busy, had virtually finished making them. Rachel and Derek had joined her and together, she and Rachel had cooked the last of the pastries and put together some fruit, yoghurt and plates of toast. The last of the bacon and eggs went into sandwiches for her, Adam, Derek and Rachel. There had to be some perks, after all, and the shock of finding Heather's body had dissipated to leave behind an almost bottomless hunger.

The kitchen was quiet for a moment as everyone ate, Heather's death still casting a long shadow over the day. But that wasn't the only thing troubling Fran. As soon as Nell left the room, Fran laid one half of her sandwich down on her plate, and reached forward to touch Rachel's arm.

'Nell mentioned something earlier,' she said. 'About your mum, and Keith... Rachel, I'm so sorry.'

Sudden tears pooled in Rachel's eyes. 'I don't know why I still get so upset,' she replied. 'She's been gone years. I think it's just everything that's happened, it's brought it all back.' Beside her, Derek leaned back in his chair, and slid his hand across the table. Rachel grasped it gratefully.

'Maybe she has,' said Fran. 'But it sounds as if a terrible wrong was done to her, Rachel. Done to you too, and things like that leave their mark. What happened?' she asked quietly.

Derek leaned a little closer as Rachel ran a finger underneath her eye. 'Me and Mum slipped under the radar,' she said. 'We lived in just another street in just another run-down neighbourhood, but it was our whole life. It may not have been much to the likes of Keith Chapman, but to us it was our home, and the place where my mum felt safe.' She swallowed. 'My dad left when I was about eighteen months old and I don't know when Mum's illness started, but as I grew up, I became aware that my mum wasn't like other mums. She didn't go out. Ever. She suffered from agoraphobia, but it was okay because there was always someone to look out for us. We knew everyone, and yes, it was a rough place and there was a ton of dodgy stuff going on, but we were one of them, we were family. I had so-called uncles and aunts everywhere, people I could turn to if Mum or me needed anything, to make sure we were all right on the days when she couldn't even make it to the little shop at the end of the road. Until the day that Keith Chapman decided our homes weren't good enough. Not even for us. Because he'd done some deal and our street was "redeveloped" to make way for people who could buy their own homes, people who had more money and bigger aspirations. We were forced to move...' She took an unsteady breath.

'We ended up miles away, in a street where no one knew us, and no one cared. There was no shop at the end of the road, even if Mum could have got there. I went out a few times on my own, but the new place was scary and I didn't like it. You can probably guess what happened next.' She looked up, smiling sadly at Derek, who gripped her hand, eyes locked on her face. 'I ended up in care and my mum had no one. She just... faded away. I didn't even find out straight away. They thought it best not to tell me, thought it would be too upsetting for me. I never even went to her funeral, never even got to say goodbye.' She smiled then, a fond smile, for the woman who had brought her into the world and made her everything she was.

'But what you have to know is that I still had a good childhood. My mum was everything to me. We were a team, just us against the world. And she taught me to be slow to judge and quick to love, to know the value of things, real things, not trinkets and baubles, but things which mattered, like home, and family. And my foster family were great too. I grew up, I was happy, but I was determined never to forget what happened to my mum and how little value Keith Chapman had given her life.'

'So you came here?' asked Fran.

Rachel nodded. 'I didn't set out to. I just spotted the advert one day. I needed a job and somewhere to live and it seemed the perfect solution. I wanted vengeance when I first came.' Rachel winced. 'Blimey, listen to me, vengeance is mine...' She shook her head as if she couldn't believe how stupid she'd been. 'Trouble was, I soon realised that wasn't really me. Maybe I did have just cause, but I'm not that kind of person – proof that my mum did instil the right values in me, after all. As time went on, I almost forgot who the Chapmans were and I guess in the end, because they'd given me a job, and a roof over my head, I settled for feeling like I was redressing the balance somehow.'

Fran nodded, giving her a warm smile. 'Except that now Nell knows about your background, you're even higher up the suspect list than I am.'

Rachel dropped her head. 'But I didn't kill Mr Chapman, Fran, I swear I didn't. I told Nell everything that happened. I even told her I blamed Keith for my mum's death, but I didn't kill him, I couldn't. That would make me as bad as he was, and Mum taught me better than that.'

Fran nodded gently. 'Nell mentioned you were a police officer, Derek.'

'For my sins,' he replied. 'I think Nell had me in the frame for Keith's murder too, but the forensic results came back on the shotguns and all of them were clean. Clean, as in no blood. If I'd used one of them to bash Keith over the head with, there would have been traces, even if I'd cleaned it. I'm not sure either of us are completely off the hook; Nell likes to keep a little doubt in reserve, doesn't she? But all we can do is tell the truth and hope it's going to be okay.'

Fran tried to smile as she picked up her sandwich. 'I hope so too,' she said, sinking her teeth into it. 'I'm sure it will be.'

16

The first couple of hours of the morning passed interminably slowly, and Fran was beginning to feel as if the day was going to be yet another during which the passage of time would be marked solely by how many cups of tea they had all drunk. In which case the sniffer dog could be said to have arrived after the third cup.

It was Derek who heard the dog first. A deep, excited volley of barks which had him crossing to the window, craning his neck to see round to the front of the house.

'Police dog,' he said. 'Drugs, most likely.'

Fran looked at Adam. 'So Nell does think that's what killed Heather then. Cocaine, she said.'

'In which case someone here must have brought it with them,' he replied.

Fran nodded. 'Or it's Mimi's...' She looked at Rachel, who shook her head.

'Not that I know of. I've never seen signs of anything like that. I wouldn't know what I was looking for in the first place, mind, but I don't think so.'

'One of the guests then,' said Adam. 'It could have been

Heather's, of course, but...' He screwed up his nose. 'She didn't
strike me as the sort. So, if not her, who else could it be? Did
anyone at the party seem high to you?'

Fran blinked. 'Don't look at me, how would I know? I'm as
naive as they come.' And it was a naivety which she knew she
ought to put an end to. She had a teenage daughter, who
possibly knew more about these things than she did. 'Probably
not Ginny, though. She's been downright miserable the whole
time she's been here.'

Rachel smirked. 'I don't know about you, but I'm not sitting
in here and missing out on what's going on. Not if things are
just about to get interesting.' She got up and crossed to the door.
'Anyone coming?'

With a look at Adam, Fran got to her feet.

They got no further than a couple of steps beyond the
kitchen, however, when the door to the main hallway opened
and a flurry of black uniform and fur barrelled through,
followed by Nell and her two detectives. She beckoned to Fran
as she passed.

'You could do me a favour,' she said, 'and get out there for
me.' She pointed back towards the main part of the house and
its reception rooms. 'I'd be very interested to know what the
reaction is to having the dog arrive. Upstairs is off-limits again
for now, and I've an officer posted on the staircase and on the
original crime scene in the study, but see if you can spot
whether anyone is overly keen for information. And listen out
too. Who's nervous, who's terrified and who's quiet as a mouse.'

Fran nodded, looking warily at the dog with its darting eyes,
panting tongue and long silky ears, flapping. It seemed far too
keen to be about its business. It wasn't that its presence worried
her, she was very fond of four-legged friends in general, it was
more that its eagerness seemed vaguely obscene under the
circumstances. That, coupled with the usual fear that the dog
would suddenly find incriminating evidence on her for no real

reason other than because it could. She really must try to stop this feeling guilty all the time when she'd done nothing wrong.

The morning room was bright, sunny and very subdued. The Dawsons sat on one sofa, unusually close. In fact, Ginny had her hand slipped inside Peter's, which was the most contact Fran had seen them have all weekend. Mimi Chapman sat in a chair opposite, looking wan and listless, and Oliver Knight sat in the far corner, arms laid expansively across the back of the chair in a pose that was meant to look relaxed, yet was anything but. Of Richard Newman, there was no sign. It wasn't until Fran walked further into the room that she realised he was sitting reading a newspaper, occupying the same seat in the corner of the conservatory where Heather had sat the day before. She had no idea whether that was relevant or not.

'Glad to see you're finally being treated like the rest of us.'

It was Ginny who spoke, staring at Fran with surprisingly hostile eyes.

'I'm sorry?'

Ginny sat forward, glancing in turn at the other guests. 'I was beginning to think there was one rule for us and one rule for you lot.'

Fran stared at her, feeling something inside of her shift. 'Us lot? Still not sure I understand. What are you talking about, Ginny?'

Fran could see that Ginny didn't like Fran's use of her first name one little bit. She wouldn't have been at all surprised to have been corrected. *That's Mrs Dawson to you...*

'The fact that while we've been kept herded in here like common criminals, you seem to have had the run of the house.'

'Oh, I see what you mean,' replied Fran, effecting a blithe smile. 'For a minute there I thought you were talking about everyday life, in which case yes, there's definitely one set of rules for "us lot" as you so eloquently put it, and one set of rules for you, and never the twain shall meet. Quite right. I know whose company I prefer.' She paused to give Ginny time to work out the meaning of her words. 'However, as you were referring to the *murder* investigation which is currently being conducted, yes, we are being treated the same as you, the only difference is that we've been sitting in the kitchen with a police officer outside the door and you've been sitting in here with a police officer out in the hallway. It's simply geography, Ginny, although come to think of it, it probably is best if we're not too far away from the *kitchen*.'

'You are a caterer.' Ginny was looking for an audience now, but funnily enough wasn't finding one.

Fran held her head a little higher. 'Yes, I am. What is it you do, Ginny?'

The two women stared at one another, and Fran found herself, yet again, in a position where she knew that, despite her words, she would still be the one to look away first.

'That's enough, Ginny.'

Ginny's eyes flicked sideways. It was Oliver who had come to Fran's rescue.

'Heather's dead for God's sake, give it a rest.'

Ginny's face flushed with anger as she sat back in her seat, pulling her hand free from her husband's. If she hoped he was about to back her up, she was clearly going to be waiting a long time. Peter Dawson looked uncharacteristically subdued, although Fran noticed he did steal a look behind Ginny's back, directly to where Mimi was sitting. Fran followed his look, a nervous half-smile, but Mimi had turned her head away.

Fran took the remaining sofa, sitting at one end so that Adam and Rachel could join her, while Derek wandered through to the conservatory to stand just inside the double doors, looking out into the garden. He was angry, Fran could tell by the stiffness of his stance, but whereas Fran preferred to sit where she could at least make Ginny feel uncomfortable, Derek preferred to remove himself from the situation altogether. He really was the most gentle of men.

For a minute no one spoke, but then Peter cleared his throat.

'You mentioned a murder inquiry just now,' he said. 'Is that what they think?'

Fran looked up. 'I believe so.' She wasn't going to elaborate.

'We were just told that Heather had been found dead this morning,' he continued. 'But the inspector woman didn't say what had happened.'

'Yes, that's right,' Fran replied. 'I found her.'

'So you know what happened then?'

'No.' She could feel Oliver's gaze on her face.

'Well, you must know something!'

'I know she's dead. And that she shouldn't be. Beyond that, no, I don't know anything. When I found her, I didn't stop to speculate what might have caused an apparently healthy young woman to die, I was rather more concerned with the fact that she had.' Fran glared at him, but she could see that he wasn't about to give up.

'So why are the dogs here then?' asked Peter. 'It'll be a gun, or drugs,' he said pointedly. 'I mean, what other things do they look for?'

'You'd be surprised,' said Derek, coming back into the room. 'The police use dogs for all sorts of reasons. It may be for firearms, or drugs, yes, but can also be for cash, explosives, human tissue too. Or, of course, they may simply want to establish where in the house Heather had been, depending on what other evidence may have been found.'

'You seem to know a lot about it,' remarked Richard, reappearing from behind him.

'I should do. I was a police officer for several years and, before you ask, I gave it up because I couldn't stand being surrounded by scumbags all day. It sickened me, the things people do to one another.'

'See, what did I tell you?' muttered Peter. 'In on it. I bet he knows exactly what they're searching for.'

A shout from the hallway outside forestalled any answer and heavy feet sounded over their heads. In a room which both Fran and Rachel knew was the one in which Oliver had been sleeping. And judging by the look on his face, he knew it too. Whether anyone else had worked out the geography of the house, Fran didn't know, but no one said a word as the noises continued. Looks were exchanged as two police officers could be seen re-entering the hallway from the direction of the stairs.

Fran had expected Nell to appear, but to her surprise it was Clare Palmer who entered the morning room first. She stood by the doorway for a moment before taking a step forward to let her colleague pass. Owen Palmer took up a stance on the far side of the room.

'Oliver Knight,' said Clare, eyes sweeping the room. She waited until she had his full attention. 'I'm arresting you on suspicion of the possession of a controlled drug. You do not have to say anything, but it may harm your defence if you do not mention, when questioned, something which you later reply on in court. Anything you do say may be given in evidence. If you could come with me, please.'

His legs propelled him halfway from the chair before his brain fully took in what had been said to him and he half lowered himself again. 'Me?' One arm fished for the chair beneath him as if seeking support. 'You're arresting me?'

'This way please, Mr Knight.'

'No, wait! What have I done? What drugs?'

'We need to do this at the police station. Mr Knight?'

The DC held out her arm but Oliver wrenched his away even though she wasn't touching him. 'No! I'm not going anywhere until you tell me what you found.'

'A quantity of cocaine, Mr Knight,' said Nell coming into the room. 'Is that good enough for you?'

'Cocaine...?' Mimi's hand fluttered to her mouth. She dropped her head as if about to weep. 'Drugs in my house, I don't believe it.'

'But I haven't done anything!' Oliver stared at Clare, his mouth working soundlessly for a moment. 'I don't know anything about any drugs. I don't know how they got there, but they're not mine.'

'Well, I hope you're not insinuating they're anyone else's,' said Peter, rising from the sofa to put a protective arm around Mimi. 'Give it up, Oliver, you've been caught plain and simple. And everyone knows you were high as a kite on Saturday night.'

'I was not!' Oliver's head spun wildly between them all, desperately searching for someone to back him up. He looked back at Nell. 'I swear, I've never touched drugs in my life.' Panic struck his face. 'Okay... a few spliffs when I was younger, but no more than that, I swear.'

Nell remained impassive. 'Possession of a Class A drug is an offence, Mr Knight, and given that Heather Walton appears to have died from a drug overdose, we're taking this matter very seriously indeed. There will be plenty of time for you to tell us everything you need to.'

'But I'm innocent!'

'Then you have nothing to worry about.' She nodded to Owen, who came forward now it was clear Oliver wasn't going to run.

He held out his arm. 'This way.'

And just like that, Oliver was gone. Fran stared in horror at Nell. Did that mean Oliver had killed Heather? That she'd just been talking to a murderer?

'Thank you, everyone,' said Nell, her face pretending to smile. 'Despite Mr Knight's arrest, the rear upstairs floor of the house is still a crime scene, as is the study area, and until my officers have completed their work, I would ask that you remain down here. Nothing has changed but I will update you when I can.' And with that, she turned on her heels and left the room.

Silence engulfed the room for a few seconds, taut and anxious, until Mimi Chapman suddenly wailed, covering her face with her hands.

'What am I going to do?' she lamented. 'How could Ollie do that to me?'

Fran glanced at Adam, but the look on his face told her he had no idea what Mimi was talking about either.

Peter laid a reassuring hand on Mimi's shoulder. 'You weren't to know, Mimi. It's diabolical behaviour, repaying your hospitality by bringing drugs here. But I must say, I had my doubts about Oliver.'

His words brought a renewed bout of tears as Mimi shook her head. 'No, you don't understand. Oh, this is horrible... with Keith barely cold. And he was a good man, a good husband in many ways, but... I feel so awful saying this. He could be very unfeeling, and he was away so much. I was lonely, you see... and Ollie... God, we tried so hard to fight it, but—'

Mimi got to her feet, steadying herself on Peter's ready arm just as Ginny held out her hands to receive her, shuffling on the sofa to make room.

'Are you saying you and Ollie were in a relationship?' Ginny asked, compassion turning her expression into one which was so at odds with her normal expression, Fran had to fight the urge to laugh. 'Oh, Mimi, you poor thing.'

'We were planning on getting married.' Mimi sniffed. 'But I had no idea about the drugs. If I'd have known then... I can't believe he could have deceived me like that.'

Peter sat down on her other side. 'Mimi, I can see what a shock this is, but... well, do you think that Ollie's motives might not have been entirely pure?'

Mimi's head shot up, her tear-filled eyes wide in astonishment. 'What do you mean?'

Peter shot his wife a glance. 'Well, Mimi, you're a very attractive woman and also... a very wealthy woman. I can't help but wonder whether Ollie might have been using you. I'm sorry, I know that's not what you want to hear, but...' He dropped his head, swallowing.

'What?' urged Mimi. 'You know something else, don't you? You have to tell me.' A tear dripped from the corner of one eye and she made no move to brush it away. 'Peter, please...'

'I have no proof of this, you understand.' He pulled at his shirt so it sat straighter over his round belly. 'But one hears things... in business. And, there's been talk for a little while that Ollie's been somewhat unlucky with his money. That, in fact, he's in rather a lot of debt. I hadn't said anything because, well, it's not sporting, is it? And I don't know for definite, but I was rather surprised when I heard he would be here this weekend.' He gave Mimi a sympathetic smile. 'I'm sorry. Perhaps I should have said something before.'

Mimi stared at him, her lip trembling. 'Oh...' A hand fluttered to her heart. 'Heather wanted to speak to me about something. She said so last night, but it was late and she... she said it could wait until the morning. I didn't think anything of it at the time, but... do you think she knew and wanted to tell me, to warn me?'

'It would make sense.' Peter turned to give Fran an accusatory stare. 'You were very thick with Heather yesterday,' he said. 'I saw you. Did she say anything to you?'

Fran flinched as all eyes turned on her. 'Not really... We were talking about what had happened more than anything.'

It wasn't exactly a lie but she wasn't about to say any more. What on earth was going on?

'I don't suppose it matters,' said Peter. 'I think it's pretty clear that the rumours about Ollie are true, especially in the light of what's just happened. And if he had a drug habit to fund, well, I probably don't need to say any more.'

You don't, thought Fran. *But I bet you're going to.*

'I'm sorry, Mimi, I hate to say this. It's awful that he's let you down like this, but by the sounds of it, I think you might be well shot of him. And you heard what the detective woman said; he could even have been responsible for Heather's death. I don't want to speak ill of the dead, but if she was silly enough to dabble with drugs as well, then—' He broke off, staring up at Richard. 'Oh my God... Do you think the police are right to suspect Heather's death might not have been an accident? Do you think Ollie might have... well, he might have wanted to stop Mimi from finding out about him.'

'You're saying you think he killed Heather?'

Peter nodded slowly. 'I think I might be. Oh Christ, this is awful. I'm so sorry, Mimi.'

At this, Mimi wailed again and pulling away from Peter, collapsed against Ginny's breast. The older woman rubbed Mimi's back, a fraught expression on her face. She looked up at Peter over Mimi's bent head as if to say, *how could you?*

Mimi's tears hiccupped to a halt. She sniffed, pulling slowly away from Ginny and looked up at the faces around her. 'But if Ollie *did* kill Heather... then what's to say he didn't kill Keith as well? I mean, think about it. If he needed money then Keith's paintings are worth a pretty penny. And if he knew that Keith was on to him then his chances of getting in on this latest project were nil, so a painting might be a neat solution. Maybe he didn't mean to kill Keith, but you have to admit that his death has done him a favour, particularly now that Heather's dead as well. He probably thought that now there'd be no one around to tell me about his debts.'

Peter looked at her, a horrified expression on his face. 'My God, Mimi, you're right...'

Ginny looked up from her task as chief comforter. 'I think

you four should go back to the kitchen,' she said. 'Gawking at poor Mimi's misfortune. It's not right that they should be listening to private family business, Peter. Besides, I'm sure we could all do with some tea. And something sweet for Mimi, for the shock.'

'I'll give her a cup of tea,' murmured Fran, moments later as they all trooped back to the kitchen. 'Only without the cup. Condescending...' She trailed off. 'And anyway, what was all that about? Was it me, or was Mimi's reaction completely over the top?'

'I don't think any of them are about to win any acting awards,' replied Rachel. 'Talk about hamming it up.'

'Which makes you wonder just who the performance was for,' replied Fran. 'Us, undoubtedly, given how quickly they got shot of us.'

'They probably think we'll go running back to Nell to tell her what we've heard.'

'Being devil's advocate for a moment,' said Derek, pausing. 'It could actually have happened the way Mimi described. It makes as much as sense as anything.' An apologetic smiled crossed his face.

'What?' said Rachel. 'You don't really believe that, do you?'

'No... like I said, I'm just floating it out there. I'm in agreement with the rest of you. There was something very fishy about Mimi's performance.'

'And, of course, now that Mimi has told everyone they're in on the new business venture, they're falling over themselves to agree with her,' said Adam. 'Talk about ingratiating—'

'Don't say it!' warned Fran.

'One thing's for certain,' finished Adam. 'I'm now pretty sure that Oliver Knight *isn't* guilty. I'm not sure who is, but—'

'Mimi's up to something,' supplied Fran.

'I couldn't have put it better myself.'

17

'You didn't hear them though, Nell,' protested Fran an hour later. 'It was like watching some awful play, talk about wooden. And the whole thing was staged for our benefit, I'm sure of it. So that they would have witnesses to attest to Mimi's emotional state and their subsequent "shock" revelations about Oliver.'

'Even so, given the *evidence* we currently have, Oliver Knight is still our best bet, for at least one of the crimes, if not all of them. I'm not saying he's guilty of anything, Fran, I'm saying the evidence points in his direction. If that's wrong, then we'll find out. But we have to start somewhere.'

'Surely the way they're all behaving is a place to start?' she replied. 'Mimi asked me to get all these parasites out of her house yesterday, and now suddenly she's promised to cut them all in on Keith's latest deal and they're all bosom buddies. Don't you think that's suspicious?'

Nell held Fran's look for a moment, clearly trying to work out what to say. 'Listen, Fran, I don't like this any more than you do, and maybe it is suspicious, or maybe it's just people behaving oddly when they're upset. That's one thing I have learned in all my years as a copper; that in extreme circumstances, folk don't always react the way you expect them to. It doesn't mean they're guilty of anything, just that we all have different ways of dealing with stress.'

Fran couldn't help the creep of her eyebrows upward. What she'd witnessed was not just odd behaviour. It was manipulative behaviour and she didn't understand why Nell was prepared to let it go. 'You don't believe that for a minute,' she said. 'You're always looking to see how people react.'

'And once we start questioning Oliver Knight again, I will be doing exactly that. Being interviewed in a police station can make a big difference to what people decide to tell us, and in Oliver's case, I think we'll find he has quite a lot to say.'

'So everyone is just free to go on their merry way, are they?'

'They are... including you, I might add.'

'Even though nothing's been resolved. You might have found drugs in Oliver's room, but being in possession of a drug is a very different thing from using it to kill someone. And we still don't know what happened to Keith, or who stole the painting.'

'Fran, I am aware of that.' Nell was using her best placatory tone. 'But I have no justification to keep these people here any longer. There's no evidence to connect any of them to a crime, and until we find some, that's simply the way it is. We won't stop looking, you know. Just because everyone is allowed to go home, it doesn't mean they're all innocent, not by a long stretch. And if they're not, then we'll find out, and they'll be charged at a later date.'

Fran sighed. 'Sorry... It just all seems so frustrating, when keeping everyone here a little longer might mean solving the whole thing. Doesn't this slow things up?'

'That's police work for you, I'm afraid. It is hugely frustrating. But the law is there to protect people and we have to abide by it. As I've said before, I need an arrest and now we have one. Let's leave it there, shall we?' She gave Fran a pointed look as if warning her not to argue. Fran guessed it was a very moot point, but she was still disappointed. 'You are also free to go however,' Nell reminded her. 'I thought you'd be glad to see the back of this place.'

For the first time since they'd started speaking, Fran allowed herself a smile. 'It's certainly been interesting,' she said. 'And it hasn't been all bad.' She slid her gaze further along the kitchen island to where Rachel was sitting. She caught her eye and nodded an acknowledgement of their friendship.

Nell reluctantly got to her feet. 'I must get going,' she said. 'Can't keep Mr Knight waiting too long and I have a very long list of other things to attend to as well. Our inquiries into the other guests are still very much ongoing and even though my team is done here, our absence doesn't mean this is over. Not at all. I'm also very grateful to you, Fran, don't think I'm not. What you've just told me could prove to be very useful information.' She glanced at her watch. 'I expect it's all going to get rather busy for a while as the guests get ready to leave, but keep in touch,' she said, turning for the door.

Fran waited until she was gone before pulling a face at Rachel, who seemed equally as subdued as she was. 'Well, we tried,' she said. 'And I guess that's all we can do.' She paused for a moment. 'Are you going to be okay?'

Rachel gave a wan smile. 'I'm going to be very busy,' she said. 'It's going to take a while to get this place sorted out.'

'Which wasn't what I asked,' replied Fran, with a warm smile. 'I rather meant with Mimi, now that Keith's dead. Is it going to make your position here difficult?'

'Who knows?' She shrugged. 'That rather depends on what Mimi has planned for the rest of her life, because I'm certain she will have it worked out. Whether that means selling up and moving on I've no idea, but if she decides to stay, I imagine life will be much the same as it has been. I hope so, for a while at least. I haven't really given much thought to what happens now. Maybe we need to let the dust settle.'

'And Derek?'

Rachel cast her eyes down a moment. 'He'll stay, if he's able. This is a big house and with all the grounds too, there's plenty to keep him occupied.'

'Well, I hope so,' replied Fran. Rachel and Derek were adults, they didn't need her to tell them they should plan a future together. They were perfectly capable of working it out for themselves. 'It's going to feel weird though, not being here,' she added. 'That's what they say about intense situations, isn't it? How they throw you together. I've almost forgotten what my old life is like.' She hadn't, but she was trying not to dwell on just how much she wanted to feel Jack's solid arms around her, or see her daughter, Martha, cavorting around the kitchen as she practised her dancing. She pushed the images from her mind. There was business to attend to yet, which reminded her. 'Have you seen Adam?' she asked.

'I think he went to find Derek,' said Rachel. 'Who has gone to see what train Richard is planning to take. He'll need dropping at the station. The Dawsons can leave under their own steam and...' She trailed off. 'Nell has asked me to collect Heather's things together. She had a sister who will be calling at some point to pick them up.'

Fran nodded, the aftermath of a death beginning to make itself felt. 'What about Oliver?' she asked. 'What will happen to his belongings?'

'That rather depends on what happens to *him*. If he's charged then, again, I'll have to pack them up so that someone can collect them. And if he isn't, he'll be back to pick them up himself.' She gave a wry smile. 'That's going to make for an interesting visit. I'd better go and make a start.'

'I could help you, if you want,' offered Fran. 'It's not a pleasant task.'

'No, you've enough to do. Don't worry. I'll be okay.'

'Well, in that case, I'll clear this lot up,' replied Fran, eyeing the array of breakfast things which had been collected from the morning room. They were still sitting beside the sink, unwashed.

Rachel flashed her a grateful look and then she too was gone, leaving Fran staring at the mess as she pondered the events of the last few days. There were still so many thoughts niggling at her, and although Rachel was right, what she should be doing was to start packing up her own things ready to leave, what she wanted to do was find Adam and run through some questions with him. There were still far too many puzzles lying unsolved within this house, and she was certain that the answers were still here.

Inhaling a deep breath, she began to stack the dishes, scraping the leftover food into the bin. A newspaper had been discarded on one of the trays and she tossed it on the side for recycling before turning her attention to the plate of uneaten pastries. There was also a quantity of fruit, equally untouched. She removed it all to the fridge and then, tucking her hair behind her ears, began to run hot water into the sink. Time for a little therapeutic washing-up and some serious thinking.

By the time she finished, she still wasn't any further forward but at least the kitchen was beginning to look more presentable. And now that it was, she could begin to think about gathering her own things. She and Adam would have to go home at some point and she couldn't think of any reason for delaying it much longer.

Scooping up the newspaper, she took it through into the utility room, laying it on the stack already there which Rachel would put out for recycling at the end of the week. It had been folded in half, midway through, and as her eyes drifted across a headline, she stopped. And frowned.

Pulling the paper back off the pile, she unfolded it,

shaking it out so she could read it more easily. Her gaze moved to the top of the page and the name of the newspaper, which was repeated on every sheet. Well, that was interesting...

She checked the date, struggling for a moment to recall what day it was, but once she had, she realised that the paper had been published on Friday, the day the guests had arrived at Claremont House. Three of them had arrived by train, and one in particular. Was this a newspaper Richard Newman had brought with him? Perhaps one he had bought from the station to read on his journey?

~

Adam caught up with Derek outside the garages, where he was giving the Dawsons' car a wash down.

'I know,' he said at Adam's pointed look. 'But if I don't do it, it will be out of spite and that makes me as bad as they are. I refuse to sink to their level.'

Adam pulled a face. 'I think if it were me, I'd *encourage* the birds to poo on it, a bit of bird seed on the roof ought to do it.'

Derek smiled. 'Don't give me ideas.'

'What time are the Dawsons leaving?'

'In half an hour or so. I'm not sure about Mr Newman, I need to find out what train he's planning to catch.'

'I was looking for him actually,' replied Adam. 'Do you know where he is?'

'No, sorry.' Derek shook his head. 'Packing, I would assume. Like everyone else, anxious to get away from here as soon as possible.'

But Richard Newman wasn't in his room, packing, because Adam had already checked. 'Well, when I find him, I'll ask him about the train.'

He was about to move off when Derek checked him, a

suspicious expression on his face. 'And are you going to tell me why you're looking for Richard?'

Adam grinned. 'Nope.' He tapped the side of his nose and with a jaunty wave, began to walk around the side of the building.

In fact, his quarry wasn't anywhere in the house, which meant that if he wasn't inside, or with Derek, Richard had to be in the gardens somewhere. And now Adam was even more determined to find him. Richard had disappeared once too often during the weekend and Adam wanted to know why. He also wanted to know why he had thrown his phone against a wall during an angry argument with someone. The answers to these questions would be impossible for him to find out once Richard had gone. It was now or never.

Adam didn't have a specific plan as such. But Richard's imminent departure at least gave him a legitimate reason to start a conversation and, as he stepped onto the terrace at the rear of the house, he could see someone sitting on a bench at the edge of the lawn. He hurried over.

Richard Newman was sitting with his eyes closed, face turned up to the sky and the warmth of the sun. He looked perfectly relaxed, not at all how Adam expected him to appear.

'Mr Newman...?' He paused, almost deferentially. 'I'm sorry to interrupt your peace and quiet, but Derek was wondering which train you'd like to catch?'

Richard squinted, his eyes taking a moment to adjust to the bright light. 'That's a very good question.' He smiled. 'I was just having a breather – it's been a bit of weekend, hasn't it? But soon, I guess.' He paused. 'Actually, I don't suppose I could ask you to check the times for me? I don't know what the problem is, but I can't seem to charge my phone and it's died on me.'

'Oh... sure,' Adam replied, trying desperately not to smile. 'Hang on a sec.' He pulled his phone from his pocket and pressed a button. 'Where are you going?' he asked.

'Euston.'

Adam nodded and waited a moment for his train app to load the information. 'There's one leaving Shrewsbury about twenty to four, gets in to London around half six. Would that do?'

'Perfect,' answered Richard, his eyes trained on Adam's phone.

'Don't know what we'd do without these,' said Adam. 'I'd feel as if I'd had my arm cut off if I didn't have mine.' He gave Richard a bright smile. 'I hope you get yours sorted quickly.' Given the number of pieces it was in, however, Adam didn't think that would be happening any time soon.

'I don't suppose I could...' Richard trailed off. 'I could do with making a couple of calls and...' He shrugged. 'Like you said, it's such a pain, isn't it, being without a phone?'

Adam stared at the oblong piece of metal in his hand. 'Oh...' he said, as if he couldn't quite make up his mind whether to lend Richard his phone. As if. 'Sure,' he said. 'Go ahead. It's not locked.'

Richard needed no second invitation and got to his feet with a charming smile. 'You're a star, thank you so much.' He took the phone and held it to his chest. 'Perhaps you could... Only they're business calls.'

Adam made a show of sudden understanding. 'Yes, of course, I'll just be...' He took a few steps backward, before stopping. 'I tell you what, why don't you just bring it to the kitchen when you're done? Would that be okay?'

'Oh, more than. Thanks again.'

Adam dipped his head and walked back the way he had come. This time he allowed a wide grin to spread across his face. He might not always understand why people did the things they did, but sometimes they were so predictable.

Derek was still by the garages as he rounded the building but it was Peter and Ginny Dawson he saw first. They were

standing beside their car, a suitcase on the gravel ready to be
stowed away, and as Adam watched, he saw Mimi approaching
from the other direction. Adam pressed himself closer to the
bushes which grew against the side of the house.

Mimi's greeting was effusive. She drew Ginny into a hug,
kissing her on both cheeks before turning to Peter and taking his
hand. She made a show of shaking it and then laughed,
throwing her head back, before pulling him forward to deposit
an equal number of kisses. Adam couldn't hear what was being
said, but Mimi's laughter was light-hearted, her face animated.
It was a far cry from the portrayal of grief-stricken widow she
had displayed earlier in the day.

The conversation continued for a few more minutes amid
much head-nodding and then Peter threw open the boot of the
car and tossed the suitcase inside as if it was a prop in a play,
empty of belongings and light as a feather. Then, with another
round of kisses, the Dawsons climbed inside their car. Adam
froze. He had no wish to be seen but, just as importantly, his
vantage point provided the perfect position to spy on the couple
as they departed from the house.

Sure enough, moments later the Dawsons' car swept past.
Adam had only a couple of seconds to view the occupants, but
Ginny's face was split wide in an expansive smile. They had got
what they wanted this weekend, after all.

Once he had relayed the details of Richard's departure time
to Derek, Adam hurried back to the kitchen.

'You'll never guess what I've just seen,' he said, moments
later. He threw a quick glance around the room to check they
were alone.

'You'll never guess what *I've* just found,' replied Fran.

They grinned at one another across the kitchen. 'You first,'
said Adam. Not that he was being competitive or anything but
he had a feeling his discovery, or should that be discoveries,
would trump Fran's.

'Judging by the look on your face, whatever you've spotted is significantly more important than my own rather small deduction. However, while I was clearing up, I came across this.' She picked up the newspaper and passed it to him. 'It's Friday's edition and judging by the scribbles on the pages and the way certain names have been underscored, I'd hazard a guess that whoever it belongs to has read the *Racing Post* on many occasions before.'

Adam flicked through the pages. There were indeed circles around the details of numerous races. 'Who do you think it belongs to?'

'I can't be certain, but Richard Newman was reading a paper this morning, and this one was left on the tray of breakfast things. Plus, it occurred to me that it's the sort of thing you might read on the train, particularly given that it's Friday's edition and we know he travelled that way.'

'As did Oliver Knight.'

Fran cocked her head to one side. 'True. But it might explain why Richard has been disappearing at numerous intervals – either to place a bet or to follow a race.'

Adam nodded. 'That's very true,' he said. 'A quite brilliant deduction.' He paused, realising just how valid an explanation it could be. 'And a hypothesis which we may be able to check any minute now,' he added. 'First things first, however. Because I've just seen the Dawsons and Mimi Chapman hugging and kissing each other goodbye as if they're the closest of friends, not people who, two days ago, had thunderous looks on their faces and were planning to pinch some of the family silver. The rats are deserting the ship and it's fascinating to see how they run. The weekend might not have turned out the way they'd all expected, or hoped, but it's clearly still been successful.'

Fran considered his words. 'And with everyone now on Mimi's side, she probably thinks she's home free. That was a clever move, cutting them all in on Keith's deal. In the absence of any other forensic evidence, as long as everyone backs up Mimi's story, she should have nothing to worry about.'

Adam blew air between his teeth. He was certain Fran was right, which made him all the more determined to find out what really happened. Puzzles, by their very nature, had solutions, and he was damned if this one was going to get the better of him. He looked up as a shadow fell across the window. It was Richard Newman and, if he wasn't much mistaken, another piece of the jigsaw.

Richard met him at the back door, full of smiles and bonhomie as he handed back Adam's phone.

'Thanks again. You're a lifesaver.'

'Everything okay?' asked Adam.

'Perfect,' came the reply. 'It's crazy, isn't it? How lost we are without our phones. How much we rely on them to do things for us.'

Adam smiled. *You don't know the half of it...*

'Right, well, I'd best go and pack up my things. The train's at twenty to four, I think you said?'

Adam nodded. 'Derek said he'd be ready to leave at three, if that suits. Don't want to risk being late.'

'No, quite.' Richard gave a warm smile and turned to go. 'Thanks for all your help.'

'My pleasure.'

Adam watched as he walked away, holding the polite expression on his face until Richard was out of sight. He let his smile fall, eyes narrowing on the phone in his hand. *Right then, let's see what you've really been up to.*

Returning to the kitchen, he laid the phone on the table and beckoned to Fran. 'Are you ready to find out if Richard is our gambler?' he asked.

She gave him a puzzled look.

'Poor Richard's been having a few problems with his phone,' he explained, 'so I did the decent thing and lent him mine.' The corners of his mouth twitched upward. 'Not sure Richard will see it that way, but then again, he's never going to find out, so...' He pulled out another phone from his pocket and laid it beside the first.

'Whose phone is that?' asked Fran, pointing to the second.

'Mine.' He grinned and tapped a finger on the handset Richard had just returned to him. 'And also mine.'

Fran stared at him, hands on her hips. 'Explain,' she said. 'How many phones does one person need?'

'You'd be surprised,' replied Adam, smiling mischievously. 'Although, essentially there's only one, given that the first is a clone of the second...'

Fran tutted. 'For God's sake, stop being so mysterious and just tell me what you've done.'

Adam picked up the second phone and navigated to an app on the home screen. 'I have an app installed on here which... let's just say it comes in handy every once in a while, and once I've opened it, we'll be able to see exactly how Richard Newman used my other phone while it was in his possession.' He scrolled for a moment, looking at the information presented to him. There wasn't much. 'Okay, so Richard visited a web page and then made two phone calls. Shall we have a listen to one?'

Fran stared at him. 'I don't want to know how we can possibly do that...' She tutted. 'But, obviously, yes.'

Adam touched his finger to the screen and, after a moment, a male voice filled the air.

'*Calmed down, have we?*'

Richard's voice was harsh. '*Stop taking the piss, Mike. You're happy enough when you're taking my money.*'

'*That I can do, my friend. What I can't do is make the gee-gees run any faster, no matter how much you want them to.*'

'*Okay, okay, I lost it, I admit. I've had a... thing going on here,*' *where I'm staying this weekend. I was stressed, that's all. It won't happen again.'*

'Ah, Richard... but that's what you always say. Still, it's your money. And I am a bookie, after all. Just don't take it out on me next time you lose. I mean that, or you'll be looking for someone else to do your bidding.' The line went quiet for a moment. 'I probably shouldn't be saying this either, but maybe you ought to scale it back a bit. That was quite a hit you took.'

'And I don't pay you for your advice, Mike. So let me worry about the money, you just do what I pay you for. As long as you're quids in, what's the problem?'

There was a long pause. 'Sure thing. So, what'll it be then?'

'The 11.35 at Lingfield tomorrow. Let's start with a grand on Jazz King. Then the same on Juniper in the 1.15 and again on Little Light in the three o'clock at Leopardstown. Got that?'

'I surely do. Pleasure doing business with you again, Mr Newman.' The line went dead.

Adam gave a low whistle under his breath. 'It would seem your hunch was right, Fran.'

'That's three thousand pounds. In a day.' She stared at him incredulously. 'What are these people like?' she asked. 'Where do they even get the money from?'

Adam was still peering at his phone. 'I have no idea, but at least that's cleared up the puzzle of why Mr Newman has been disappearing all weekend. And what he's been doing when he has. There's nothing sinister about it at all.'

Fran nodded. 'We're pretty sure he's innocent of anything untoward then?'

'Yeah,' agreed Adam. 'I think we can rule him out.' He screwed up his face. 'Argh... we're so nearly there, Fran. But there's still so much we don't know about all of this, or can't categorically prove. And until we have all the answers, there's nothing more we can do.'

Fran's mouth settled into a hard line. 'Then we just have to keep going until we do have all the answers. Mimi is banking on us being no threat to her. And I think we should pose a *very* large threat indeed. Something extremely nasty has gone on here and I want to know what it is.'

'Hold that thought,' replied Adam.

'Why, what are you going to do?'

'It's just occurred to me that Rachel is gathering Heather's things together, and I'm quite interested to see whether she brought a laptop with her. If she did, well...' He let the sentence dangle.

'Adam, you can't do that. The poor women's dead, you can't hack her computer.'

'Not even if it can help prove who killed her?' he said. 'If there's any information on there about Oliver, then—'

'Be respectful,' said Fran. 'That's all. Don't go poking around in anything which is obviously personal.'

'I won't,' said Adam. 'Promise. I liked her too.'

18

Once Adam was gone, Fran stared around her at the kitchen. She needed to pack up her things and sort out the details of all the extra food she'd had to produce. There was no way she would be leaving Claremont House out of pocket, and the way she was feeling about Mimi, she'd rather enjoy working out how much extra she was owed. But she was torn. Their time here was coming to an end, but there was still much to resolve and they were so close, she could feel it. Trouble was, close was nowhere near enough. She had a decision to make, and soon.

'Where is Rachel?'

The voice from behind her was so unexpected that Fran nearly dropped the packet of flour she was holding. It was Mimi, an impatient expression on her face.

'Oh... upstairs, I think.' Fran didn't want to mention Heather by name. 'She's in the rear guest bedroom,' she added.

'Never mind.' Mimi looked around the room, blankly. 'I shall be requiring dinner this evening... that's all. A Caesar salad will be sufficient.'

Fran wasn't sure whether her statement was a request to relay the information to Rachel, or meant for Fran herself. It was almost as if Mimi had forgotten that Fran didn't work here all the time. 'Yes, of course, I'll let Rachel know straight away.'

Mimi had changed clothes since the last time Fran had seen her and was now wearing a plain white tee shirt with straw-coloured jeans. Gone were the silk blouse and trousers and, with them, her very formal appearance. Now Mimi's hair had been released from its chignon, tumbling onto her shoulders. Her feet were also bare. It wasn't this that most surprised Fran however, but the fact that Mimi left the room exactly the way she had arrived, absolutely silently.

'So, Keith *did* know about Oliver's financial situation,' said Fran some hours later. 'You're sure about that?' It was early evening and Adam was sitting beside her in the kitchen, a plate of toast and jam in front of him. Behind him, Rachel was busy whipping up a Caesar dressing for the salad which Mimi had requested for her supper.

'As certain as I can be. The email from the forensic accountant on Heather's laptop was pretty explicit. I didn't read the full report that was attached but I can guess at its contents. I'm pretty sure what Heather told you was true.'

Fran took a deep breath. 'So what are we saying?' she asked. 'Do we think Keith told Mimi, or Heather did? In which case are we also saying we think Mimi killed Keith?'

'Hold that thought,' said Rachel, pouring dressing over the salad she had already prepared. 'Let me just go and take this up. Mimi is dining in her room this evening – she couldn't bear to be downstairs apparently, not where she can see the—' Rachel held her hand to her forehead in a mock swoon. 'Not where she can see the room where her husband died.' She pulled a face. 'Sorry,' she said unnecessarily.

Fran stared at the slice of toast which still lay on Adam's plate. 'Can I pinch that, I'm starving? All this talk of dirty deeds is making me hungry. I suppose we should think about getting ourselves something to eat.'

Unusually, Adam looked a little reticent. 'Can I just check something?' he asked. 'Only... Aren't we supposed to be going home?'

Fran could feel heat flooding her face and she bit her lip. 'Um... swear to me, Adam,' she said. 'Swear on your mother's life that you won't tell Jack. But I've told him we've got to stay here until at least tomorrow.'

'Francesca Eve, I'm shocked at such behaviour.' He grinned. 'But that's wonderful news. We can crack this, Fran, I know we can. So, what do we do next?'

'I think we need to draw up a list – everything we know, and everything we don't know. Because if we want to pin this on Mimi we have to work out all the details and I'm worried we've overlooked something vital.'

'Okay... But there is one other thing we need to do first.'

Fran narrowed her eyes, pretty sure she knew what Adam's answer was going to be. 'How about egg and chips?' she said. 'I've just had a sudden yearning for some.'

'Perfect,' replied Adam, beaming.

An hour later, Rachel and Derek having joined them, all four sat around the table expectantly. Their dirty dishes were still piled by the sink and the remnants of an apple crumble which Rachel had fetched from the freezer sat between them. As did Adam's laptop and a notepad and pen.

Adam slid the latter towards Fran. 'Right then, chief note-taker. What do we know? Let's start at the beginning with Keith's death.'

'Okay,' said Fran. 'Well, he was killed in the early hours of Sunday morning, hit over the head with something solid, possibly something with a square base. However, whatever was used hasn't yet been found, despite an extensive search of the whole house.'

'And a search of the grounds hasn't turned anything up either,' added Derek.

Fran nodded. 'And, as far as I know, or have managed to overhear...' She paused to give a wry smile. 'No other forensic evidence relating to Keith's death has been found outside the study. In fact, Nell said there was a distinct lack of forensics, which puzzled her. Nothing in anyone's rooms, or on the clothing they wore the night of the party. The study looked like there'd been a struggle, and Keith's prize painting had been stolen, but again there's no sign of this anywhere, even though no one had left the house.'

Adam leaned forward. 'Fran seemed to have been the last one to see him alive, and you said he was very drunk.'

'Yes, and morose too; melancholic, although that was very probably the whisky. When Rachel and I first showed Nell into the room, she remarked that there was a damp patch on the floor and there was an empty glass on the desk. I think he either spilled his drink or it was knocked over. In any case, I'm honestly not sure how much of a fight he could have put up; he could hardly stand.'

'Which is odd, given the state of the room,' put in Adam.

'And also the fact no one heard a thing. Both Heather's room and mine are directly over the study, and neither we, nor anyone else, reported hearing anything. No shouting, sounds of a struggle, no noise of the room being trashed, nothing. No one saw anything suspicious either.'

'Apart from me,' said Adam. 'I saw someone walking up the garden, don't forget. Stark naked. Whoever it was looked like she had wet hair too. So, either this person had been for a swim, which is possible, it was a very hot night, or they'd had a shower down in the cabin. One of them looked like it had been used when I went to check the next day. It's possible that the shower was still wet from when Ginny and Heather had been down at the pool with Mimi on Saturday morning, but the more I think about it, the more convinced I am it was Mimi I saw. It couldn't have been Ginny, she's... well, she's just the wrong shape. The night was moonlit, enough to see curves and things and...' He broke off, embarrassed. 'Anyway, if it wasn't Ginny, then it could only have been Heather or Mimi and somehow I don't think it was Heather. She was much shorter than Mimi for starters.'

Fran made a another note on the pad. 'Okay, so is there anything we've missed about Keith's death?'

'Only that Mimi had a very red hand the morning after he was killed,' said Rachel. 'Remember?'

'It looked like a burn to me,' said Adam. 'But I even checked down at the wood oven by the pool, and I couldn't see signs of anything having been got rid of there. And the fireplaces in the house would all have been checked as part of the search process.'

'Burn to hand...' murmured Fran, as she committed it to paper. 'Right, so what do we know about everyone here? Let's start with the Dawsons. They were the first people I heard arriving on Friday and made a great impression when Ginny Dawson said she intended to milk Mimi's hospitality for all it was worth. There certainly didn't seem to be any love lost between them, and Ginny was downright furious at the arrangements for the spa morning. She also made reference to the "mess" she and Peter were in, which we now know to be financial. They were obviously incredibly keen that Peter secure the deal with Keith this weekend, and when it seemed as if that wasn't going to happen, they outright said they should nick something to recoup their losses. They have to be the number one suspects for pinching the painting. Even though Mimi subsequently promised them in on Keith's deal, they didn't know that at the time.'

'I agree,' said Rachel.

'Hey, I've just had a thought,' said Adam. 'We've been

thinking that the Dawsons had cheered up noticeably when they left because of the deal Mimi offered them, but what if they did pinch the painting? That might also explain why they were in a particularly good mood, because they were also going home with it.' He scratched his head. 'But heaven only knows where they hid it, if they were.'

'Was their car searched?' asked Rachel.

Fran nodded. 'Yes, nothing.'

'Which brings us neatly to Richard Newman,' said Adam. 'Who at one point was seen having a row with someone on his phone, which he then threw against a wall in a fit of rage. Yet, just before he left this afternoon was relaxing in the garden looking as happy as Larry. I wanted to know who he'd argued with, and why he'd been disappearing at odd intervals all weekend, so, knowing he was without his phone, I offered to lend him mine. Once he'd given it back to me, with a little bit of "technical" help, we discovered that Richard had made a phone call to his bookie.'

'I found a copy of the *Racing Post* when I was clearing up,' added Fran. 'It had been left on a tray with the breakfast things and I wondered then whether it belonged to Richard. His phone call confirmed it. And it also told us that his bookie had been the one he'd been yelling at. He'd lost his temper because he lost a load of money on a race.'

'So what are you saying then?' asked Derek. 'That Richard is innocent?'

Adam nodded. 'His behaviour all weekend looked suspicious, but I don't think it was, really. Out of all the guests I think he's the least likely to have killed Keith.'

'Trouble is though, that eliminating Richard doesn't prove that Mimi killed her husband,' said Fran. 'And there's still the possibility that it was the Dawsons, even though that looks less likely.'

'Okay, so let's think about Heather for a moment,' said Adam.

Fran wrote Heather's name on a clean page of her notebook and stared at it briefly. 'She was very scared,' she said, underlining the name.

'Yes, she was,' replied Adam. 'We know from Heather's emails that she didn't find out about the truth about Oliver's finances until Saturday afternoon. And if you think about it, that would make sense too, given that Heather had a private conversation with Keith down in the cabin by the pool. A conversation that by all accounts started off well but then left Heather preoccupied almost to the point of being frightened. Fran, you spoke to Heather and found out that she was guilty of passing on inside information to Keith very early on in her career. It was a mistake which has given him a hold over her for years, knowing full well that if that information came to light, Heather would not only lose her job, but very likely end up in prison too. That's what she and Keith had been discussing. Perhaps Keith promised that after this latest deal was struck, he would let Heather go. Except that Keith would never really do that. I think he told Heather his intentions on Saturday afternoon and that's what freaked her out. She realised that, although technically, Keith being *her* client, she could rescind that agreement, the reality was that she would never be free of him.'

Fran looked at the expression on Rachel's face. 'Is something wrong?'

'Only that what you've described might well have given Heather cause to take her own life, if it was suicide, that is.'

Fran thought for a moment. 'It does... but I really don't think that was what happened, and neither do the police. It sounds callous to say it, but I think Heather's death is just another piece of the puzzle, one which fits into a much bigger picture. Heather *was* upset after her conversation with Keith, she may even have been fearful that she would never be free of him, but I don't think she became *really* scared until much later, after Keith had been killed and she guessed that Mimi must have known about Oliver's finances. That's when she realised Mimi had a motive for killing Keith, that's when she worked out that Mimi was the killer. Heather wasn't just scared, she was frightened for her life.' Fran's hand went to her mouth as she stared at Adam.

'But Mimi claimed she didn't know about Oliver's lack of money,' said Rachel.

'Exactly,' replied Fran. 'It was something she was very anxious to tell us. Why else stage that ridiculous piece of theatre this morning? She wanted us to believe she was the innocent party, caught up in Oliver's lies and deceit when, in fact, it's the other way around.'

Adam's breath caught audibly in his throat. He'd been quiet while Fran had been speaking, his eyes fixed on her face, and Fran knew his mind had been running ahead of her words, computing scenarios, checking the logic.

'You're right,' he said. 'It's the timing of Mimi finding out about Oliver that's important here. That single fact changes everything.' He laid his palms flat on the table. 'Think about it... The weekend starts off and Mimi and Oliver are thick as thieves. Maybe she was playing him, I don't know, but on the face of it at least, they seemed very friendly. Then, late on Saturday afternoon, Fran, you heard Keith and Mimi arguing and him telling her she would be hearing from his solicitor. The consequence of which was that Mimi had a face like thunder all evening. And I think that's the point at which she found out, some time during that afternoon. That's when it all changed for Mimi, because suddenly the future she had planned out for herself fell into jeopardy. I haven't quite worked this bit out yet, but when Keith threatened Mimi with divorce it would have made her angry, sure, but she still had Oliver to fall back on, her knight in shining armour, a knight who also had pots of money. So, when she subsequently discovered that those pots were empty, she realised that her plan to run away with Oliver wasn't going to work either. She'd be divorced and left penniless, so what could she do? And then it came to her, Keith had to go...

'What if, she kills him, and then late on Sunday night when Heather asks to speak to her, she realises that Heather has her sussed, and kills her too? If she's clever, she can make it look like it was Oliver's hand at work all along, and while she's at it, pin Keith's death on him as well. Oliver was broke, and he would have been desperate to keep that information from Mimi, he'd probably guessed that she wouldn't look at him twice if he was penniless. And with Keith dead, there was only one other person who knew about his financial predicament: Heather. So there's your motive right there, and Mimi had worked that out too. Plus, she also has a house full of people who, with a little manipulation, could become willing to back up her story. So she offers them all what they wanted, a cut in on Keith's deal, hoping that will secure their loyalty to her. So today, having possibly planted drugs on Ollie, Mimi acts all distraught when the "truth" about him comes out and weeps in despair because they had planned to be together, and how could he do that to her? And so on and so on...'

Fran looked at each of them in turn, but it was clear they were thinking exactly what she was. 'But to do that you'd have to be... ruthless... and very clever.'

'You'd have to be a survivor,' replied Adam. 'And I think Mimi's background gave her exactly the skills she needed. We have to find proof that Mimi knew about Oliver's situation – it's the one thing which makes everything else fall into place.'

19

Fran stared in dismay. Where did you even begin?

She pushed open the door to the study a little wider, swallowing as she recalled the last time she had done so. It had been Sunday morning, the day Keith's body had been found, and since that time no one had been allowed near this room. Now, two days later, with Adam standing beside her, the only thing missing was the body. Everything else was exactly as it had appeared then. Furniture overturned, books hurled from the shelves, curtains torn down from the window and, almost in the centre of the room, the picture frame which had once held Keith's priceless painting. Since that time, however, the forensic team had scoured every inch of the room and left their mark; almost every surface was covered with fingerprint powder and it would take a lot of work to make the room presentable once more.

'I don't know what you expect to find,' said Fran, taking a step inside. 'Anything that was here is now long gone.'

'I'm just curious,' replied Adam. It was the first time he'd set foot in this room and Fran could see his eyes roving over every detail.

'So nothing has been moved?' he asked.

Fran shook her head. 'No... only Keith.'

Adam looked to where the carpet was still stained with blood. 'And he was where exactly?'

Fran moved forward and pointed. 'There. He was lying almost face down. His head this way, feet that way.'

For a few moments, Adam remained silent, his eyes focused on the chair where Fran had last seen Keith, nursing a glass of whisky. She had a feeling he wasn't really seeing it though; his focus had shifted to the thoughts inside his head. He came to with a start, as if suddenly understanding what he was seeing.

'God, why didn't I think of it before! Keith's computer...'

It was a study, a place where, among other things, Keith came to work. It was obvious there'd be a computer here but, up until now, Fran's thoughts had skated over it, far more concerned with what else the room contained. She pulled a face.

'It wouldn't have done you any good if you had,' she replied. 'Nell was hardly going to let you in here to check it.'

Adam looked puzzled. 'So why didn't they?' he asked.

She shrugged. 'Presumably they didn't see any need to. But I have a feeling they might come back for it, and soon. I guess it rather depends where their inquiries lead them and how quickly they work out the significance of Oliver's financial situation. But once they do work it out, then...' She gave him an anxious look. 'You'd best get cracking,' she said.

Adam nodded and hurried to the desk.

Fran drifted about for a couple more minutes, before realising that there was little she could do to help. And there was one thing she did need to attend to. 'I'll be in the kitchen,' she said. 'Let me know when you find something.' But Adam didn't even look up, intent on his task.

The kitchen was as they'd left it, untidy, and still piled with their dishes from the night before. Overwhelming tiredness had hijacked them all, and the task of washing up had been abandoned in favour of getting some sleep. Some hope of that though, and all of them had got up early this morning. Fran had waved away Rachel's offer of help to set the kitchen straight, telling her that she would see to it. That way Rachel was free to make a start cleaning the guest rooms. Mimi would expect nothing less.

Even though it wasn't Fran's kitchen, it was still the place where she knew she would do her best thinking. Mundane domestic tasks allowed her brain to slip its gears and freewheel. It was amazing what came into her head at such times, and she had learned to go with it over the years – some of her most useful insights and inspiration had come to her in this way. And she could certainly do with them now.

Today would be her and Adam's last day at Claremont House. She couldn't put off the return to her own life any longer, and what they didn't uncover today would stay hidden. It was an odd feeling, bittersweet. On the one hand she was desperate to see Jack and Martha again. She had thrust thoughts of them from her head over the last couple of days, but now that the prospect of seeing them again was so tantalisingly close, their presence was beginning to loom large. But there was still the pull of a mystery unsolved, the sadness of two deaths to extract justice for and there was also this place, which had wormed its way under her skin.

The kitchen was a pain. It was just as Rachel had declared it to be; ill-thought out and difficult to work in. Fran had walked miles navigating her way between cooker, sink and fridge this weekend, but it had also provided something unexpected; the friendship of Rachel and Derek, and, given the situation they'd all found themselves in, Fran was eternally grateful for it.

She picked up a bowl and carried it to the sink, smiling to herself at her thoughts. The dinner on Saturday seemed like a lifetime away, so much had happened since, and unless they uncovered the truth of what had gone on here, she would have to walk away leaving everything unresolved and she hated doing that. She must make the most of every minute they had left.

As she filled the sink with water, her thoughts turned to Mimi, wondering how she was feeling. Was she lying upstairs even now, a growing excitement inside of her at the thought of a new life which lay ahead? Or was she racked with guilt and remorse over what had happened? Terrified of being found out? Fran was pretty sure she knew the answer. Mimi was too cunning, and too manipulative ever to doubt her actions. Right from an early age she had set her sights on the future she wanted for herself, and she hadn't let anything get in the way of that, even turning her back on her family to achieve it. Mimi wasn't the sort to suffer from introspection. No, women like her were just like the proverbial leopard; they never changed their spots. She frowned as the flicker of a thought hovered at the edge of her mind, but it was gone before she could catch it.

The sink filled, she immersed the bowls in soapy water and began to wash them, letting her thoughts drift. She could easily have used the dishwasher instead, but that wasn't nearly as therapeutic.

A little while later, with the kitchen set to rights, there was nothing else for Fran to do but to start packing up her things. And alongside that was the small matter of her bill to adjust. There was no way she was leaving without working out exactly how much she should charge Mimi for all the extras she'd had to provide, both in terms of the cost of the food and her time involved in making it. Flicking the kettle on to boil, she sat down to make a list.

Her mobile rang just as it began to bubble, startling her.

'Nell, hi... I wasn't expecting to hear from you again.' She paused, thinking that sounded rude. 'At least not so soon, anyway.'

There was an equal pause from the other end. 'Yes, well, that's because... Anyway, I thought you'd want to know that we've charged Oliver Knight with Heather's murder and—'

Fran couldn't help her gasp, and she could almost hear the reproach in Nell's voice as she stopped speaking.

'There's the possession charge for a start and... look, I can't give you the details, but this isn't the first time he's been involved with drugs. And he's admitted they're his. He made a simple mistake, he says. Said he bought them for Keith, to offer as a sweetener if you like, for goodness' sake. Only he didn't realise it wasn't Keith's thing. We didn't find out until late yesterday and it changes things...' She trailed off. 'I'm under a lot of pressure with this one.'

'Which means?'

There was a large intake of breath. 'He still says he had nothing to do with either Keith or Heather's death, but withholding this kind of information from us hasn't gone down well. I still think he's hiding something, and he's fudging questions about his financial situation for one.'

Which didn't answer Fran's question.

'He's probably just terrified that Mimi is trying to fit him up,' replied Fran, wondering why Nell couldn't see that. Or was refusing to. 'I would imagine Oliver doesn't want you to find out about his financial situation because he knows it paints him in a very bad light and he's still trying to work out what Mimi might have said about him. I mean, one minute the man is planning to run away with her and the next she appears to have dropped him quicker than the proverbial hot potato. If he's being cagey about what he tells you it's probably because he's scared of what could happen.'

'Nevertheless, he is still our main suspect, he has to be. Just because you didn't approve of Mimi's so-called theatrics yesterday morning doesn't mean she wasn't right. And the fact that you don't like her doesn't make her a killer either.'

'Yes, but you didn't see what happened yesterday.'

'Exactly, Fran. I didn't. I've obviously taken into account what you've told me, but may I remind you again that you and Adam aren't the police.'

Fran couldn't believe it. Did Nell really think that Oliver was guilty? 'But you're going to charge the wrong man!' she protested.

There was an irritated huff. 'You don't know that. Look, Fran, I didn't have to tell you what I have, but I just thought I should, out of courtesy because it's a situation you were involved in—'

'So, what about Keith then? How do you explain his death? We've been led to believe that Mimi didn't know about Oliver's financial situation, and that she's only just found out, in other words *after* Keith was killed. That obviously throws suspicion onto Oliver. But if Mimi knew *before* Keith was killed then the situation is very different, and it puts Mimi very firmly in the frame.'

'Perhaps it does, but either way whatever Keith was hit over the head with should have been easy to find given the circumstances, as should the painting, and we've drawn a blank with both. In fact, we have so little forensic evidence it's bizarre. Nothing in anyone's room, on their clothes and—' She came to a sudden halt. 'Anyway, that's *my* problem, not yours.'

'And are you going to tell Mimi that you've charged Oliver?'

'She'll be kept informed, yes. Our family liaison officer will be updating her in due course.'

'I can tell her myself if you like. See what kind of a response she has to the news.' Fran was shamelessly fishing now, but she couldn't believe that Nell was seemingly prepared to overlook her doubts about Mimi. She must be under more pressure from above than Fran realised.

'Fran, what possible reason do you have for going back to the house...?' Nell fell silent, and Fran could almost hear the cogs whirring in her mind. They were followed by an irritated tut. 'You're still there, aren't you?' she said. 'For goodness' sake, Fran, what are you doing? You've no need to be there any longer. Go home to your husband and daughter.'

Fran baulked. That was a low blow.

'Listen, Fran, I have to go, but you are not to say anything to Mimi, leave that to my officer, okay? In fact, make sure you leave everything to my officers, Fran. And that goes for Adam too. Especially Adam. I appreciate your wanting to help, but I... I'll speak to you soon.'

Fran was left staring at her phone in frustration, irritated by Nell's attitude. She and Adam had been clearly warned off from 'meddling' as Nell would put it. *Well, bad luck, Nell,* she thought, *because now you've made me even more determined.* Fran hadn't taken a particular liking to Oliver Knight but that didn't mean she wanted to see him charged for a crime he didn't commit. More to the point, she *had* liked Heather, and whoever had caused her death needed to atone for it. And if Nell and her team weren't going to find out for certain, then perhaps it was up to her and Adam to find out what really happened. The way things were going, she was sure they were close.

She thought again about what they had already learned. No matter how hard she tried, she couldn't connect the deaths of Keith and Heather in her head; it simply didn't seem to make sense. She was certain they were two separate things. And when it came down to who killed Keith, two questions still remained. Where was the painting? And where was the weapon which had struck the fatal blow?

Fran glanced at her watch. There was little point in wasting time looking for either of these things. Trained police officers had been over every inch of the house and grounds, and they knew where to look. They knew where people were in the habit of hiding such things. On the face of it there seemed little chance that she and Adam could find anything they hadn't. She pressed the heel of her hand against her forehead. It wasn't leg power which was going to solve this, but brain power instead. *Think, Fran, think...*

But ten minutes later, as she took Adam a cup of tea, she was still none the wiser. He didn't seem to be having much luck either. He growled with frustration as Fran entered the study.

'This is going to take longer than I thought,' he said. 'And is making me even more convinced that Keith's deals were dodgy. No innocent person would have files hidden within files and password protects the way he has. Which also makes me wonder who he was hiding things *from*, given that only he and Mimi lived here.'

'Rachel and Derek?' suggested Fran.

'Possibly... but I can't really see it. More likely to cover his tracks should he ever be investigated. I'll find something, don't worry, but it's going to take a while.'

Fran flashed him a smile. 'Crack on then,' she said. 'Nell has just been on the phone, informing me they have Oliver firmly in their sights. They've charged him with Heather's murder, and from the sound of things they're going to do their damnedest to link him with Keith's death too.' She gave him a direct look. 'She also firmly warned us off the case, which is precisely why we need to double our efforts.'

Adam grinned back, waving his hands at her. 'Go on then, shoo.'

It was as Fran was walking back to the kitchen that a sudden thought came to her and she hurried up the back staircase. Rachel was still in the room which Richard had used during his stay at the house.

'Does Mimi have a computer?' Fran asked. 'A laptop, or tablet perhaps?'

'She has both,' Rachel replied, holding a pillowcase in her hand. 'Keith was the only person who used the study, but Mimi was constantly online. Social media is more her thing, as you might imagine. Why are you asking?'

'Only that we need proof Mimi knew about the state of Oliver's financial affairs. Adam's looking at Keith's computer now, but it's proving harder than he thought. I wondered if Mimi's laptop might be an easier nut to crack.'

Rachel's eyes widened. 'Adam can do that?' she asked.

'Hmm...' Fran frowned. 'Adam can do a lot of things he's not supposed to, but I admit they do come in handy sometimes. Do you know where Mimi is?'

'In her room, I think. She's just been for a swim.'

'And her laptop?'

'Will also be in her room. Why, what are you thinking?'

'That we lure her somewhere else for long enough to get Adam in there so he can take a look.'

Rachel shot a glance out into the hallway. 'I don't know, Fran. It seems a bit risky, and if Mimi catches us... I could lose my job. I might anyway, but if I'm fired, bang goes any chance I have of a reference. Wouldn't it be easier to wait until Mimi goes out?'

'Probably, but we're up against time, Rachel. Finding that proof is only one step of the way towards finding evidence that Mimi had anything to do with either Keith or Heather's death. If she doesn't go out, or not until much later, we'll lose the only chance we have. And we'll make sure we keep you out of it, I promise. If anyone gets caught it will be Adam or me.'

Rachel studied her for a moment, indecision written across her face. 'Okay,' she said finally. 'What do you want me to do?'

'Just let me know when Mimi goes back downstairs,' Fran replied. 'And leave the rest to me. Oh, and one last thing – do you know where exactly Mimi keeps her laptop?'

Fran hurried back downstairs and into the study to relay her idea to Adam. 'And Rachel says Mimi normally leaves her laptop in the sitting room of her suite, which is the first room you enter, her bedroom is behind it. There's a side table to the left of the sofa – try there.'

'How long will I have?'

'As long as I can give you,' replied Fran grimly. She met Adam's look. 'It might be the only chance we get.'

'No pressure then.' He cracked his knuckles, making Fran wince, and she hurried back to the kitchen.

She needed to think of some way to keep Mimi talking and away from the main part of the house, even if that meant Mimi might ask her to leave. The weekend was over, the other guests had gone, and there was no reason for her or Adam to stay.

She picked up her notebook. Her bill would be a legitimate thing to discuss and she sat down to continue where she had left off. She just had to hope that Mimi would want to go through things with a fine-tooth comb. Somehow she didn't think so.

Nearly an hour went by before Rachel came by the kitchen. Fran had long since finished making her notes by then, but at least if her ruse didn't work, she now had a detailed record of just how much she should be invoicing Mimi for. Rachel's expression, however, was troubling.

'She's in the morning room,' said Rachel. 'But she's got her laptop with her. That isn't unusual but it's going to make it hard for Adam to get in and out easily. You know how that room gives a wide view of the hallway. If Mimi is anywhere nearby she'll spot him, no problem.'

'Then I'll just have to do a good job in keeping her attention, won't I?' replied Fran. She grimaced and took out her phone to message Adam. That done, she offered up a silent prayer, and went to intercept Mimi.

'Mrs Chapman?'

Mimi turned, a query on her face. She looked at Fran as if it were the first time she had seen her. After a moment a distant memory stirred. 'Shouldn't you have gone by now?' she asked.

'Yes, I... things got a bit delayed, what with...' She trailed off. 'So I stayed on a bit to help Rachel clear up.'

'Rachel is paid to clear up,' she replied. 'I do hope you're not going to charge me for your—'

Fran could feel resolve stiffen her spine. 'And I just wanted to say, I'm so very sorry for your loss, Mrs Chapman.'

Mimi stared at her, opening her mouth to speak but then clearly changing her mind about what she wanted to say. 'Thank you,' she said instead, a cool expression on her face. She was barefoot again, Fran noticed, wearing a similar outfit to the day before.

'Is there something you wanted?' Mimi asked.

'I'm sorry, I know this isn't a good time, but since you mentioned my charge I really do need to speak to you about it, given that things have altered since we first agreed a price. I haven't had a chance to look at it before now, but would you have a minute so I can discuss it with you before I leave?'

Mimi's eyes were wandering, through the adjoining conservatory windows and out into the garden. The last thing she wanted to do was talk to Fran.

'Perhaps I can make you a coffee, and get you a little something to eat? I know you won't have felt like eating the last few days, but I'm sure I could find something you might fancy.'

Mimi still wasn't convinced.

Fran decided to be blunt. 'Because I've incurred quite a lot of additional costs over the weekend and I'd rather not send you an invoice without going through these things first. That doesn't seem fair.'

Mimi's eyes slid back to her, assessing her from head to toe. 'Very well, but I don't have a great deal of time.'

Fran couldn't help but wonder what she had to do that was so pressing. 'Thank you. I have everything in the kitchen if you'd like to come and have a look.'

Walking ahead, Fran idly pulled out her phone as if to

check the time. A simple touch sent a pre-written text message to Adam, letting him know the coast was clear. As soon as Mimi had reluctantly followed her through the door to the rear of the house, Adam would slip down the hallway and into the morning room.

'Can I get you a coffee?' Fran asked, once they were in the kitchen. 'Or something else to drink, perhaps?'

Mimi shook her head, eyes roving the paperwork on the table.

'Something to eat then? There are some fresh figs left. Perhaps you'd like them with some Greek yoghurt and a little honey?'

Mimi at least thought about it, but the answer was still no, and now Fran was all out of ploys to delay her even longer. She'd have to resort to plan B, something she really didn't want to do. It was tantamount to picking a fight.

'Let's just go through things then, shall we? I have everything here and—' She broke off. 'Oh... I thought I had a piece of paper there which...' She turned around. 'I wonder what I've done with it?'

Mimi sighed. 'Ms Eve, did I not make it clear enough when I said I didn't have much time? If your paperwork isn't in order then perhaps you could make sure that it is before you speak to me about it.'

Fran held out her hand. 'No, wait...' She rifled through the papers. 'It's here, sorry. I have it now.' She smiled in encouragement. 'There.' She laid down the piece of paper on the table and indicated that Mimi might like to take a seat.

Adam's heart sank. Mimi's laptop was on the coffee table in front of the armchair. An armchair which faced the hallway and was in almost the worst possible place it could be. But dwelling on that fact was time he couldn't afford to waste and he immediately sank to his knees beside it. If ever there was a need for a God of laptops it was now; he could use a little divine intervention. He opened the lid, peered at the screen, eyes narrowing, and sighed. He might have known there'd be no such help afforded him.

'This is what we originally discussed,' began Fran. 'So, starting on Friday...' She pointed to the first item on the list as Mimi sat down. 'We have the evening cocktail reception, then on Saturday a breakfast, followed by—'

'Yes, thank you, I can read.'

Fran swallowed. 'However, when I arrived, I discovered that afternoon refreshments were required on both days, for guests arriving on Friday and then again to bridge the gap between the picnic lunch and the evening dinner on Saturday.' She lifted another sheet of paper. 'And this is a list of what was provided. Because this wasn't discussed during our initial conversations I couldn't factor it into my original quote, which would have been the most cost-effective way, so I decided that the fairest way was to charge you as if I was providing a stand-alone afternoon tea. You'll see from the list that it's effectively what it was. I've multiplied the standard charge for this by the number of guests and again on the Saturday, which brings us to this total here.'

Mimi glanced at the figure. 'Yes, and...?'

'So that's the figure for Friday then – the afternoon tea, and the cocktail reception with evening buffet.'

How many minutes had elapsed? Had Adam even had time to access Mimi's laptop? She cleared her throat.

'Moving to Saturday... There weren't any extras other than the afternoon tea, so that's the figure here, plus the two picnic lunches, sundry refreshments and then in the evening...' She passed across another invoice. 'This is for the ice sculpture, as discussed.'

Mimi picked up the paper and tossed it back towards Fran. 'Go on.'

'And then, dinner, which was all as expected. But it's when we come to Sunday that, er...' Mimi's eyes were fixed on hers, Fran couldn't possibly utter the words which finished the sentence. 'So, I wondered, how you'd like me to go about billing for that?'

Mimi's lips twitched upward into something approaching a half smile. She raised one eyebrow. 'As I recall, although my memory is rather hazy, I don't believe we really ate anything for breakfast, or lunch on that day. Those were the meals which you were engaged to provide, I think.'

'Yes, they were, but—' Fran's insides began to churn.

Adam drummed his fingers on the table and shifted position. Why did things take so long when you had so little time? Mimi's laptop was pretty new but it was taking an age to reboot. Maybe that's what the problem was: it was pretty, but had the processing power of a gnat on a bicycle. *Come on, come on...*

The screen flickered into life and Adam's fingers flew over the keys. *Administrator...* and he was in. Now he just had to figure out what he was looking for.

Fran hated situations like this at the best of times, and in this case her actions were designed to not only ensure she wasn't left out of pocket for the weekend, but to provoke a reaction in Mimi, one which might take a little time to resolve. She had to give Adam as much time as she could.

'The thing is, whether people eat the food or not, it costs the same amount to provide it. And Sunday turned into Monday and then Tuesday morning. After the provision of the midday meal on Sunday, everything else is extra.' She passed Mimi another piece of paper, giving her a few moments to digest the figures.

'But I already pay Rachel to provide meals. She's not up to much beyond basic dishes but if I pay you also, doesn't this mean in effect that I'm paying twice?'

'I was simply trying to help out,' she replied, bristling on Rachel's behalf, and knowing that she needed to push Mimi even further. 'I knew that you wouldn't have wanted standards to fall below the level you deem *acceptable*. Besides, Rachel was kept very busy attending to other things. She provided ongoing hospitality to your guests but also looked after the, at times, quite large numbers of other people who were in the house. It was a difficult situation and we worked together to ensure it was made as comfortable as possible. I'm sure you agree that was only right.'

A pout was beginning to creep onto Mimi's face. 'It's hardly my fault I had to have those people in my house, for days. You think I wanted them here?'

Oh, I think it all turned out for you very nicely indeed, having those people do your bidding and corroborate your story... Fran pushed the thought away. 'No, understandably. But the fact of the matter is that they *were*, and I *did* cater for them. And you'll notice we're not talking food of the same standard I provided for you on Saturday evening. I've made an adjustment for that, but even so, extra provisions had to be brought in and although I tried to be as economical with ingredients as possible, there was an additional cost which had to be paid for.'

Fran paused a moment. Had Adam found Mimi's laptop? Did he need to connect it to a power source? Was it slow to boot up? Was it password protected? The list of potential opportunities for things to go wrong was huge and every extra second she could give Adam could be critical. Even when – if – he managed to access it, he would still have to find the proof they were looking for. And she had no idea how long any of that might take.

Mimi sighed, waving a limp hand over the sheets of paper on the table. 'This is all so... I can't be bothered with such trifling things. Really, it's ridiculous that you think...' She sighed again. 'Very well, add all these things to your bill.' She ran a hand over her immaculate hair, smoothing it down, the large diamonds on her ring finger glinting in the sunlight. It struck Fran as a very calculated movement, designed to draw attention to the differences between them.

Fran waited while Mimi got to her feet, while she turned the bracelet on her wrist, freeing it from the confines of her shirt sleeve, while she drew a finger along the table surface, while she demonstrated her position as mistress of the house with every move she made, and all the time Fran's heart began to beat faster and faster. She waited until Mimi had almost reached the door and then fired her last attempt at detaining her.

'Oh, sorry, Mrs Chapman, there is one other thing—'

Mimi was becoming intensely irritated now.

'It's just that, and this is a little awkward, the figures I've given you for the extras since Sunday lunchtime only account for the cost of what was purchased in order to provide the meals. They don't account for any of my time.'

Both of Mimi's eyebrows shot skyward.

'Naturally, when I charge for my services the details of any quotation include not only the cost of raw materials but also payment for my expertise and skill in providing the food, the length of time it takes me and—'

'Yes, I get the picture, Ms Eve. You feel I should pay you for your time here, even though you were a murder suspect just the same as anyone else.'

'That's hardly the point,' blustered Fran. 'I was engaged to provide a service to you for the duration of the weekend and I have done everything asked of me to the highest of standards. I don't think you can disagree with that, but I have incurred other costs by being here longer than planned. Namely, work I would have undertaken over the last couple of days but which I've had to cancel. There's a cost to that not only in terms of income lost, but also damage to my reputation and—'

'So, what are we talking here? I take it you have a price. Perhaps you should just tell me what that is.'

Fran was lying through her teeth of course, she had no jobs on until the end of the week but Mimi wasn't to know that. Besides, the haughty expression on her face made her palms itch and Fran wasn't someone usually given to violence of any kind. She lifted her chin a little higher. She still needed to buy as much time for Adam as she could. A nice healthy argument ought to do it.

'I thought rather than charge you on an individual basis for each additional element I provided, a lump sum might be a fairer way to go about it.' Fran's head scrabbled about for a figure so preposterous that Mimi would have no choice but to laugh with incredulity. 'So, I'm proposing a sum of seven-hundred-and-fifty pounds be added to the total.'

Adam had no clue what he was looking for but he headed straight for Mimi's emails. He was looking for evidence that she knew about Oliver's financial situation, and given that Heather's report from the forensic accountant had come to her via email, it seemed logical that this is also how Mimi would have received the information. He checked the email address she was using – MimiClaremontHouse – a little formal perhaps but... he started scrolling: Tuesday, Monday, Sunday... Saturday. He slowed down, eyes whizzing over the detail in front of him, checking the subject line of the emails, trying to spot who they were from. He stopped, and peered closer. Nothing. Keep scrolling...

This was useless. He'd had his doubts the moment he'd started checking. These were the wrong type of emails. Adam didn't know what they were, but they were formal, too impersonal, nothing that looked to be from friends, or family. And now he was into Friday's messages. Too early... He groaned in frustration, there was nothing here. *Think, think, where else could he look?*

Fran held her breath, waiting for the explosion.

'Oh, for goodness' sake... Do you think I'm made of money?' Mimi tossed her hair. 'Fine, fine! Seven hundred and fifty pounds... just do it.'

Fran was so surprised she almost forgot what Mimi's flouncing exit meant. *Shit...*

She snatched up her phone, hastily jamming her fingers on the keys to send Adam a message. *Move* was all it said.

Adam swore, clamping his mouth shut. The internet was his last hope. If Mimi didn't use a web-based email then he was scuppered, but if she did then he might just have time... He opened all the tabs from Mimi's last browser sessions. Dear God, didn't she ever close anything down? And then he saw it, the tiny multi-coloured letter 'M' that signified an open Gmail account. He prayed and clicked...

The email that Mimi had received on Saturday afternoon was still open. Adam barely had time to register what it said, but two names leaped out at him. One was Keith and the other was Oliver. He lifted his phone to snap a picture just as it buzzed with a message and Adam's pulse rate went through the roof.

He jabbed at the keys, slammed the laptop lid shut and scrabbled to his feet.

Fran paced the kitchen, ears straining for any noise. She had no doubt that if Mimi had caught Adam looking at her laptop then she'd yell loud enough for the whole house to hear. But there was nothing. Not a murmur. She was about to go and stand by the swing door through to the main hallway when the corner of her eye caught movement outside.

Moments later, Adam appeared through the back door. He was flushed, his hair sticking up on end, and she had a sudden image of him pushing his hand through it in frustration. He was also walking with a limp.

She touched his arm as he drew level with her. 'Is everything okay?' she asked. 'Did Mimi see you?'

Adam shook his head, his face annoyingly expressionless. But she'd seen that look before. He strode to the table, pulled out his phone from his pocket and flicked at something on the screen. He peered closer, frowning for a moment, before turning it around so that Fran could see the screen. A broad grin began to creep up his face as if in slow motion. His eyes met Fran's.

'Got her,' he said.

20

'What?' asked Fran urgently. 'What did you get? And what have you done to your leg?'

'Never mind that now. It's an email from Keith,' replied Adam. 'I haven't even had a chance to properly read it yet, but I saw Oliver's name and that was it.' He lowered the phone. 'God, my hands are shaking. You have a look.' He passed the phone to Fran. 'I couldn't find Mimi's emails at first, she has more than one account so I only had time to take a quick snap of it. I was terrified it would be blurry, but I think it's okay.'

Fran quickly read what was on the screen, her heart beginning to pound.

'It's more than okay, Adam. Listen to this: "So you can forget any hopes of living happily ever after with Ollie. He's skint, Mimi, and I have the accountant's report to prove it. In fact, forget any hopes of living happily ever after, full stop. I've been taking some advice and remember that prenup you signed? Seems you won't be getting a penny after we divorce. Have a lovely evening, darling."' She looked up at Adam. 'This is it! The smoking gun, it's exactly what we've been looking for!'

She cleared her throat and lowered her voice. Mimi mustn't

know what they'd uncovered or they could fall at the final hurdle. 'This email not only proves that Mimi knew about Oliver's lack of money, it also proves that Keith was about to start divorce proceedings, leaving her penniless. If that's not a motive for murder then I don't know what is.'

Adam's eyes were twinkling but she could see that he still hadn't fully grasped what the email revealed. 'I feel I should know the answer to this,' he said. 'But, what's a prenup?'

Fran smiled. 'Prenuptial agreement,' she replied. 'Basically, it's an agreement you sign before you get married, which sets out the terms for what happens when you divorce. It's such a romantic gesture.' She held a hand to her heart. 'It gets me every time.'

'So Mimi really would have got nothing if she and Keith divorced? There's no way she could have contested it?'

Fran shook her head. 'None. It's a legally binding document. And despite what it means, I can only assume that Mimi would have been more than eager to sign it. A young girl, from a not very nice background, with everything that Keith was offering her up for grabs? She'd have signed it in a heartbeat.'

Adam's face registered his dismay. 'And by all accounts, Keith was a very canny businessman. He wouldn't run the risk of losing his fortune for something as inconsequential as love, would he?' His face fell even further. 'That's if it even was love in the first place.' He looked up at Fran. 'You were right. Being around the Chapmans and their ilk is not healthy, is it? Their damaged way of looking at the world is infectious. I knew there was a reason I try to avoid folk as much as I can. People really aren't very nice, are they?'

'*Some* people, Adam,' Fran reminded him. '*Most* people are very nice, despite seeming evidence to the contrary. I firmly believe that. Don't let people like Mimi and Keith colour your view of the human race.'

But Adam wouldn't be convinced. His face was pale as he

stared back at her and Fran touched his arm, looking at him with concern. 'Come and sit down before you fall down,' she said. 'Are you okay?'

He swallowed and pulled a wry face. 'I think so, sorry. Just a bit overwhelmed, I guess. Plus, I don't recommend speed hacking of computers, it doesn't do your nerves much good. I was terrified I was going to get caught.'

Fran bustled over to a cupboard. 'Let me find you a biscuit... Something sweet should help.' She watched as he hobbled to a chair and sat down. 'What did you do to your leg anyway?'

Adam smiled, but it lacked his normal ratio of cheek mixed with joy. 'Fell over. I'd been kneeling on the floor to look at Mimi's computer, and when I saw your text I jumped up, got hit by that weird blood pressure thing that happens when you stand up too fast, staggered to the patio doors and all but leaped through them, not realising that my foot had also gone completely numb from where I'd been sitting on it.' The corners of his mouth twitched. 'So just my usual combination of style and grace under pressure.'

Fran grinned, pleased to see a little more colour returning to Adam's cheeks. Colour and his more usual sense of humour. She had got so used to it she missed it when it wasn't there. She pulled the lid off a Tupperware box and laid it on the table, directing Adam to it with a nod of her head. 'Get stuck in,' she said, helping herself to a piece of shortbread.

'I think it's just hit me what I'd actually gone looking for and, indeed, what we've now found,' said Adam. 'This *is* it, isn't it? Proof that Mimi felt justified in hitting her husband over the head with a... with a what?' He groaned. 'Are we even any further forward?'

'Yes,' said Fran firmly with several nods of her head. 'We are further forward because we now have proof that Mimi knew about Oliver's financial situation. It's proof yesterday morning's little show was exactly that, and also that Keith *was* planning to divorce Mimi. He planned to cut her off without a penny and she couldn't even run off with Oliver and not give a damn. Well, she could if she loved him, but I think we both know what she loved, and it wasn't Oliver's personality. So, what we have in a nutshell is proof of Mimi's motive to kill Keith. What we still don't know is how she did it.' Fran sighed. 'And then there's the theft of the painting, which makes no sense at all.' She bit the end off another biscuit. 'There has to be something...'

'I don't see what,' said Adam, and Fran could see how frustrated he was. 'Maybe it *is* just time to admit we're not going to solve this one and go home, leave it all to the police.'

'You don't really believe that, do you?'

'Well, unless one of us has a eureka moment, I don't see what else we *can* do. We can't stay here forever.'

Fran screwed up her nose. Adam was right, she just didn't want to admit it. 'I got everything pretty much packed up here this morning while you were poking about on Keith's computer. Plus, I got Mimi to look at all the invoice details...' She broke off to indicate all her notes on the table. 'That was my ruse to buy you some time just now. She's agreed to everything, so I guess there really isn't anything else we need to stay for. I'm sorry, Adam. I really thought we were going to crack this one but maybe we're just a one-hit wonder.'

Adam was staring morosely at the table, eyes roaming the bits of paper on it aimlessly. Fran wasn't sure he was even seeing them. She began to collect them together, no point leaving them where they were.

But, as she picked up an invoice his hand suddenly shot out. 'What's that?' he asked.

'The bill from Mac, for the ice sculpture.'

Adam was studying it, she couldn't think why. It was just a few lines and a total.

'Have you got a photo of this?'

'What, the invoice?'

Adam rolled his eyes. 'No, the ice sculpture. I can't really remember what it looked like.'

Fran picked up her phone. 'Um... I didn't take any on the night of the party, I forgot, but Mac probably did. He said he wanted to use it on his website. I could ask him for one, if you like?'

'Please... will it take long?'

Fran had caught the sudden interest in his voice. 'I have no idea.' She narrowed her eyes at him. 'What are you thinking?'

'Maybe nothing... probably nothing, just...'

But the light was back in his eyes, Adam wasn't fooling anyone. She opened the emails on her phone. 'Okay, let me send Mac a message.' Her thumbs paused. 'Oh...' she said, eyes widening. 'There's this, I've just remembered.' She scrolled through one of Mac's previous messages; communication they'd had when she was first enquiring about his services. 'He did some sketches for me so I could see what he was aiming for with the sculpture. Here, it's not exact but it gives you an idea.' She laid the phone on the table between them.

Adam drew two fingers across the photo to zoom in on a detail. The seconds ticked by in excruciating silence as Fran stared at him, waiting for him to say something. And then she saw it; his eyes suddenly opening wide as the longed-for eureka moment hit. 'Dear God,' he said. 'I know how she did it!'

'But we have no proof!'

'Exactly,' replied Adam, his eyes burning. 'That's why it's so clever.'

Fran tore after him down the hallway. 'But you can't just go waltzing in there,' she hissed, dipping her head towards the morning room. 'Mimi will make mincemeat of you and we'll be no further forward. All she has to do is say you're wrong and that's it. Game over.'

Adam stared at her. 'There has to be evidence somewhere. No murder is that perfect. Besides, I don't reckon Mimi's as clever as she thinks she is. She'll slip up, I know she will. Plus, she hasn't got a cohort of cronies with her this time, doing her bidding and being paid off for their services. This time it's just her and us. And my trusty phone of course, on which I can record the whole thing.'

'You can't do that!'

'Why not?' asked Adam. 'It worked the last time.'

Fran blinked. They were going to get in so much trouble, but she knew Adam was right. 'What are you going to do?'

Adam took another step towards the morning room. 'Get her talking and hope she trips herself up.'

'That's not really a plan.'

'Got a better one?'

Fran shook her head, wincing. 'Nope...'

'Come on then.'

Adam strode into the morning room with Fran scurrying after him. Mimi was sitting on one of the sofas, a glossy magazine in her hand.

'Mimi? I'm just wondering...' began Adam. 'Why *did* you kill your husband?'

Mimi looked up, hand frozen as she turned a page.

'I beg your pardon?' Her voice was loud, indignant. She stared at Fran and then looked back at Adam. 'What are doing here? And take that ridiculous hat off your head.'

Adam smiled. 'If it's all the same to you, I reckon I'll keep it on, thanks. Anyway, why did you kill him? I'm just curious to know if we were right.'

Mimi smoothed down her hair. Buying time as it's otherwise known. 'I don't have to sit here and listen to this,' she said calmly. Her voice was like ice, which Fran thought was rather funny under the circumstances. 'You are in *my* house. And you've no right to be here any longer. Get out. Get. Out. Now.'

'Ooh, or what? You'll call the police?'

That got her. She wasn't expecting sarcasm. A moment's panic lit her eyes. 'What, and waste their time on the likes of you?'

Clever, thought Fran. *Not a bad answer.*

Adam wrinkled his nose. 'Still going to have to be the police, I'm afraid, because I'm not going anywhere.'

'Derek?' Mimi's voice was suddenly strident in the quiet room. 'Derek!'

Adam cocked his head as if he was listening. 'Don't think he heard you. I tell you what though, until Derek gets here, why don't I just go ahead and tell you how I think you killed Keith and you can stop me when I get it wrong?'

'I did *not* kill my husband.'

'Oh, but you did, Mimi. And I have to hand it to you, it was bloody clever. Inspired. What I don't know though, is whether it really was one of those spur-of-the-moment things when the perfect opportunity just seemed to land in your lap, or whether it was something you planned.' He shook his head. 'Never mind, we can leave that little detail for later. So, where was I? Ah, yes, killing Keith...

'I can't believe it took me so long to work it out, but like I said, who would have thought it, eh? And I should have guessed really, right from the minute when Keith's body was found, because I saw you, that night, when everyone else was sleeping off the effects of the party. Of course, you protested that you hadn't seen anything the night of Keith's murder, that you'd been asleep all night, but—'

'Because I had!'

'Are you sure about that, Mimi?' He paused to let her answer.

'Ah, she remains silent... Okay, so does that mean you're not sure? Or that you don't want to answer me? Either way, I'll assume it means that you *were* up in the night. Something I know to be true, actually, because I couldn't sleep that night either, and I just happened to be looking out of my window, getting some fresh air, and what did I see? You, walking up from the garden.'

'It wasn't me. How on earth could you be sure of that, when it would have been dark?'

'True. But it was such a beautiful night and the moon was almost full. I could see you clearly.'

Mimi made a derogatory noise. 'It could have been anyone.'

'Possibly. But not really. You see, whoever I saw was naked and...' He broke off to give a smirk. 'With the best will in the world, are you really saying that Ginny could be mistaken for you with no clothes on? I hardly think so. It was definitely you, Mimi. Odd thing to do though, go for a walk at night, totally naked, when you had a house full of guests.'

'It was hot, there's no harm in that. I'm not ashamed of my body.'

Adam paused. 'Ah, okay... so you *are* admitting that you went for a walk then? Great, that's good. It *was* a hot evening, you're right. It wasn't raining though.'

'Raining? For goodness' sake, what are you talking about?'

'Well, your hair was wet, but it wasn't raining, so... How did your hair get wet, Mimi?' He stared at her, waiting for an answer, letting the silence stretch out. 'I thought maybe you'd been for a swim.'

'Yes, that's it. I'd forgotten, I had been for a swim, to cool down.'

Adam nodded. 'Okay, that makes more sense.' He smiled. 'Still think it's odd though, going out starkers, even if you did want a swim. It makes more sense when you realise you left your clothes inside, very deliberately.'

Mimi's eyes shot to his.

'I say deliberately, because of course that was a lovely dress you wore the night of the party. I can understand you not wanting to get it wet. I can also understand you not wanting to get blood all over it. That's why you slipped it off, just before you went into the study to kill Keith.'

'I did what?' Mimi half rose to her feet. 'This is ridiculous, I don't have to sit here and listen to this.'

'No, you don't, but aren't you just a teeny bit curious?' He studied her face. 'You are, aren't you? You can't help yourself, you want to know whether I'm right.' He grinned. 'And it was the perfect dress for it, wasn't it? No underwear for it to snag on. No belts, buttons, fastenings of any kind, except for a simple clasp on one shoulder. Undo that and the whole thing simply slithered to the floor so you could step out of it. I did wonder whether Keith would have been surprised to see you entering his study naked, but then I think he'd had a little too much to drink, hadn't he? So much, in fact, that he was fast asleep. That, or passed out. Not that it really matters, but it's what made it so much easier to kill him. He didn't put up a struggle at all.'

Mimi barked incredulous laughter. 'So what did I kill him with then? The incredible vanishing hammer? The police have searched every inch of this house and found nothing.'

'No, well, they won't, will they? That's where this gets really clever. I hate to use the word genius, Mimi, not where you're concerned, but it really was.'

'What are you talking about?'

'Oh, didn't I say? The ice sculpture, Mimi. I can show you a picture if you like, but basically, the police knew they were looking for a weapon that was heavy and possibly had a square base, the corner of which being the bit that did all the damage to Keith's poor head. And it just so happens that the spire of the church from the ice sculpture had such a square base, where it joined the top of the tower. Absolutely brilliant! And of course, once Keith was dead, you simply dropped the chunk of ice on the floor, where it melted. Come morning, there was hardly even a wet patch; it was, after all, a very hot night. Or maybe Keith had just spilled his drink. Which one was it? Mimi?'

'You have absolutely no proof of that.'

'Possibly not, but then again... You hurt your hand, didn't you?'

'What?'

'On Sunday morning, when you became the grieving widow, several people noticed you'd hurt your hand. At least it looked like you'd hurt it, it was very red. Stupid of me, not to realise the significance of that, but there you go.'

He waited for her to say something, but Mimi simply sat and glared at him.

'How *did* you hurt your hand, Mimi?'

She looked at him coolly. 'I had a reaction to some cream I used.'

Adam nodded. 'I see, and what cream was that?' he asked.

'I can't remember.'

Adam wrinkled his nose. 'Hmm... would you not remember? I don't think so. I mean, if I'd had a bad reaction to a cream, I'd sure as hell remember what it was because I'd want to make sure I didn't use it again. And it must have been new, otherwise you'd have had a reaction before.' He cocked his head at her. 'Thing is, Mimi, I don't think that's the truth. You see, I was forgetting that it isn't only hot things which burn, but very cold things too. In fact, holding something frozen for any length of time hurts like hell, and you had to hold that solid lump of ice really tightly, didn't you, to get a good grip? So you didn't just drop the ice, you were desperate to get rid of it and it probably stuck to your skin as well. I don't think you bargained on that, but I guess it was a small price to pay.'

Mimi closed the pages of her magazine thoughtfully and tossed it onto the sofa beside her. 'You know, you're hilarious, but aren't you forgetting something?' she sneered. 'The state of the room. There were books on the floor, the curtains were torn down. Someone had been fighting with Keith.'

'No, they hadn't. You simply wanted everyone to think that's what had happened. See, that was the other aspect about all of this which confused me, because no one heard a thing in the night. No sound of shouting, or arguments, no furniture being overturned, no books being hurled from the bookcase, nothing. And the reason for that is very simple. And it's because, as I've already said, Keith wasn't in a fit state to fight with anyone that night. So, after you killed him, knowing you had to disguise your involvement in his death, you very carefully, and *quietly*, arranged the room to look like Keith had interrupted a robbery and got beaten over the head for his trouble. After all, what possible reason could you have for stealing something that was already yours?'

'This is crazy.'

'No, it isn't, Mimi, it's what happened that night, it's just taken me far too long to see it. I had all these little pieces of information in my head, but I didn't know how they all fitted together. Not until I saw the pictures of the ice sculpture, that's when it all made sense. So just to recap – you approached the study, knowing that Keith was inside, probably that he was asleep – you undid the clasp on your dress, stepped out of it – snapped off the church spire from the sculpture and murdered your husband. You flung away the icy weapon, knowing it didn't matter because it would melt anyway, rearranged the room and calmly walked from the house, naked, to the pool, where you either went for a swim, or more likely had a shower to wash away any traces of icky stuff on your skin. You walked back to the house, skin drying in the warm night air, slipped your dress back on, went back to bed and, bingo, by morning, the rest of the ice sculpture had melted and had already been cleared away by an unsuspecting Rachel. Did I leave anything out?'

Mimi clapped her hands together. 'Quite a show,' she said.

'Quite a little invention... And I can see how much you want to believe it's true, but you're forgetting one thing. Why on earth would I want to kill my husband?'

Adam tapped a finger to his head. 'Ah yes, motive. I'm glad you brought that up. Oldest motive there is, Mimi. Money. All a bit pathetic really, but you don't come from a very nice background, do you? So when Keith came on the scene, promising riches, what were you to do? You threw yourself at him until, unable to resist your charms, you got what you wanted: marriage and money. But Keith always liked to have an insurance policy, so he got you to sign a prenuptial agreement before you got married. Divorce, and you got nothing. Bit problematical that, but not if the replacement you lined up for Keith was also loaded... Shame Oliver's skint, isn't it? He could have been quite a catch.'

'But I only found that out yesterday!' protested Mimi. 'You were there when it happened, for goodness' sake. That's why I think Oliver killed Keith. Keith knew he was broke, you see, and Oliver wanted to stop me from finding out. He's the one who's been deceiving everybody.'

'Nice try, Mimi. But we have proof you knew about Oliver's financial affairs *before* Keith was killed. In fact, that's *why* he was killed, obviously, because you suddenly realised that dead, you didn't have to divorce him, you just inherited all his lovely money instead.'

Two spots of colour had appeared in Mimi's cheeks, but her eyes were blazing. 'Well, bravo, well done you... It's a great story, I'll give you that. You seem to have thought of everything, except the fact not a word of it is true. Even if I did know about Ollie's state of affairs, that doesn't mean I killed Keith. I might have even thought about it, but as long as I didn't do it, that's all that matters. And I didn't kill him. For all your wonderfully vivid imagination, and ludicrously implausible suggestions, you cannot prove a single word. Can you?'

Adam darted a look at Fran. A look which, of course, Mimi spotted.

'Hah! There, not so bloody clever now, are you?' Triumph burned in her eyes and Fran felt physically sick.

Mimi couldn't be allowed to get away with this, but she was right and she knew it. They had no proof. Fran knew Mimi wouldn't ever simply give up and admit Adam was right. Because Mimi was a fighter and a survivor, and people like her didn't roll over and take stuff, they fought back. Leopards didn't change their spots— The thoughts in Fran's head crashed to a sudden halt. And resolve burned through her.

'You're not wearing your jewellery,' said Fran. 'Yesterday, you were wearing several rings, but not today.'

Mimi stared down at her hands. 'So? I must have forgotten to put them back on after dressing this morning.'

'Back on?'

'Yes, after showering.'

'So you take off your jewellery when you shower?'

Mimi sighed with consternation. 'Ms Eve, I don't expect you to understand.' She stared at the thin gold band on Fran's hand. 'But my rings are worth tens of thousands of pounds. I really wouldn't want to take the risk of losing a diamond down the drain.' Her supercilious smile made Fran want to slap her.

Fran held Mimi's look, a serene expression on her face. 'So when you showered on the night of the party, to wash any trace of Keith's blood from your skin and hair, you would have taken off your necklace first, wouldn't you?'

'What necklace? Don't be so ridiculous.' But a flicker of fear had shown itself on Mimi's face, and Fran knew she was right.

'The leopard head necklace you were wearing,' she replied. 'It really is true what they say, leopards don't change their spots and a necklace like that, a very *intricate* necklace, will have traces of blood on it. I have no idea what the stuff is called that the police use to find trace evidence, but I know it's incredibly good. They'll not only find traces of blood on your necklace, but no doubt in the shower tray as well, down by the pool. The shower you used after you'd killed Keith.'

'Incredible...' Mimi rolled her eyes. 'You can say what you like, who on earth is going to listen to you? More to the point, believe you? A *caterer* and a...' She glanced dismissively at Adam. 'Whatever it is you are...'

'They don't have to believe us,' replied Fran. 'There just has to be the tiniest seed of doubt sown. The police will follow it up, you can be sure about that. And when they do, they'll find exactly what we've said they will. And evidence doesn't lie, Mimi.'

'Yes, but you have to find it first. Do you really think I'd be stupid enough to let you get your hands on it? Just try it, and I'll accuse you of trying to steal it. The painting too, don't think I've forgotten about that. Who will the police believe? Someone like me, or someone like you? They'll just think you said what you have to cover up attempted theft.'

'Maybe they will,' said Fran. 'But they'll still test the necklace. Tiny seed of doubt, Mimi, that's all it takes.' She eyed her stonily. 'Do you really want to run that risk?'

'You'll never get your hands on it. How on earth do you think you're going to stop me?'

Fran looked at Adam. 'Well, *one*...' He picked up his phone from the table. 'I've recorded everything which has been said. 'And *two*...'

'Sorry, I was just outside pruning the roses,' said Derek, stepping in through the patio doors. 'I couldn't help overhearing. Do you guys need any help?'

21

Of course, Derek didn't just 'happen' to be anywhere, but Fran had to admit his timing was spectacularly good. Mimi's mouth dropped open and, realising that it was now essentially three against one, she slumped back on the sofa, her mouth drawn into a thin line.

'I'm not saying anything else,' she said, scowling. 'And I'd like you all to get out of my house.' She directed a look at Derek. 'I should fire you,' she said. 'Seeing as you've obviously teamed up with *them*.' She spat the last word with distaste.

But Derek ignored her, merely eyed her stonily, with equal disdain. He might be a lowly caretaker and she a socialite with pots of money, but it was very evident who was the more worthy. Fran wanted to hug him.

She smiled sweetly. 'Excuse me one moment, I just have a phone call to make.'

Nell answered in her usual brusque fashion. 'I'm very busy, Fran,' she said. 'What is it?'

Fran took a deep breath. 'Hi Nell... you're not going to believe this.'

The series of expletives which followed assured Fran that

Nell absolutely believed her, all too well. 'I'll be there in half an hour,' she said. 'Will you be okay until then?'

'Oh yes, we have Derek on guard duty.'

She could hear the smile in Nell's voice as she answered. 'I do like that man,' she said.

'Me too,' replied Fran.

'Don't let Mimi touch anything, or go anywhere. She mustn't have any opportunity to destroy or remove evidence. I'll be as quick as I can.'

It took Nell twenty-eight minutes to reach them, arriving with Clare Palmer in tow. A forensic team arrived three minutes later. Shown into the morning room by Rachel, Nell found all four of them virtually unmoved. During that time, Fran had looked at Adam, who had looked at Derek, who had looked back at Fran, and all of them had stared at Mimi, whose expression remained precisely as it was half an hour ago. It was the most excruciating half hour Fran had experienced. She could feel Mimi's loathing for them, seeping into the air like a noxious vapour.

Nell broke the silence.

'Mimi Chapman, I'm arresting you on suspicion of the murder of Keith Chapman.'

Even Fran flinched. Blimey, Nell didn't mess around.

'You do not have to say anything, but it may harm your defence if you do not mention, when questioned, something you later rely on in court. Anything you do say may be given in evidence. Do you understand?'

Mimi got to her feet, straightening her tee shirt. 'Perfectly,' she said, turning her head away from Fran.

'I would also like you to tell us the location of your leopard head necklace, Mrs Chapman. The one you were wearing on Saturday night last, the evening before Mr Chapman was killed.'

Mimi turned her gaze on Nell, looking her up and down. 'I don't think I can remember where I put it,' she replied.

'It will be in the safe,' supplied Rachel. 'It's where she keeps all her jewellery.'

'Thank you,' said Nell, smiling. 'You can show us where it is, can you?'

Rachel nodded.

'Then all I require is the code to open it, Mrs Chapman.' She waited a moment, eyes unwavering. 'It will make no difference if you don't supply it,' she added. 'I'll have a team come out and take it apart, along with half the room probably. They're not the most subtle group of people. Your choice. I might add, however, that I don't like people who play games and waste my time. If, as I'm sure you're claiming, you have nothing to do with your husband's death, then you won't mind us taking a closer look at your necklace, will you? It will be returned to you, obviously.'

'Three-two-five-v-s,' said Mimi. 'Lower-case letters.'

Nell smiled. 'Excellent. Rachel, would you mind showing Detective Constable Palmer where she can find the safe? And Derek, while that's happening, could you show the forensic guys down to the pool? Specifically, to the showers located in the cabin.' She dipped her head. 'Thank you.' She smiled at Fran. 'We'll just wait here until DC Palmer gets back and we'll be on our way.'

Twenty minutes later and they were gone, leaving Fran, Adam, Derek and Rachel staring at one another.

'Blimey,' said Rachel, breaking the stunned silence first. 'Just like that, and it's not even eleven o'clock yet. What do we do now?'

'Throw a party?' suggested Derek, who then pulled a face. 'Sorry, that sounds horrible. It's actually the last thing I want to do, but I'm struggling to find any sympathy for Mimi. I didn't approve of a lot of the things Keith did, whether they were in the name of business or not, but he didn't deserve to die.'

'No, he didn't, and I agree with you; I don't think I'm going to be in the mood for a party any time soon. I do think, however, that you two should just enjoy having the run of this place for a while. You've more than earned it.'

'What will happen now?' asked Rachel. 'To the house, I mean?'

'I've no idea,' replied Fran. 'But the police will be able to advise you. As will Mimi's lawyer. I'm sure someone will be in touch, but it's going to take a while before anything gets sorted so I should just enjoy it while you can.'

Fran glanced at her watch, feeling sadness looming. Her and Adam's time at Claremont House was coming to an end and, despite everything that had happened, Fran would miss their shared friendship with Rachel and Derek. 'We should get out of your hair too,' she said with a soft smile. 'Just in case my husband forgets what I look like.' She turned to Adam. 'Are you all packed?'

He nodded. 'I didn't bring as much as you, obviously,' he replied with a cheeky grin. 'I'll go and get my bag. Shall I fetch yours down too?'

'It's on the bed,' Fran replied. 'I've pretty much finished in the kitchen,' she added. 'Just a couple more bits to shove in boxes and then I'm done.'

By the time she'd gathered together her things, Adam had reappeared and they couldn't put off the moment any longer. Fran hated goodbyes.

'I'll just put our stuff in the car,' she said. 'And I'll come back to say cheerio.'

'You'll do no such thing,' replied Derek. '*I'll* load it and then I'll bring it around. You'll be leaving via the front door.' He held out his hand for her keys with a broad smile, which she returned.

Rachel grinned at them. 'Come on then, front door it is.' She held out her arm. 'After you.'

Fran pushed open the swing door to the main part of the house for one last time and looked to her left. The morning room was still glowing with sunshine and, holding the door open for Rachel and Adam, she took a couple of steps forward. For all that had happened, she would miss this place. She smiled to herself and turned away. *Don't be so silly, Fran, it's just a house.*

Even so, she couldn't leave without taking one last look at the dining room. The dinner had still been a triumph and she was proud of what she'd achieved.

She paused by the doorway. It seemed an age since Saturday night, and almost ever since, the room had been out of bounds, turned into a police incident room. There had been computers and equipment, people and noise, but Rachel had managed to reset the table and, today, it lay waiting for the next meal, the next party. Fran had a feeling it would be waiting a very long time.

She took in the huge bowls of flowers which still looked lovely, the finest china and crystal, the deep sheen of the beautiful mahogany table and she nodded. This was certainly one dinner she would remember for quite some time to come. She turned away, and then looked back, frowning gently. Something was different about the room, but she couldn't say what. Perhaps, simply that it was no longer dressed as she had last seen it. No matter, it was still a beautiful room, even if not quite returned to its former glory.

She held out her arms towards Rachel for a hug. 'God, I'm going to miss you,' she said, pulling her close.

'Me too,' said Rachel, hugging her back and laughing. 'Miss you, that is. And you,' she added, turning to Adam. She held out her arms. 'Tiny hug?'

Fran smiled as Adam submitted to what turned into a very

big hug indeed. He didn't know whether to be delighted or squirm with embarrassment, and settled somewhere in between the two.

'And keep in touch, please,' said Fran, smiling as Rachel opened the front door. 'I want to know what happens to you two. It's going to take some time for everything to be sorted out, but I hope you'll be able to stay here for a while, at least. And if you do get looking for other jobs, just remember me. I'll be more than happy to give you a reference.'

Rachel nodded. 'I will, don't worry. For now, I think we'll just see how the land lies.' She turned at the sound of tyres on gravel. 'And enjoy a bit of peace and quiet.'

Fran waited until Derek climbed from her car.

'I do hope you're going to leave that,' she said, pointing at the driveway. 'And not get raking it the minute we're gone.'

He laughed. 'I might have to sit on my hands. It's kind of an automatic reaction now, but I'll try my hardest.' He held out a formal hand. 'I probably shouldn't say it's been a pleasure, given what's happened over the last few days. But it *has* been a pleasure meeting you and Adam. And thank you.'

Derek pulled Fran into a hug as she took his hand, his intention all along, she realised, and she returned it, pulling away laughing.

'Right, come on, Adam. Let's get going before I get something in my eye.'

Adam flashed her a smile and with a wave at Rachel and Derek, ran for the car. He didn't like goodbyes either.

Fran kept one eye on her rear-view mirror the whole way down the drive, grinning as Rachel and Derek stood waving on the front steps of Claremont House. They remained there the whole time, and it wasn't until the driveway turned as she approached the road that they disappeared from view. She took a huge breath and concentrated on the road ahead of her.

Well, Adam,' she said, 'I guess that's that.'

. . .

Fran put the last of the boxes down on the table and stared around her kitchen. Oh, how she'd missed this: the warmth, the familiarity, the calm but not necessarily always ordered space of her happy home life. She'd been gone far too long and, standing here now, it felt like years had gone past instead of just a few days. And something felt odd... She was trying to ignore it, putting it down to the intensity of the last few days which had pulled her so far from her ordinary everyday reality that she felt like a stranger here. Once she started work again the feeling would go, she was sure of it. Jack would come home from work, Martha would return from school and she'd be caught up in the wonderful domesticity she had missed so much. Except that...

'You're awfully quiet,' said Adam, looking at her from across the room. 'In fact, for someone who has just solved another murder, I'd say you were bordering on morose. When what you should be feeling is jubilant, triumphant, vindicated... other adjectives are available.' He smiled at her, with the look on his face which Fran knew meant he wasn't going to leave it alone until she told him what was bugging her. Trouble was she didn't really know what was.

'It's the painting,' she said. 'The fact that it's still missing. It's niggling me for some reason and I can't work out why.'

'Fran, don't pay it any mind simply because Mimi drew your attention to it, she was just clutching at straws. She knew she was in a corner, and saying anything which might get her off the hook.'

'But that makes no sense either. She can't be in trouble for pinching her own painting, can she?'

Adam grimaced. 'Good point.'

'So why say what she did? Unless...'

There was something here, something Fran was missing. The theft of the painting had niggled her right from the start, when it became clear that the police couldn't find any trace of it. Keith's untimely death as a result of an interrupted burglary made sense – it threw suspicion away from Mimi and onto other people – because why would Mimi pinch her own painting? So, if that was the case, why would she deny stealing it now?

And then it came to her. The answer was very simple. Because Mimi hadn't stolen the painting, someone else had.

Fran bashed a hand against her forehead and growled in frustration. How could she not have seen what was so obvious?

'Adam, we've been looking at this the wrong way! We've been going along with the scenario we thought Mimi had fabricated – that Keith had been killed because he interrupted a burglary in progress. So we treated the death and the theft of the painting as one and the same crime. But that's where we've been going wrong. We shouldn't have been thinking of it as just one crime, but instead, *two*... The theft of the painting is entirely separate from the murder. Which means there are two guilty parties here and not one.'

Adam stared at her. 'But that could also mean that whoever took the painting might have done so after Keith was dead, or at the very least, lay dying. What kind of a person would do that?' He thought a moment. 'Or, they could have taken it beforehand and when Mimi entered the study to kill Keith, she saw it was missing. That's what gave her the inspiration for the interrupted burglary scenario.'

'Hmm, that's possible, but it doesn't seem right. Stealing the painting by itself, when the weekend wasn't even over, seems far too risky for any of the guests to have attempted. But if you could make the theft look as if it was part of another crime, well then you had far more chance of it getting away with it. The police would obviously focus on solving the murder first because it's a far more serious crime, especially if it looked like the theft was connected.'

'Then who did it?' Adam's face was a mixture of emotions.

'And more to the point, is there anything we can we do about it? You saw the speed with which all the guests left Claremont House, the painting will be long gone by now and—' He was studying her face quite intently. 'There's something else, isn't there?'

Fran gave him a sheepish smile. What Adam said made sense, but there was still something she couldn't put her finger on, something she'd seen or heard which didn't add up. And she'd felt this way before – during their last case – and it wasn't until she had figured out what was bugging her that everything had fallen into place. Was the same true now? If only she could work out what it was.

She shook her head. 'Just a feeling that I've missed some-thing,' she replied, smiling. 'Don't worry about it, it'll come to me.' She brightened her smile. 'Anyway, you must be desperate to get home, Adam. Thanks for helping me unload everything.'

He dipped his head and then looked up, a resigned expres-sion on his face. 'I'd almost forgotten what I was supposed to be doing last weekend, but computer games don't write them-selves, I suppose I ought to go and get some work done. It's funny 'cause it's usually the worlds I create in my games which seem more exciting than real life. This time, though, it's the other way around.'

'Exciting? That's not quite the word I'd use. But I guess I know what you mean. It has been a very weird few days, but I'm quite looking forward to things calming down, and oh... the thought of sleeping in my own bed tonight: heaven.'

Adam grinned. 'I shall miss the food,' he said, fishing in his pocket for his car keys. 'You will let me know if you hear anything from Nell, won't you? And when you remember what's bugging you.'

'Of course I will. We can't leave this last piece of the puzzle unsolved.'

Adam tapped his head. 'And I shall set my little grey cells to work as well.'

Once he had gone, an unwelcome feeling of anticlimax settled round Fran's shoulders. It was only to be expected. The high drama with Mimi had been the culmination of another very unusual period of time; her and Adam's second murder case no less, although she wasn't sure Nell would see it like that. And while she was looking forward to the return of normality, Adam was right, there was an element to it which Fran did find exciting, even if she gave herself a hard time admitting it. She drew in a deep breath and looked around her. It was time to put her own house in order.

A short while later, with her kitchen equipment unpacked and her suitcase emptied, Fran had put a wash on, made a cup of tea and emptied the dishwasher. Jack was very good at taking care of business while she was away and she was eternally grateful that things still ran like clockwork even when she wasn't there. But there was nothing like a few domestic tasks to make her feel at one with her house again. She fetched the vacuum cleaner from the cupboard under the stairs and parked it in the centre of the kitchen floor. She would drink her tea, check her work emails and then set to it.

She always felt humbled and incredibly thankful that her business continued to flourish in the way that it did. Word of mouth accounted for a huge portion of her work, and while it was a sobering thought that all her efforts over the weekend wouldn't be earning her any recommendations from Mimi, at least there were still enquiries coming in and jobs to be planned for. And a couple of the new emails looked very promising. One was from a guest who had attended a wedding Fran had catered for the previous year and was now looking to book Fran for her own. She checked the address the prospective client had given and then called up Google Maps to check its location. It wasn't a million miles away either, which was helpful. She was about to click off when an open internet tab caught her attention. It was the search results she had called up when checking on Mimi's background a couple of days ago.

It was interesting to wonder whether recent events had been the culmination of those which had been set in motion all those years ago. When Keith Chapman had used his wealth and power to achieve exactly what he wanted, even though it had meant destroying lives in the process. For hadn't the exact same thing just happened now? Wealth and power taking another life, except, ironically this time it was Keith's, and taken by a woman who had turned those same weapons against him for *her* own gain. All that money, a life that was envied by many, and yet neither of the Chapmans were happy. In the game of life, neither of them had won.

She read through the article again, thinking about the toll the Chapmans had taken on people's lives, changing them irrevocably, and she shivered. Perhaps, finally, justice had been served. With a sigh she got to her feet and went to plug in the vacuum cleaner.

Smiling, she swept a handful of crumbs from the table. It brought to mind a picture of Martha munching slice after slice of toast, something she often did on arrival home from school. No doubt, when the same thing happened later that afternoon, Fran wouldn't find it quite so endearing, but for now she would enjoy the thought. Without thinking, she reached for the lever underneath the table which would allow the leaf to drop on one side. The join always harboured crumbs which had stuck in the crevice and she knew from experience that this was the only way to get rid of them. She brushed them away with her hand and—

A sudden image filled her head. Of the dining table back at Claremont House, and the moment just before she left when she had looked at the room. She had been remembering how beautiful it looked on Saturday night, just hours before tragedy struck, but she knew there had been something odd about it. And now she knew what it was.

She straightened up, thoughts whizzing through her head, scenes replaying, conversations rewinding. And for the second time she groaned at her stupidity. How had she not seen the connection? But the answer, she knew, was because she hadn't been looking for it.

Picking up her laptop, she snatched up her phone and dialled Adam's number. He answered almost straight away.

'Have they definitely got her?' he asked.

'What?' She frowned. 'Oh, Mimi... I don't know, I haven't heard from Nell yet. But listen, Adam, that isn't why I'm ringing. Are you doing anything?'

'What, now? Um... just having a bite to eat.' She could hear the amusement in his voice. Knowing Adam, a bite to eat meant he was eating a foot-high sandwich.

'Well, finish it quickly. I'll pick you up in ten minutes.'

'Why, where are we going?'

'You'll see,' she said.

22

'I can't believe we're going back there,' said Adam, half an hour later. 'Are you going to tell me what this is all about?'

'Nope. But I know someone who can.'

Fran drove the car straight around the back. They may have just left Claremont House via the front door, but this time it was very definitely a back-door visit. She had no idea whether Rachel and Derek would even be in, but something told her they would be – they had quite a lot to talk about, after all...

Sure enough, as Fran rounded the corner of the house, both the housekeeper and caretaker could be seen through the kitchen window, sitting side by side at the island unit; the place of a fair few important conversations. It seemed appropriate somehow.

It was Rachel who yanked open the door, having already spotted Fran's car.

'What are you doing here?' She laughed. 'Blimey, Derek, they can't keep away.' She stood back from the door, allowing Fran and Adam into the room. 'We were just having yet another cup of tea,' she said. 'Actually, Derek found a tub with the last few Florentines in it, and it seemed a good enough reason to down tools and have a break. I don't think either of us can quite get over the fact that we can do this anytime we like. It feels so weird.'

Fran smiled across at Derek. 'Don't get up,' she said. 'There's no need. But there's been a development in the case and we thought we might as well come and tell you in person.' She grimaced at Adam. 'I don't know about you two, but I can't seem to settle. It seemed as good an excuse as any.'

'Come and sit down then. We're just the same, sitting here mulling over all that's happened. Wondering what's going to come next. I don't think either of us knows what to do.'

Fran took a seat opposite Derek, leaving Rachel to return to her original place. 'Well, I think the two of you should take a well-earned break; you deserve it. Bugger what needs doing in the house. Take a few days out, enjoy the beautiful weather. And each other's company,' she added with a soft smile.

Derek returned it. 'Aye, we were thinking that. Comes hard though, switching off, I mean. When you're used to working all the time.'

'Make the most of it,' replied Fran. 'And fingers crossed, things don't change too soon.'

Rachel nodded. 'It doesn't take a genius to work out that they will though. Keith's dead, Mimi's most likely going to be charged with one, if not two murders. I don't think she's going to be coming back here any time soon. Which means the house will have to be sold and... that's us out of jobs, I guess.'

'Oh, I don't know,' mused Fran. 'I'm a firm believer in everything happening for a reason. Maybe this is a good opportunity to think about what you both want from the future and maybe... maybe start doing things for yourselves for a change. Both of you, *together*...'

Rachel's eyes widened. 'How long have you known?' she whispered, blushing in a most becoming way. Derek smiled, his eyes soft on hers.

'Longer than the pair of you, probably,' said Fran. 'It was obvious to me the first time I saw you both together. Plus, given your history and the fact that you had every right to hate Keith for what he did to you and your mum, I couldn't work out why Nell seemed to discount you from her inquiries. That didn't seem like her, she's pretty tenacious, as you'll have seen. You had an alibi, didn't you? For the night of the murder?'

Rachel dipped her head. 'We were together. In fact, it was the first time we *had* got together. And I know that Nell didn't have to take Derek's word for it that I was with him, but thankfully she did. Maybe she's a sucker for a good love story.'

Fran smiled. 'Maybe she is. But I think she can also spot the real deal when she sees it. You know, if any happiness can come from all this horrible business then I'm glad. Because it couldn't happen to two nicer people.' She gave them both a knowing smile.

'So, have you had any thoughts yet about what you might do?'

Derek's eyes were firmly on Rachel. 'A change of scenery might be good,' he said. 'Away from here and all the... memories. I'm not quite sure yet, we're still trying to figure out what might be possible.'

'Well, the money will help at least. I'm glad about that.'

'What money?' asked Rachel.

'From the sale of the painting. You will sell it, I hope?'

There was a shocked pause before Derek scrambled to his feet, colour draining from his face. 'Fran, please, it's not what you think, we—'

Fran held up a quick hand. And smiled. 'No, you misunderstand...' She looked between the two of them. 'We're not going to tell a soul you stole the painting.'

'Aren't we?' Adam's head shot up, a bemused expression on his face.

'No, Adam, we aren't. Because if anyone deserves it, it's

these two. People who never ask for anything, who never believe that anything is automatically their right. Besides, there are some things in life that are simply destined to remain a mystery.' She gave Rachel a coy look. 'I am a little intrigued to know how you did it though.'

Rachel pulled a face. 'You're going to laugh at this but I don't really even know why I took the painting. Except that when I went into the study first thing on Sunday morning and saw what had happened, something inside of me snapped. Mimi had been particularly vile all weekend, and Keith was drunk, worse than usual, making lewd suggestions when he thought no one was listening. So when I saw him lying there, even though I didn't know who had killed him, I was glad. I thought the Chapmans had finally had their comeuppance. So I took the painting. It was the one thing Keith really loved, and some part of me wanted him to know what that was like, having someone take away the thing you loved most in the world. It didn't occur to me until afterwards that he was dead and wouldn't be thinking anything of the sort, but...' She shrugged. 'It made sense at the time.'

Adam stared at her. 'But what did you do with it?' he asked. 'No, don't tell me...' He'd hardly said a word since their arrival at the house, but now he threw Fran a look. 'You know, don't you? Intrigued to know how you did it, my eye, you've got it all worked out, I can tell.'

'Makes a change, doesn't it?' she said, smirking. 'For me to beat you to the solution. Although, obviously, you solved the murder. Compared with that, this is just a little side dish.'

Adam shook his head. 'I'm going to kick myself,' he said. 'But come on then, tell me where the painting was hidden. I haven't a clue.'

'That's the very best bit,' replied Fran. 'Because it was right under the police's nose the whole time.' She looked at Rachel, who was still gripping Derek's hand, a shell-shocked expression on her face. 'I'm right, aren't I?'

'I nearly died,' said Rachel. 'But as it turns out, it was probably the very best place I could have hidden it. How on earth did you guess, Fran?'

She tapped her head. 'Photographic memory,' she said. Beside her, Adam was positively squirming. 'Shall I show you?'

Fran got to her feet and led Adam out of the kitchen and into the main hallway, with Rachel and Derek following on behind. The bemused expression on his face made her want to howl with laughter. He really was going to kick himself when he found out the truth.

'I don't believe it...' he muttered, when they arrived at the room in question. 'It was in the dining room the whole time? But the police were in here for days. They've only just left.'

'I know,' replied Fran, nodding. 'So where do you think it was hidden then?' She was teasing him, but she couldn't help herself.

'Just show me, Fran,' he replied, eyebrows arched. 'I'm not falling into that trap, I'll never hear the last of this as it is.'

She grinned and crossed to the table. The beautiful mahogany table she had admired so much. Of course, it was far too large for just Mr and Mrs Chapman, or the number of people who had dined with them on Saturday night, but that wasn't the point. No doubt Mimi liked that its size gave the impression that they regularly entertained in much larger numbers.

Carefully, Fran picked up the large bowl of peonies that sat in the centre of the table and, moving the mat from underneath, relocated it a little distance away.

'The table is one of those which extends,' she said. 'And if you slide one half of the table away from the middle, what you find is a dropped leaf. They're very clever actually. See, the centre piece folds in half and sits neatly underneath the main table. Once it's revealed, all you do is lift one edge and the sliding mechanism allows you to open it out flat.' She broke off to demonstrate. 'And when you do that...'

Beside her, Adam gasped as the painting was slowly revealed. 'But that's... that's...'

'Genius?' finished Fran. 'It is rather, isn't it? Because once the extension leaf is folded away again... like so... Hey presto, the painting disappears once more. And the best bit is that, even from underneath, you can't see anything. Everything is hidden within the table.'

Adam stared at Rachel. 'How on earth did you think of that?' he asked. 'Come to think of it, how did you get the painting out of the frame?'

She blushed. 'I panicked, that's all. I knew I wouldn't have much time, so I snatched up the letter opener that was on Keith's desk. I say letter opener, it's actually an old knife, heavy silver and still pretty sharp, and I just cut the painting from the frame. When I walked out of the study with it in my hand, I knew I'd made a mistake, and I panicked, I didn't know what to do. So I shot into the room opposite – the dining room. At least then no one would see me from the hallway, even if they did happen to pass. I wiped the knife clean with one of the silver polishing cloths we use and then threw it in a drawer with the rest of the cutlery. Mimi hasn't a clue what's in there, so I knew no one would be able to tell it apart from the rest of the knives. Then, still clutching the painting, I stared around the room. That's when I realised I hadn't reset the dining table, and that if I dropped the inner leaves and then re-laid the whole thing, no one would notice. Or, I hoped they wouldn't anyway.'

'The police certainly didn't,' finished Fran. 'They searched the room, but they never thought to look *inside* the table. And once the room had been given the all-clear, they covered the table with their equipment and got down to work, never suspecting for one minute what lay underneath it.'

'I can't believe you worked that out,' said Adam. 'It must have been a lucky guess.'

Fran grinned. 'Partly it was. But that was the thing which was bugging me earlier. The last thing I did when I left the house before was take a look at the dining room. And because the room had been out of bounds since Keith was killed, it was the first time I'd seen it since Saturday. Something must have struck me about it, but I couldn't put my finger on what. It wasn't until I brushed some crumbs from my table back at home, dropping the leaf to clean it, that my brain made the connection. Everything about the table here looked exactly the same as it had on Saturday, it was just *smaller,* that was all.'

'So what was your plan, Rachel?' asked Adam.

'I don't think I had one. Although I blabbed of course, straight afterwards. Told Derek everything. But there was nothing we could do, there was no way we could move the painting, and so that's where it's stayed. Until now.'

'But you could have moved it once we'd left,' said Fran.

'And do what with it? I don't know, somehow it just seems safer to leave it there... for the time being at least,' she finished, a faint flicker of something crossing her face. Just for an instant.

'It's a bit of a problem, all right. Although...' Fran gave Rachel and Derek a gentle smile. 'It's easy to forget about your past, isn't it? When you're standing in a house like this, surrounded by opulence and luxury. It's easy to forget that it wasn't always like this and that, in fact, the place you grew up in was very different indeed. A similar area in fact to the one where Mimi grew up. Having a background like that makes you a survivor, doesn't it...?' She let her sentence hang in the air for a moment. 'And if it were me, and I had in my possession a painting that was worth a lot of money, then I might be able to think of someone who could fence it for me... And if not that, then perhaps an ex-police officer might just know a few crooks who are into that kind of thing...' She cleared her throat. 'That's what *I'd* do anyway. If it was *me*...'

Rachel gave Derek a nervous look. 'But are you really not going to tell anyone about the painting?'

Fran gave her a soft smile and folded up the extension so that it disappeared from sight, sinking back into place beneath the table and taking its precious cargo with it. She carefully slid the table back together again and replaced the flowers. 'What painting?' she asked. 'Oh, you mean that one that was stolen. No one knows what happened to it, do they? I should think it's long gone by now.'

She turned slowly, giving the place one last, lingering look. 'You know, this really is a beautiful room.'

23

TWO DAYS LATER

'Do you suppose we'll ever hear from Rachel and Derek again?' asked Adam. He was sitting in Fran's kitchen, eating a bowl of lemon meringue pie.

'I think so. I hope we do anyway,' she replied. 'Although in a way I hope it's not for a little while. Once they're settled somewhere, in place of their own, maybe even married.'

'And living happily ever after?' He smiled. 'That's a nice thought.'

'I think so.'

Adam stuck out his tongue and licked his spoon clean. 'I'm still surprised at you though,' he said. 'I mean, *me* doing what you did, that would make sense. But *you're* supposed to be the sensible one, Fran. The one who does things by the book. Not that I don't approve, of course I do, it's just that...' He trailed off, grinning.

Fran lifted her chin, narrowing her eyes at Adam before plunging a spoon into his bowl and stealing a chunk of pie. 'It's just that...' she said, popping the spoon in her mouth. 'Sometimes the little people have to win.'

She swallowed, closing her eyes in pleasure just as her

mobile trilled from beside her on the table. She started guiltily. 'Oh God, it's Nell,' she said, panic filling her. 'What do I say?'

'Try hello,' replied Adam, with a smirk. 'And then just listen. And remind yourself that she does not know a thing about the painting. And neither will she.'

Fran swallowed again and picked up her phone, putting the call on loudspeaker.

'Hi, Nell, how are you?'

'Fine, Fran, just fine.' Nell's sharp voice rang out around the kitchen. 'Busy. You know how it is... Anyway, I just rang to say that we've formally charged Mimi Chapman with two murders. Forensics came back, and you were absolutely right. Adam was too. Blood all over the necklace, and in the shower tray. And once we put that to her, the rest of her sorry little story came tumbling out. It was a pure fluke that in her anger at Keith the ice sculpture was the thing she snatched up to kill him. She hadn't planned it at all. Course she was clever too, that helped. She realised almost immediately how much of a perfect weapon it was. But anyway, job done, and obviously we're very pleased.'

'But that's brilliant news,' replied Fran. 'I mean, obviously it isn't, but... And you've let Oliver Knight go?'

'We have. He's up to his neck in debt, and there's the question of the drugs, but he's not a murderer. In fact, curiously, I almost feel sorry for him. He really did love Mimi and was convinced they had a future together. He's devastated that she tried to pin the whole thing on him. Mimi, however, as we know, loved her money and not a lot else.' She paused a moment. 'Thing is...'

'Yes?' replied Fran, rolling her eyes at Adam in amusement.

'I just wondered if—'

'Nell, it's perfectly fine,' interrupted Fran. 'I know how it works. You're obviously very grateful to us for sussing out whodunnit, but officially it was down to the concentrated efforts of your team. Exactly as it should be.'

'I'm very grateful to you, Fran... and Adam, please don't think that I'm not. But this was a very high-profile case, as I said, and the powers that be need to see proof of the taxpayers' money at work. That's not me talking though, you do know that, don't you?'

Fran smiled. 'Of course I do, Nell. I understand perfectly. And it's fine, really. Actually...' She broke off, smirking. 'It's probably better if no one else knows Adam and I were involved in this. I haven't exactly mentioned it to Jack, you see. And Adam hasn't told his mum either, so really, as far as anyone needs to know, we were just innocent bystanders.'

'Excellent. Well, I'm glad we've sorted that out.' There was a muffled pause. 'Fran, listen, I'm sorry, I've got to go, but... I have no doubt we'll be speaking again, so take care, both of you, won't you? Until next time then...'

Fran smiled. 'Bye, Nell. You look after yourself too. Until next time.'

A LETTER FROM EMMA

Hello, and thank you so much for choosing to read *Death at the Dinner Party*. I hope you enjoy reading my stories as much as I enjoy writing them. So, if you'd like to stay updated on what's coming next, please do sign up to my newsletter here and you'll be the first to know!

www.bookouture.com/emma-davies

I had huge fun writing this book, wandering around the rooms of Claremont House in my mind and imagining my characters doing just the same. Of course, a murder mystery can't be all about imagination, and so when I came to the nitty-gritty details of this particular murder, I knew I needed professional help. To this end, I am indebted to Detective Constable Lyn Roberts and the CSI team at the Wrexham division of the North Wales Police for answering all my questions, particularly as Lyn never seemed to mind when I had 'just one more!' Although she also mentioned that their CIO would have heart failure investigating a case of two murders within days of each other, and both in the same house. Thank heavens for fiction! Any factual inaccuracies therefore are mine alone.

I'm also incredibly grateful to my wonderful publishers, Bookouture, for enabling me to bring you these stories and for their unfailing support. Thanks also to my wonderful team of editors and in particular Susannah Hamilton for her sage advice.

And finally, to you, lovely readers, the biggest thanks of them all for continuing to read my books, and without whom none of this would be possible. You really do make everything worthwhile.

Having folks take the time to get in touch really does make my day, and if you'd like to contact me then I'd love to hear from you. The easiest way to do this is by finding me on Twitter and Facebook, or you could also pop by my website, where you can read about my love of Pringles among other things.

I hope to see you again very soon and, in the meantime, if you've enjoyed reading *Death at the Dinner Party*, I would really appreciate a few minutes of your time to leave a review or post on social media. Every single review makes a massive difference and is very much appreciated!

Until next time,

Love, Emma xx

www.emmadaviesauthor.com

facebook.com/emmadaviesauthor

twitter.com/EmDaviesAuthor

instagram.com/authoremmadavies

Made in the USA
Las Vegas, NV
09 January 2023

65301218R00173